SHARK COVE

PARADISE CRIME MYSTERIES BOOK 15

TOBY NEAL

Prov. 17:17~ A true friend loves regardless of the situation, and a real brother or sister shares the tough times. (The Message)

CHAPTER ONE

NOTHING interesting ever happened to Stacey Emmitt. "Seriously. Why is my life so boring?" The fifteen-year-old walked home from Maui High School, muttering to herself as the hot afternoon sun beat down on her head. She kept her eyes on her phone as she read posts from her favorite student gossip site, Wallflower Diaries. The kids written about on the site, especially homecoming king Blake Lee, seemed to have nonstop action going on in their lives.

"Ouch." Stacey tripped on a tussock of untrimmed grass, catching herself on some thorny, overgrown bougainvillea spewing out of a nearby garden—there was no sidewalk in this run-down part of Kahului. "Ow!"

"Need a ride?"

Stacey glanced up, startled, sucking on her pricked thumb.

A guy was speaking to her.

"Uh . . . I'm okay." Guys just didn't pull alongside her in fancy cars and speak to her; she didn't attract attention, hiding any looks she had under baggy jeans and oversized tees out of shyness. But yep, a guy was speaking to her: a hot guy, in a cherry red Mustang.

She shouldn't get into a car with a stranger, no matter how cute he was, or how nice the car.

"You sure? You look awfully *hot*." He drew the word out flirtatiously.

Stacey blushed. "I'm not supposed to accept rides from strangers. My parents would kill me."

"Do I look like a serial killer?" The guy had a dimple, perfect teeth, and nice muscles. He laughed. "C'mon. I'm just trying to do a good deed here." He told her his name. "What's yours?"

"Stacey," she stammered.

"See? Easy. We're not strangers anymore." The guy pulled the beautiful car into the grass ahead of her, jumped out, and opened the passenger door. "Your chariot awaits, Stacey."

She got in, hugging her heavy backpack. "Thanks."

He ran back around to his side, got in, and pulled the car onto the road. "I just went by the store and bought some cold sodas." He dug in a small cooler at her feet and pulled out a bottled Coke. "Can you open mine since I'm driving? You're welcome to one, too."

"Sure." Stacey unscrewed the bottle and handed it to him, then took one herself. She drank thirstily, draining it halfway, then hid a burp behind her hand. "You're so nice."

"That's what all the girls say." Hot Guy winked.

Five minutes later, Stacey Emmitt had passed out, her head slumped forward to rest on her backpack. The red Mustang drove out of her neighborhood, heading in another direction entirely.

Something interesting had finally happened to Stacey Emmitt, and she would never be the same.

TWENTY-FOUR HOURS LATER:

Teen girls were disappearing on Maui. The broad daylight abduction of fifteen-year-old Stacey Emmitt was the latest in a case that had been going on for months.

"I have to find whoever is doing this," Sergeant Leilani Texeira muttered aloud to her partner, Pono Kaihale, frustration tightening her jaw as she pushed through glass doors into the urban ugly rectangle of the Kahului Police Department building. "We have to get a handle on where these girls are going!"

"We're doing all we can," Pono said. "It's not all on you."

"I know." Lei blew a curl off her forehead. "I have to drop this info off to Gerry and Abe."

Usually, Lei headed straight for the elevator to the third level, where she and her partner were lucky enough to have an office on the same quiet floor as her husband, Lt. Michael Stevens—but today, she had to stop by her teammates' cubicle.

"I'll get your computer started," Pono said. Lei's aged desktop was the butt of continual jokes.

"Thanks, bro." Lei peeled off from Pono and headed onto the open 'bullpen' area, where Maui's detectives worked on everything from vice to homicide in a maze of modular units.

Gerry Bunuelos was in his unit with Abe Torufu, and Lei paused in the doorway to smile; she always enjoyed the sight of her mismatched friends together.

Bunuelos was a little over five and a half feet and a hundred and fifty pounds of wiry Filipino; he couldn't have been more different physically than massive Tongan Abe Torufu, who topped six and a half feet and two hundred fifty pounds of solid muscle. The two were engaged in animated conversation with a tall, slender, dark-haired woman wearing a detective's badge on her belt.

A visceral sense of recognition hit Lei as she gazed at the unknown detective, but when the woman turned to her, Lei couldn't place her face. "Sorry for interrupting," Lei said. "I can come back if this is a bad time."

Bunuelos stood up. "No, we were just finishing up. Lei, have you met our newest detective, Harry Clark?"

"You look familiar, but I don't believe so." Lei advanced, her hand out. "Sergeant Lei Texeira, Homicide." Clark's grip was cool and strong; her honey-brown eyes and angular face still seemed familiar. "Have we worked a case together?"

Clark winked and smiled. "As a matter of fact, we have, Lei. About sixteen years ago."

Lei stepped back, her brows snapping together. "Harriet Vierra? That Harry?"

"The very same."

Lei swallowed as her throat went dry. She had a history with this woman—a history that came back in traumatic flashes of memory now and again, the stuff of nightmares and bogeymen under the bed. Her mind buzzed with questions, none of which she could ask in front of their eager audience.

Torufu was the first to break the awkward silence. "Sixteen years ago . . . that would put you both at about legal drinking age. I wouldn't have minded meeting you girls back then."

"I'd love to hear that story!" Bunuelos chimed in.

Clark grinned. "A girl's got to keep some secrets, right, Lei?"

"Right." Lei felt wobbly, ambushed, and a little bit terrified. "We'll have to catch up sometime."

"Yep, but now is not the time or place. See you around the office!" Clark sashayed off.

Lei turned to stare after her, watching the brunette enter one of the cubicles on the other side of the room. "She's working in Vice?" Lei's voice cracked on a high note.

"Harry and her partner, Pai Opunui, just got promoted to Homicide; she came over to pick our brains about it. She transferred here from Oahu about a year ago. She's got a good reputation." One of Bunuelos's eyebrows quirked up in question. "Spill, Texeira. Did you party together back in the day?"

Best to fend off more questions with a version of the truth, rather than stoke her friends' curiosity with secretiveness.

"As a matter of fact, we did," Lei said. "One crazy, unforgettable week down in Mexico. But I haven't seen Harry since. I'm just surprised to see her again, especially as a detective—and no,

I'm not telling you why." She waggled a finger at their loud groans. "On a bummer note, I came to bring you an updated file on the latest missing girl." Lei removed a folder from under her arm and handed it to Bunuelos. "I just interviewed Stacey Emmitt's parents and searched her room—they don't have a clue what might have happened to her on her way home from school. I'm not happy there's another girl gone, when we hadn't made any progress on the one before. Stacey's details are in the folder."

"I hate this case." Bunuelos's mouth tightened; he was a proud and protective father of five. "Who knows what's happening to these poor kids."

"Those 'kids' have reached the age of being totally freakin' annoying to their parents and the community in general." Torufu swiveled his chair back and forth, beefy fingertips forming a triangle that echoed the tattoos running down his ripped forearms. "Every time I haul in some brat for tagging walls, ripping off cars, or panhandling, I remember why CJ and I decided not to have kids." The thick gold wedding band on Torufu's finger was still shiny; he and their station's chief, Captain CJ Omura, had recently married.

Lei shook her head, smiling. She had two children at home and, like Bunuelos, loved her rich family life. "Thankfully, we haven't had to cross the teenage hormone bridge yet, though our son is not far from that milestone." She sobered. "I'll be in touch after you read Emmitt's file and we can set up a case review to make sure we've got everything covered and divided up."

"Got it. I'll pass this on to Abe after I read your notes." Bunuelos was already studying the folder, topped by a school photo of fifteen-year-old Stacey that the parents had provided.

Lei waved to the guys and headed for the elevator. Her gaze flicked over to Harry Clark's office in the corner of the room. Whatever had happened to the woman's adopted daughter, Malia? The baby they'd found in Mexico during that "crazy week" they'd spent together would be about the same age of the missing victims—maybe now was a good time to warn Clark about the disappearances.

Lei changed direction and headed for Clark's cubicle. She rapped on the thin, hollow-core wooden door that gave an illusion of privacy in a network of open-ceilinged modules. "Come in!" a woman's voice called.

Lei opened the door and peered around it. Pai Opunui, a lean, shaggy-haired Hawaiian man she knew from a few cases, sat across from Clark. "Hey, Pai! Can I get a private word with Harry?"

Opunui stood up. "Perfect timing. I needed to refresh my coffee anyway." He picked up his MPD mug and left, brushing past Lei.

Lei slipped inside and shut the door, sitting on Opunui's still-warm seat. She met the brunette woman's light brown eyes. "I want to tell you about the case I'm working on."

"I thought you might want to talk about our *original* case." Harry reached for a silver-framed photo set near her computer monitor, turning it toward Lei. Inside the frame, two young girls smiled. The older one was dark-haired, brown-eyed, with tawny skin and a curvy build. The younger, almost the same height, had rippling light brown hair, hazel eyes and a freckled nose. "Malia, who you met as a baby, is on the right. The one on the left is my biological daughter, Kylie."

Lei took the frame into her hands to look at the picture more closely. "They're beautiful!"

Harry leaned back in her chair, smiling. "They're my reason to get up in the morning."

Lei glanced at Harry's left hand—no ring. "Not married? Your last name didn't used to be Clark."

Raw pain showed on Harry's face for a moment as her full mouth turned down. She shrugged, a fake-casual movement. "My husband left us about a year ago. He's a lawyer and lives in California now."

"Oh, that must be hard."

Harry nodded. "The girls have taken it badly. Particularly Kylie —she adored her dad. Malia and I . . . we're still close."

Lei set the photo frame down. "I thought I should tell you that Malia is the prime age for a ring of human traffickers that we think are operating in Hawaii. We're coordinating efforts with the FBI on all four of the major islands since every county is experiencing the disappearance of teen girls, mostly runaways. Yesterday, a girl was snatched on her way home from school."

Harry's eyes widened. "Yeah, I heard about the runaways. How is it a homicide case, though?"

"We found a body—one of the runaways who disappeared washed up in Kahului harbor with restraint marks on her wrists a few months ago. Like I said, we suspect these girls are being trafficked. I just wanted to warn you—now's a good time to keep a close eye on Malia, as well as Kylie."

Harry frowned. "Why isn't the case in the news?"

"We didn't realize this was such a big problem until recently, but with this latest disappearance, a 15-year-old on her way home from school . . . the time's come to go public. I'm bringing it up to Captain Omura in our next team meeting."

The color had drained from Harry's cheeks. "I guess human trafficking isn't just happening in Mexico." The experience they'd shared in Mexico lay between them—a dark secret Lei had done a good job of trying to forget.

Lei shook her head. "No. Unfortunately."

"Well, my girls go to a private school, Paradise Preparatory Academy, and it has pretty good security. They take a bus to and from campus. Neither of them goes anywhere alone in the community, and their father and I have drilled stranger danger into their heads as well as self-defense techniques. I'm sure they're as safe here as they would be anywhere."

Lei stood up. "I just thought I should mention it, considering Malia is close to the age of the victims."

7

"Thank you," Harry said. "Hey, any chance you want to come by our house after work? You can meet the baby you first saw sixteen years ago and see how she's grown up."

Lei took her phone out of her pocket and checked it. "As a matter of fact, I *can* stop by. My husband is picking our daughter up from preschool, and our son has a ride home from his soccer game with another mom. I can come by for a few minutes, sure, provided you don't live too far away."

"No. We are right up near Wailuku. Not far at all."

"Then it's a date. Give me your contact info." Harry's address and phone number were soon added to her contacts. "I'm looking forward to meeting both of your daughters."

MALIA HUNG her backpack on the hook on the wall, toed out of her shoes, and lined them up beneath it. She shrugged out of her favorite giant black hoodie, hanging it over the backpack. She still had some homework, but she'd get to it later after she checked the Wallflower texts and put some new things up on her secret gossip site.

Her sister Kylie had been dropped off earlier by a friend rather than riding the bus, and Malia spotted her backpack, thrown behind the couch. Muttering, she picked it up and hung it on the hook, then retrieved the eleven-year-old's shoes, kicked across the room, and set them next to hers. If she didn't, tomorrow morning would be awful with Kylie running around looking for missing items.

It wasn't just that her little sister was messy—it was as if she shed everything when she reached home, peeling herself like a banana and leaving the skin for Malia to slip on.

"Kylie!" Malia hollered. No answer.

She found Kylie upstairs, lying in the middle of Mom's bed, eating a bag of popcorn as the sixth grader watched a teen reality show.

"Did you hear me call you?"

"No." Kylie shoved in another handful of popcorn, chewing, her cheeks bulging like a hamster's—and she still looked way cuter than Malia would ever be.

Harry had adopted Malia in Mexico and married Peter Clark a year later. They'd thought their family complete until Kylie had come along, a total surprise. It had always given Malia a secret comfort that Kylie didn't look like Harry; their mom had Hawaiian blood that showed up in olive skin, brown hair and bold features, and Malia looked more related to her than Kylie did.

What had Malia's birth parents looked like? Who had she inherited her short stature and curvy build from? There was no one to ask; according to her mom, she'd been abandoned at an orphanage as an infant. Meanwhile, looking related to Harry saved a lot of the "I'm adopted" questions, while Kylie was the image of their good-looking dad.

"Homework before screens." Malia turned the TV off. Kylie threw a handful of popcorn at her, scowling. "Have fun picking that up." Malia turned and headed back downstairs.

Annoyed guilt, the usual feeling Kylie brought out in her, dogged her steps. It sucked to be saddled with babysitting a sister who'd been mopey and sassy ever since Dad left. No secret that Kylie was his favorite; she'd been devastated by his departure, and Malia shouldn't have to pick up the pieces he'd left behind when her own heart was bruised.

Malia had caught her parents kissing or snuggling numerous times when she was younger—but after Harry was promoted to detective and often worked twelve or more hours a day, their parents had cooled down to roommate status. Dad got more and more into his spirituality, going on "juice cleanses" and "silence retreats" and practicing meditation on the deck outside their former house on Oahu, until finally, in the kind of well-planned lawyer move Peter Clark was known for, he'd filled two suitcases and left. Just weeks later, a packet of divorce papers had arrived in the mail.

Harry had been blindsided by the whole thing. She had refused to sign the papers. They'd fought bitterly on the phone. Malia still remembered overhearing her mom imploring. "I can't raise the girls without you! Give me another chance. I'll change my job if that's what you want!"

But he hadn't believed her, and in her heart of hearts, Malia didn't either.

Harry loved her job. She ate, slept, and breathed law enforcement. Home and family were her retreat, her nest, her recharge station; she'd just taken them for granted a little too long.

"Damn you, Dad," she said aloud, taking a baggie of chicken thighs out of the freezer. Mom bought them in bulk at Costco and then separated them, just enough for each meal. Malia put the meat in the sink and glanced at the clock—4:00 p.m. Hopefully her best and only friend, Camille, would be able to talk soon.

Peter Clark used to come home from his law practice right around now, and "keep his girls company" until Mom arrived, whenever she came home.

Now it was just Malia, covering for both parents and getting popcorn thrown at her for thanks.

Kylie came schlumping down and dribbled into her chair, reluctance oozing from every pore as she opened her homework. Malia ignored this, already deep in burner phone text messages sent to the number for posting on Wallflower Diaries, her anonymous gossip blog. According to sources, Blake Lee, the homecoming king, was seeing at least three different girls. That had been three too many for the Homecoming Princess, who'd canceled their date to prom—and their confrontation made a juicy post.

Her fingers flew on her laptop's keys as Malia entered first names in conversation balloons that she pasted onto cutout yearbook photos of the girls in question and loaded into a meme maker video template. She finished the update: *"Blake L man-slut status confirmed!"*

Malia squashed the dying quiver of her own crush on Blake as she posted the graphic. Making posts into GIFs and cartoons was part of the site's appeal. To keep the material from circulating and getting her in worse trouble if she were ever tracked, Malia encrypted the posts so the address was concealed; people could see the content and leave comments, but nothing more.

Epithets began appearing right away from Blake supporters, along with angry denials from friends of the girls. *Good.* This was a hot post. She rubbed her hands together with glee.

"What are you doing over there? Watching porn?" Kylie's eyes narrowed and her chin thrust out as she glared at Malia over her math book.

Malia snorted. "Very funny."

She shut the laptop and filled a pan and set the chicken thighs in it, adding teriyaki sauce. She took out frozen broccoli and a rice cooker, glancing at the clock. Maybe Camille would be done by now. She called her friend's cell, but it went immediately to voice mail.

An hour later, Malia turned all the food off, waiting for Mom to get home. Kylie had finished her homework and gone back upstairs by then.

She tried Camille again—no answer.

Maybe Camille's mom had taken her phone away. That had sometimes happened, like when Camille wouldn't submit to the chemical peel her mom, Regina William, had scheduled for both of them—never mind that you weren't supposed to do things to a sixteen-year-old face that you did to a fifty-year-old one.

Malia tried Camille's house phone, which rang with a sound like celestial chimes. That device was a piece of polished sculpture, a shape that didn't even look like a communication appliance. Malia could picture it there on the shiny dining room sideboard, the light of a crystal chandelier falling around it like frozen rain.

"Hello?" Regina William's breathless voice.

"Hi, Ms. William. This is Malia." Camille's mom didn't like

her, so Malia was surprised when she cried, "Oh, thank God! Do you know where she is?"

"Where who is?"

"Camille! Camille's gone!" The woman's breathy voice had climbed to a screech. "She wasn't home when I got here with Pierre to do electrolysis. She's with you, right?"

"No." Malia's heart thumped with alarm. Camille was well-liked, but she was a homebody and didn't have a lot of friends she saw outside of school. Generally, she was either at her own house or Malia's. "I called this phone because she wasn't answering hers."

"But she must be with you!" Ms. William was pacing; she'd seen the elegant blonde woman do it often enough before, striding back and forth on the deep carpet of the dining room, or multi-tasking around the big showy house with a phone to her ear. "I can't believe this. Camille packed a bag and left a note saying she'd had it with me and the beauty treatments. She's run away!"

"What? Camille would never do that." Camille loved her mom; she might someday refuse to let her force her into a beauty queen mold, but run away? *Never.* Camille didn't like adventures. Where would she go, if not to Malia's house?

Malia felt a terrible feeling: a sock to the gut, actual nausea. What if Camille really had run away, and run away from her best friend, too?

CHAPTER TWO

MALIA WAS ASSEMBLING the teriyaki chicken, rice and broccoli for dinner when she heard the sound of a key in the lock. "Hey, Mom," she called.

"Hey, Malia," Mom called back. "Where's Kylie?"

"On your bed. Eating popcorn." She heard her mother hang her purse on the hook beside their backpacks next to the stairs. She'd usually go upstairs next and lock up her gun and badge in the safe in the nightstand by her bed, but instead, Harry said, "I've brought someone home to meet you."

Malia frowned as she set the casserole dish of chicken down on the table. No one ever came over to their house!

Mom walked into the dining area, a bump-out off the kitchen, as Malia glanced worriedly at the table set for three—there wasn't enough food for a fourth. "Malia, this is an old friend of mine. Lei Texeira. She's a homicide detective."

Malia wiped her hands on a dish towel, stepping forward with a hand extended. "Hi." Lei was a pretty mixed Hawaiian/Asian woman with curly brown hair, large tilted brown eyes, and an athletic build. "Nice to meet you."

"You're lovely, Malia." The detective smiled, holding Malia's hand in both of hers for a brief squeeze. "I knew when I met you as a baby that you'd be a beauty."

Malia started. "What?" She glanced at her mother. "You knew her back then?" Malia'd never met anyone who'd known her as a baby.

"Lei and I were crazy college girls back then." Harry smiled, but Malia read worry around her eyes and in the lines bracketing her mouth. "We met in Mexico when I adopted you."

"You were such a sweet baby," Lei said. "I totally understand why Harry had to keep you for her own."

Malia and Harry snorted in unison. "Not sweet anymore," they said, in perfect sync.

Lei laughed. "If I didn't know better, I'd swear you were related."

"We absolutely are related." Harry slid an arm around Malia, pulling her close, and kissed her forehead.

Malia's heart swelled with love, but she scowled for form's sake. "Quit it, Mom."

A clatter of footsteps came from the stairs—Kylie must have heard their voices. "And right on cue, Lei, this is my other daughter, Kylie."

"Hello." Kylie put her dimples on display. "I'm not adopted, though. Mom's my real mom." *Why did she have to brag like that?* Malia's smile died. "You knew Malia when she was a baby?" Kylie asked.

"You heard right. Your mom and I met in Mexico when she adopted Malia. Great to meet you, too, Kylie." Lei's phone beeped, and she glanced at it. "Oh, shoot, I can't stay after all. I've got to go pick my son up from soccer practice; his ride fell through. He's a few years younger than you, Kylie, and plays for the Haiku Chargers."

"I'm not into sports," Kylie said in her sassy way. Malia wanted to slap her.

14

Harry drew Kylie in for a kiss, anyway. "And that's an eleven-year-old for you. Sure you can't stay for dinner, Lei?"

"I thought I could, but parenthood calls." Lei gave Harry a direct look. "Be sure to tell your girls what I told you at the station. It's important."

"I will," Harry said. "I'll walk you out."

Mom followed Lei to the front door. Malia heard their murmuring voices on the front porch as she turned back to the stove to drain the pot of broccoli.

A moment later, Harry returned.

"Can I talk to you a minute, alone? It's important," Malia was dying to tell her mother about Camille's disappearance.

"Oh, honey. Can't I eat first? This looks so good." Harry pulled Malia into her arms, rested her cheek on Malia's head. "What would I do without you?"

Malia shut her eyes for a second, feeling her mom's strong arms around her, the tiredness in her lanky body. She savored being needed, belonging. Only Harry really made her feel that way. *And Camille.*

"Group hug!" Kylie yelled, clearly feeling jealous. She body-slammed the two of them, embracing from the outside.

Laughing, Harry pulled them both into her arms for a big squeeze. "Okay, let's eat. Thanks for making dinner, Malia."

They sat. Malia dished up the food, noticing dark circles under Harry's eyes. Harry was still a good-looking woman, and she had a way that put people at ease and made her well-liked on the job. Still, their father's desertion had left scars that weren't healing quickly. Her mother was smoking again; Malia could tell by the tiny tremble in her hands and the way her mouth pinched when she chewed, as if longing for the shape of a cigarette.

"Now can I talk to you?" Malia asked when they were mostly done.

Kylie looked up. "So, talk."

"Not in front of you," Malia snapped.

Kylie looked at Harry. "Mom! Malia's being mean."

"Only because you make me have to boss you around by not doing what you know perfectly well you need to do."

"Girls, please." Harry set down her fork. "Are you going to make me handcuff you again?" She'd handcuffed the two to each other for an entire day to curb their bickering—and it had worked for a while.

Malia looked down at the remains of her meal. "I wanted to talk to you alone because it's none of Kylie's business, but I guess it doesn't matter if she knows." Malia took a fortifying sip of water. "I called Camille this evening and her mom says she's missing. She was super freaked-out and thought Camille was with me. Said she packed a bag and left a note, and if she wasn't with me, she must have run away."

"Hmm. That doesn't sound like Camille." Harry finished her meal. "That was delicious. Tomorrow night, Kylie, you get to fix dinner since you ate popcorn on my bed and gave Malia a hard time."

"I don't know how!" Kylie folded her arms and pushed her lip out.

"Well, it's time you learned. We'll pick a recipe and make a plan tonight."

"I don't want to!" Kylie flounced out of her chair and ran upstairs.

"Alone at last." Harry winked at Malia.

Malia wanted to smile but couldn't. "Mom. This is serious. Camille would never run away."

"You think that, but that mother of hers pretty much tortures her daily. I'd have run away long ago." Harry helped herself to seconds.

"Mom, really. If she was going to run away, she'd have told me." Malia touched her mother's arm to make sure she had Harry's attention. "She was irritated with her mother and all the beauty treatments, but she would never run away. She's not the angry rebel type. She loves her mom, even if Ms. William is a psycho bitch."

"Language." Harry sat back, crossing long legs in their worn black jeans, kicking a foot thoughtfully. Even at the end of a long day, her thick hair in a simple braid, makeup worn off— Harry had a style that made striding around with a gun taking down bad guys easy to imagine. Malia glanced down at her own full chest and rounded thighs. She looked like the Pillsbury Dough Girl next to her mom. Obviously, they weren't biologically related.

Harry got up and looked around to make sure Kylie had gone upstairs; Kylie hated Mom's smoking and got dramatic when she caught Mom with a cig. Mom cracked the window and fetched a battered pack of Virginia Slims and worn gold lighter from her purse. Dad had given Mom that lighter when she got her detective rank, and it always made Malia a little sad to see it. "I have to talk to you about something serious," she said.

"Nothing is more serious to me than Camille disappearing." Malia watched her mother tap the cigarette on the table, light it, inhale, then let the smoke trickle out of her nostrils as she gazed at the ceiling. Harry'd often said she did her best thinking when she was smoking; it was part of why she had a hard time giving it up.

Mom took another drag, blew the smoke in a concentrated stream in the direction of the open window. "Lei told me about a case she's working on at the office. Someone's abducting teen girls here on Maui. She wanted me to caution you; you're right in the age bracket that's getting kidnapped. Kylie's a little young, but I want both of you to be on alert."

Malia clapped her hands to her cheeks. "Maybe someone took Camille!"

"Not likely if she packed a bag and left a note. These missing girls have been street kids— and just recently, a girl who was walking home alone. Doesn't fit the situation you described with Camille."

"There's something wrong, Mom. Camille would tell me if she was leaving." Malia's eyes teared up.

"Maybe there's a boy involved." Harry narrowed her eyes to squint at Malia through a curl of smoke. "Yeah. My vote is a boy, or the dad. Isn't he some shipping magnate? And who was she going out with?"

"Camille had someone she liked, but I don't think she was actually going out with him, yet," Malia said. Blake Lee, the man-slut homecoming king, was the guy Camille liked; good thing Malia had exposed him for the jerk he was, never mind that she was secretly crushing on him herself. "Run off with a boy?" Malia shook her head. "That's just not Camille."

"What about the dad, then? Doesn't Leonard William live on a yacht?"

Malia paused, thinking about her friend's relationship with her father. Camille hadn't talked much about William since he left, roughly at the same time as her own father had. "Camille complained about her mom's beauty fetish, but I never heard her say she'd rather be with her dad. From what I can tell, she's a little afraid of him."

"I'm not surprised. Leonard William has a reputation for having a bad temper as well as some shady business dealings." Harry got up and went to the sink, where she crushed out the last of her cigarette, then dropped it in the garbage disposal and ground it up. "I better go shower before I deal with your sister." She kissed the top of Malia's head and squeezed her hunched shoulders. "Hang in there. Camille will probably turn up tomorrow and have a story to tell you about how she'd had it with her mom."

"I hope so." Malia watched Harry walk away, then opened the window wider, turned on the overhead fan, and cleaned up the rest of the dinner mess, phoning Camille's cell one more time.

Still no answer.

Later that night, Malia stared at the ceiling. She'd texted a few kids she thought might have heard from Camille, fishing to find out if her friend was with them—but no one had seen her since that afternoon.

She tossed and turned.

Had Camille decided she couldn't trust Malia because of the Wallflower website? Because she'd posted about Blake? Had she been dumped as a friend?

The door squeaked as it opened. Malia sat up in bed, recognizing Kylie's shape, ghostly in a white sleep tee. "What do you want?"

"I can't sleep." Kylie came to stand next to the bed, her shoulders slumped and eyes dark shadows in the glow from a nightlight, her old bear Doodlebug clasped in her arms. "Can I stay with you?"

Malia tried to hold on to being annoyed with her sister, but couldn't. She slid over without a word. Kylie climbed into bed beside her, settling herself like a chick fluffing its feathers in the nest, plumping a second pillow and snuggling close against Malia's back with the bear in her arms. Malia smiled in the darkness, and finally her own eyes grew heavy.

CHAPTER THREE

THE NEXT MORNING, Lei poured a cup of the station's inky black coffee into her favorite, only slightly chipped MPD mug. She stirred in powdered creamer with a red plastic stick as she headed for the conference room.

Captain CJ Omura was seated at the head of their table, early as usual. Her sleek laptop was open, her pretty, manicured fingers flying across the keys. The captain's sharp dark eyes flicked up from typing to take in Lei's appearance.

Even after all their years working together, Lei's stomach tightened reflexively under the Captain's laser like gaze. Had her hair escaped its ponytail? Was her polo shirt tucked into her jeans?

"Looks like your daughter shared some of her breakfast with you, Texeira," Omura said.

Lei glanced down. Sure enough, a large blob of oatmeal clung to Lei's right breast.

Lei grabbed a paper napkin off the table and scrubbed at her shirt. "Thanks. I'll have to change at some point." Lei eyed a platter of beautifully arranged vegetables and cut tropical fruit on bamboo skewers that pierced a small, upside-down watermelon half to make a porcupine shape. "Love the food, Captain."

Omura rolled her eyes. "You know my mom and her healthy snacks."

"And I'm grateful. She's so sweet to do this for us every week." Lei picked up an artistically cut radish and crunched on it. "The kids got fed and off to school on time, and I reached the station before the meeting. Did I get breakfast? You know the answer to that."

Omura sniffed. "That's what you get for being a parent."

"Abe tells me you guys aren't having kids."

Before that thorny topic could go any further, Lei's partner Pono entered, carrying a mug of coffee and his laptop, talking over his shoulder to Torufu. Other than Torufu's greater height, the two men could have been cousins with their brown skin, shoulder and arm tats, and thick black hair buzzed into order.

Bunuelos followed them, carrying a pink bakery box. He plopped the box down next to the beautifully arranged platter. "In case anyone needs a sugar dose. I know I do, before we tackle the specifics of this case."

"All right, everyone. Five-minute break for food, then we need to get moving on this." CJ Omura might be married to Abe Torufu, but in any given meeting, there was never any question of who the boss was.

Once the team had talked story and filled their paper plates with a combination of tasty upcountry malasadas from Komoda Bakery along with fruit and vegetables, Omura got the meeting underway. "Texeira, why don't you keep us organized on the whiteboard."

Lei got up, advancing to the board holding copies of case notes that she had made for convenience. She'd carried in the coordinated case jacket holding paperwork related to the matters at hand; it rested in the middle of the table for all to refer to.

Pono, Torufu and Bunuelos all opened their laptops to look at the online version of the case record, along with Captain Omura, who made a call to the Coast Guard Investigative Service (CGIS) agent helping with the case, putting him on video via her laptop. "Glad you could tune in, Agent Thomas."

Special Agent Aina Thomas, who had become friends with Lei when assisting on past cases, nodded. "Wish I had some of your snacks, people."

"Make it down here to our station and you'd be welcome," Lei said. She cleared her throat, shifting gears. "We have a new disappearance as of yesterday: Stacey Emmitt, age fifteen. She usually walks home from Maui High School, and she never made it to the family house. Not a runaway, according to the parents, and friends who knew her." Lei wrote the girl's name on the whiteboard along with her physical statistics: five foot six in height, blonde hair, blue eyes, weight one-twenty. "Stacey has no history of at-risk type behavior, such as drug experimentation or being out past curfew." Lei turned to face the team. "Up until now, our other victims were runaways or living on the streets, so verifying who their associates were, and when exactly they disappeared, has been more difficult. Stacey Emmitt's disappearance has a clear timeline."

Pono tapped the folder. "I'll talk about the others so we can look for any patterns."

He reviewed stats on the five other missing Maui girls, all in the age range between fourteen and sixteen years old, gone missing over the last six months. "As we already know, runaways tend to congregate in Lahaina. We shut down a house where a perp was grooming them a couple of years ago, and we hoped we had that operation buttoned up after we busted the pirate ring."

Omura poured herself fresh coffee from a silver carafe and passed it on to her right. "I've checked with our Lahaina detectives to ensure that this is an entirely new situation, and so far, we believe it is."

Lei nodded. "We think the kids are snatched and held somewhere before being sent, probably on a boat, to Oahu. From there, they are likely shipped overseas. Michelle Ho'opua, the homicide victim found in Kahului Harbor, showed evidence of restraints; as we've reviewed before, we believe she was trying to escape and drowned."

"This is all review," Captain Omura said. "I thought you were going to talk to Emmitt's parents yesterday?"

"I did. They're terrified for Stacey. They're hoping for a ransom demand, but we don't think they will be getting one," Lei said.

"We didn't want to spook them further by speculating that Stacey could be part of this larger case, since they weren't aware of it," Pono rumbled. He rubbed his mustache, a characteristic gesture, and picked up a carrot stick, crunching it loudly. "We let them hold onto hope that their daughter was kidnapped, but the family has little to no financial assets so that's unlikely."

Omura shuffled through the pages of the case file, frowning. "We should be coordinating with the FBI on this. They can then take the lead on warning the public." Omura glanced up at Lei. "Texeira, you're our FBI liaison. Why don't you make a call to Waxman on Oahu? We can conference him in right now."

Lei had been waiting for this, and she was ready. She'd touched base with Omura yesterday about this after their talk with the Emmitt parents. "I'll get him on the line."

Everyone waited and refreshed their snacks as Lei used the conference calling phone in the center of the table to reach Special Agent in Charge Ben Waxman, a starchy and well-groomed man whose appearance reminded Lei of Anderson Cooper. Waxman soon came on audio feed. "To what do I owe the pleasure, Sergeant Texeira?"

"Aloha from Maui, SAC Waxman," Lei said. She pushed the button on the triangular speaker. "You are on speakerphone with a team meeting regarding the kidnap disappearances of five girls from our island."

"Yes, we've been monitoring your cases. We're working on disappearances here on Oahu and the other outer islands, too. We were waiting for you to loop us in on what's happening over there," Waxman said. He rattled off their open case number and the names of the agents that were already working on the disappearances and Lei scribbled notes, trying to keep up. "According to protocol, unless we have evidence that this crime has crossed state or international lines, we wait upon local law enforcement to ask for help."

"Well, that moment has come, Ben," Captain Omura said. "Let's officially proceed. Now that they've taken to grabbing girls on their way home from school and we still have no leads, we need all the help we can get."

"Happy to hear it. Our agents will liaise with you tomorrow. I'll assign Ken Yamada and Marcella Scott, already working on the disappearances here."

Lei's face broke into an involuntary smile. She hadn't seen her friend Marcella or her ex-partner Ken Yamada in months, and it was always a treat to work with them. After briefing SAC Waxman on the latest disappearance, Captain Omura expressed her desire to see some sort of curated announcement about the disappearances on the media. "We are working on that, in connection with the governor's office," Waxman assured her. "A press conference is scheduled for tomorrow, so island wide, young women can be on alert."

"I'll call Special Agent Scott ASAP to coordinate our efforts. Thank you, SAC Waxman. We look forward to solving this together." Lei ended the call to the FBI cordially, then sat back in her chair after grabbing a malasada from the pink box. "I think we are finally going to get somewhere with this. Happy that Agents Marcella Scott and Ken Yamada will be assigned to the case. I can vouch for their effectiveness from our shared work in the past."

Omura steepled her shiny nails. "Glad we will have the resources of the FBI, too, because I need to reassign Torufu and Bunuelos to the County Council murder."

Lei opened her mouth, preparing to protest, but Omura held up a finger. "As you may know, Mayor Costales was asked to set up a committee tasked with developing ways to diversify the economy on Maui away from tourism, and to replace the sugar industry in the use of open lands. That committee's work has been derailed by Councilman Agora's recent hit-and-run death, and last night Councilwoman Tavares was found dead in her bed, cause unknown. Dr. Gregory's preliminary review says it looks like a medication interaction accident, but I'm worried that there's a trend here— someone doesn't want anything but tourism driving our island's economy."

Lei frowned as both Torufu and Bunuelos burst out with protests about where they were on the case, and the need for boots on the ground finding the girls missing here on Maui.

A knock came from the door, interrupting the spirited discussion, and Detective Harry Clark stepped inside, closing the door behind her. "I hope I'm not interrupting. I have some information I'd like to share with the team."

Lei's heart did a little skip of alarm at the sight of the other woman; clearly, Harry had not slept well. Dark circles ringed her eyes, and her thick hair was every bit as rumpled as Lei's. The life of a single mother, even with older kids, seemed to leave a bodily impression.

"Welcome, Detective Clark," Captain Omura said. "You're a good distraction right now. Have a seat and help yourself to something to eat. You look like you need a little nourishment."

Harry smiled, but it was more of a twitch of her lips than positive emotion. "Thanks. No time for breakfast." She grabbed a paper plate and helped herself. "I want to let the team know that my daughter is concerned because her best friend Camille is missing. Camille William is sixteen, right in the age range of disappearances that have been occurring. Camille wasn't at home when she was supposed to be, and when I talked to her mother, Regina, she said that she arrived home from school because Camille's phone was left on her desk. She left a note, though, and clothing is missing." Harry paused to chomp down a malasada and chase it with a gulp of coffee.

"Sounds like a runaway, then," Lei said. "Not that she won't be in danger because of that."

"Regina isn't convinced that her daughter ran away, and neither is Malia, my daughter. She says, 'Camille just isn't the type.'" Harry paused to cram another malasada into her mouth, chewing rapidly. "I actually agree with Regina and my daughter; from what I know of Camille, running away is uncharacteristic. Malia says Camille would never go anywhere without telling her." Harry picked up several skewers of fruit and slid their contents off the bamboo and onto her paper plate; she was fueling her body out of sheer necessity. Lei could relate to that style. "Anyway, I told Regina I would bring it up with the team and fast-track a missing person report for Camille if you agreed, Captain. But I didn't let on to Ms. William that we had a pattern of missing girls on the island."

Omura was typing rapidly on her laptop, her nails clicking like delicate castanets. "We just got off the phone with the FBI. They will be putting on a press conference to warn the public about what's been going on with these disappearances, and then the cat will be out of the bag. I'm sorry to hear that another girl is missing for whatever reason, but we should be cautious in jumping to conclusions. If the girl left a note and her clothes were missing, then there's a viable possibility she left on her own. She's not necessarily one of our victims."

"Being a runaway does put her at risk," Lei injected. "I agree with Harry that we should treat her disappearance with urgency."

"Yes." Harry polished off her plate and wiped her fingertips with a paper napkin. "Lei told me yesterday to keep an eye on my daughters, who are in the age range to be targets, and I appreciated the heads-up, especially when I came home to hear about Camille." She poured herself a clear plastic cup of water and chugged down a few gulps. "Camille is a beautiful girl. She is also from a wealthy and well-connected family, not that it helps at all in this situation."

Omura frowned. "How well-connected?"

"Her mother is a successful art gallery owner, and her father is a shipping tycoon. Leonard William is also rumored to be an arms trafficker, though I don't believe there has ever been an official investigation into his activities. Camille is their only daughter, and Regina is the type to shout her news from the rooftops. It would behoove us to get out in front of it."

"Here we go with the racist, classist imbalance of law enforcement and the justice system," Pono said, eyes narrowed. "No one has cared this much about local kid runaways getting nabbed."

"I didn't say all of that to perpetuate some racist double standard," Harry snapped. "I'm half Hawaiian myself. My daughter Malia is Mexican, adopted at birth. I'm just telling you background that could be pertinent in moving forward."

"And I appreciate the perspective," Captain Omura said. "We need to have as much information as we can. I'd like you to work on this case with us, Detective Clark, and liaise with Lei and Pono about anything you need to know moving forward. Pai Opunui can pick up your current cases if it gets to be a full-time commitment."

"I would appreciate you letting him know that," Harry said. "He might not like getting left holding the bag on our current investigations."

"Consider it done. Detective Clark, why don't you meet with Lei to make an action plan to follow up on the situation with Camille William, then divide up who does what, since Bunuelos and Torufu are being reassigned. Lei oversees this investigation. You should also be aware that there are teams on each of the islands, and this case has now moved to the FBI level."

"I'm glad to hear that." Harry's voice vibrated with emotion. "I have a particular hatred for sex traffickers."

Lei met her newly rediscovered friend's beautiful, light brown eyes and nodded. "You and me both."

CHAPTER FOUR

MALIA WOKE up the next morning with a crystal-clear intention: *she was going to find out what had happened to Camille.*

After their usual hurried morning routine, Harry left for the MPD and Malia tried Camille's phone.

When her friend still didn't answer, Malia grabbed one of Harry's personalized notecards from her desk and forged a note from her mom for a dentist appointment. She changed, dressing for comfort in a tank top, shorts and sneakers. She threw her big black hoodie on to cover everything up.

Soon the bus, a sixteen-passenger van, dropped Malia and Kylie off at the gracious turnaround of Paradise Prep, and, after making sure her grumpy sister had headed off to the middle school area, Malia hurried into the main school office. She handed over the notecard to Mrs. Spelling, the front desk clerk, a papaya-shaped lady with pillowy hips and too-tight skirts in upholstery fabric. "I have to leave right after homeroom. Don't know why Mom bothered to have me come in."

Mrs. Spelling eyeballed Malia over half-glasses and nodded. "Okay. Who's picking you up?"

"Mom—but she said she's in a hurry. Can I just sign out now and meet her outside the gate?"

"That's not protocol, but your mom's a policewoman." Mrs. Spelling sniffed to show she was allowing Malia latitude because of her mother's important job. Malia signed the logbook and Mrs. Spelling paper-clipped the note to the page. Malia thanked her, walked out, and checked in at homeroom, turning in her homework from the day before and grumbling to the teacher about the dentist. When the bell rang for classes, Malia looked both ways to make sure the coast was clear and then hurried down the gracious drive planted with swaying palms.

Her school, in its own little cup of valley in central Maui, was near the island's oldest town of Wailuku. Surrounding the campus, grassy former sugar cane fields bent and danced in the ever-present trade winds. Malia exited through a magnetic one-way gate beside the main entrance gate designed for cars and walked down to the two-lane highway.

Cars and trucks swished by as Malia plowed through sweet-smelling uncut grass on the shoulder. Above her, the clear blue sky raced with puffy cotton candy clouds, as if there couldn't be anything to worry about *here*. Malia knew better. Paradise was full of problems; the islands just had a prettier backdrop for them.

She had a long way to go to Camille's neighborhood—too far to reach the William house in a reasonable amount of time on foot. Steeling herself against every threat and warning her parents had ever given her, Malia stuck out her thumb to hitchhike.

If only she had her own wheels. She had her learner's permit and almost enough hours logged behind the wheel to take her license test, but that wouldn't do her much good with no spare car to drive; Harry drove their one car, a Honda CRV with a license plate reading MAMACOP.

A battered tan pickup pulled over onto the grass ahead of Malia. She jogged up to it, glancing inside to make sure the driver didn't look too much like a rapist or murderer. An old guy in a paint-speckled aloha shirt with antennalike whiskers protruding from his eyebrows hunched behind the wheel. "Whatcha doin' out of school?" he asked as she opened the door.

"Mom's car broke down and I'm hitchhiking to the dentist in Wailuku." The lie rolled easily off Malia's tongue; a story that was consistent and simple was the easiest to remember and maintain, her mom had told her once.

"I can get you to the dentist at least," the old guy said. "But a young girl like you shouldn't be hitchhiking. It's not safe." The man insisted on driving her all the way to her destination, which she made up as an office building in downtown Wailuku where her mom's oral surgeon was located.

That address still wasn't close enough to where Malia was really going, but the old guy's lecture rattled Malia so much that she walked the rest of the way.

Forty-five minutes later, sweaty and bedraggled, Malia headed up a semi-steep incline into the development of two-acre lots where a ten-foot-high decorative wall bisected by an artificial waterfall and clump of palms marked the Valley View Estates. Malia discovered a faint trail cutting through the open meadows that marked unsold properties and hurried on.

Finally, she stood at the bottom of Camille's driveway.

More decorative palms arched over a driveway leading to a Mediterranean style mansion complete with a red tiled roof and bougainvillea plantings. Verandas surrounded an expanse of brick courtyard bordered by potted hibiscus. Malia trotted up the driveway and peeked into the glass insert set into the garage—Regina William's BMW SUV was gone, but Camille's car, an older silver Toyota Prius, was still inside.

If Camille had run away, wouldn't she have taken her car? Who would have picked her friend up and taken her somewhere? It just wasn't Camille's style to hitchhike or walk a long distance and get all sweaty like Malia had done.

The spare house keys were hidden under a rubber rock in a

little decorative Japanese garden near the stairs; Malia found them, unlocked the front door, and deactivated the alarm with her friend's birthdate.

"Camille?" Malia called, looking around inside. Here in Camille's house, with her friend's car in the garage, it seemed impossible that Camille wasn't in her room upstairs, that this whole thing wasn't some big mistake. Malia unslung her backpack and dropped it by the shoes she toed out of by the front door. "Camille?"

The big antique grandfather clock in the front hall ticked and tocked, the heartbeat of a couple of hundred years, a creepy backbeat as Malia padded in her socks down the tiled hall, reaching a sweeping staircase rising to the next level of the house. She glimpsed herself in the mirrored wall alongside the stairs: cheeks red with sun and exertion, hair unraveling from her braid, eyes squinty with worry.

Malia hurried up the treads, calling once more, "Camille? It's Malia."

Camille's room was closed; but her friend rarely locked the door. Malia turned the handle, heart thumping.

Camille would be in her bed sleeping, and she'd sit up and blink in surprise at Malia.

But Camille's bed was unnaturally perfect, the way it looked after the maid had cleaned, with three lacy throw pillows balanced in a pyramid against a matching peach satin headboard. Malia's stomach plummeted in disappointment.

She put her hands on her hips and looked around, trying to remember her mom's comments about assessing a crime scene.

"I go slow." Harry had blown a plume of smoke at the ceiling. "I let my eyes relax and scan back and forth thoroughly, covering every section of the room in a grid pattern. I try not to focus on any one thing too soon, just let things flow by, until something 'blips' in my vision, something that's out of place or might be a clue."

Malia walked slowly forward, letting her eyes tell her about the room without focusing on any one thing. Fresh vacuum tracks on the floor would reveal her footprints, so she stayed on a runner rug, and then hopped onto the sheepskin next to the bed.

Camille loved that sheepskin; someone who enjoyed sensations on her skin, Camille liked soft fabrics, silky clothes, fuzzy things. Sinking her feet into the rug reminded Malia of how Camille always sighed happily as she put her feet on it.

Malia's eyes prickled. "Where are you, Camille?"

She blinked to clear her vision; she was here to figure out what had happened, not get mopey.

Malia frowned as she surveyed Camille's desk. Her friend's closed laptop rested on it; Camille would never run off without her laptop, her link to the world. *But maybe she was using her phone?* And Malia's heart sank even further: Camille's phone was plugged into the charger where she always put it when she got home from school.

Nothing short of a natural disaster would make Camille leave her phone behind. Something was definitely wrong.

Malia hopped off the sheepskin rug and tiptoed over to her friend's closet.

The walk-in was packed with gorgeous clothes, sorted by color, all of it the work of a consultant who had pronounced Camille a "spring" and proceeded, with Regina William's help, to stock Camille's closet with outfits that were coordinated and photographed on a ring of laminated reference cards hanging on the closet door.

Camille had dealt with this by going shopping at a discount superstore with Malia, and making herself a 'favorites' section way in the back of her closet. She'd hung pairs of Seven7 jeans, simple tanks, and a couple of colorful zip-front hoodies back there. Underneath those clothes rested three pairs of bright Converse sneakers that Camille liked better than any of the designer shoes nested like art objects on a nearby tiered shelf.

Someone had gone through the closet, pulling out clothes and leaving gaps of rattling hangers—*but that someone wasn't Camille.*

"I have to find the note you left." Malia's voice sounded small and scared in the big, luxurious room. "But where is it, Camille?"

Malia backed out of the room, erasing her footprints with one of the pillows, until she realized, at the door, that the pillow was supposed to be on top of the pyramid on the bed. "Crap."

No help for it. She'd have to vacuum when she was done searching.

Malia padded across the room, set the pillow in its proper place, and glanced over at the phone. The little icon with "messages" pulsed in the corner. Probably Malia's own messages, and if Camille was declared missing, they'd be listened to by law enforcement.

Had she said anything incriminating? Perhaps a mention of the Wallflower Diaries website, but that could be explained away. Could the phone tell her something? Since she was going to have to vacuum her tracks now, she might as well see if Camille had been talking to someone.

Malia sat down on the bow-backed desk chair Ms. William had covered in peach fabric to match the bed. She inputted Camille's password—but now she was really getting into her friend's privacy, and her fingers paused above the phone's screen.

Camille's favorite clothes left behind in the closet decided Malia: someone who didn't know Camille had packed her things and tried to make it look like Camille had done it. That couldn't be good.

Malia checked Camille's text messages, and immediately spotted one from Blake: *"Hey Cam, did you see that nasty post about me on that damn Wallflower website? Don't believe everything you read! I can't handle one girlfriend, let alone three!"*

Malia's stomach wound tighter than a Boy Scout knot. For whatever reason, Camille hadn't told her she and Blake were anything but friends, but Blake's messages, as she scanned them, sounded like he had feelings for her.

Blake and Camille had something going. Malia had a responsibility to find out more, since she, the Wallflower, had passed on unfiltered intel about Blake from potentially unreliable sources. She would answer back as Camille and put Blake out of his misery—after all, Camille had believed that he "wasn't the type" to be a man-slut.

"Hey Blake, it's all good. You know I don't believe everything I read, and the Wallflower has been known to get it wrong once or twice. Ha, ha." Malia hit Send.

Malia moved on to check e-mail, but Camille hardly used it. She saw a few *"Dear daughter, how are you?"* stiffly worded e-mails from her father, with no mention of a visit. She then checked her friend's social media page: no new posts since yesterday. Camille posted up positive thoughts or little arty photos she took with her phone and then wrote things like "Have a great day!" next to them.

Nothing. And no hidden boyfriend except whatever had been going on with Blake.

Malia powered down the phone. Now her fingerprints were on it. She pulled some tissues out of a rhinestone-covered box and wiped down the phone and the area.

Had she forgotten anything?

A spike of panic that the maid would come, or the yard guy, or God forbid, Regina William herself, accelerated Malia's heart rate again. She pushed the chair in and ran out and down the hall to the utility closet, getting out the vacuum. She'd have to vacuum the hall too, because there were her footprints leading in and out of Camille's room—and she still hadn't found the note.

She abandoned the vacuum and hurried into Regina William's gigantic bedroom.

The room ran the length of the whole upper floor of the house and was separated into sections with screens and furniture groupings: a seating area in front of French doors leading onto the deck in front of the house. A dressing area with one of those "vanities" where you sat down to primp, a TV and exercise bike, and a walk-in closet. Finally, at the back, the inner sanctum where Regina William's bed was robed in ivory satin with—Malia's eyes goggled —a white fur throw that looked like real mink draped over one end of it.

The whole expanse of fancy shag carpet had been recently vacuumed, and Malia's footprints showed as clearly as if they'd been left in sand on the beach.

Malia spotted the note on the bedside table, in an envelope with '*Mom*' on it. She ran over—and stopped. What if they found her fingerprints on the note? She grabbed a tissue from a dispenser and eased the folded cream paper out, holding it with the tissue.

"Dear Mom: I've had it with all the beauty treatments. I'm running away to somewhere where I can be myself. Don't bother looking for me and don't worry, I'm safe. Love, Camille."

Malia rocked back on her heels. It was Camille's writing all right. There was even the little heart she dotted the 'i' in her name with.

Camille really had run away, and she hadn't told Malia a thing. Where was this place where she 'could be herself'? Wherever it was, Malia wanted to go there too.

Malia had to find more clues, and be back at school by two o'clock, which was going to be challenging. She slid the note back into the envelope and set it back the way it had been, scanning the unfamiliar space.

She'd only ever been in Regina William's room as far as the seating area, where a couch and armchair were grouped with a standing lamp.

Maybe there was some evidence of what was going on in the bathroom.

Malia padded into that area, and, using a tissue, opened the various cabinets. She found bottles and bottles of pills, everything from things she recognized like Xanax to things she didn't, like dextroamphetamine. She used her phone to take pictures of the bottles in their rows, and then opened the cabinet under the sink.

A bright yellow box of rat poison rested there, as out of place as a neon sign.

Rat poison.

Why would Ms. William need rat poison, and why keep it here?

Six months ago, Camille had been so sick she'd had to go to the hospital and have her stomach pumped. They'd found traces of rat poison in her system, and no one knew how it had got there, least of all Camille.

Regina Wiliam had been in a tizzy. She'd sent Camille to all sorts of doctors and psychologists and blamed her ex for pushing Camille to attempt suicide.

But what if Regina William had poisoned Camille herself, to try to show that Camille was disturbed, and to get back at Leonard William even more?

Malia took a picture of the terrible yellow box with its crossed-out rat on the front.

Camille had eventually gotten rid of the doctors and psychologists by being her usual sunny self, but after that, she had never wanted to eat at home. She wouldn't eat what her mom cooked, always making excuses that she was counting calories or had just eaten—but never once had she said a word against her mom.

Camille was loyal like that.

Malia's stomach churned. Everything in the room looked suspicious: the bottles of Xanax and Ambien to drug somebody. A missing satin cord hanging from the drapes could have been used to tie Camille up. The rug was gone—what if Regina William had killed Camille herself, or drugged her and taken her somewhere? Camille had always been an "illness-prone" kid. How many of those illnesses and accidents might have been caused by Regina William?

Malia was so spooked that her hands were shaking, but she made sure the bathroom looked like it had originally. She almost dropped the vacuum cleaner as she lugged it out of the closet, remembering to hold the handle with the tissue. The tissue promptly shredded once she started vacuuming, stopping to turn the machine off every few minutes to listen, terrified someone would approach and she wouldn't hear them coming.

Finally, Malia'd vacuumed all her footprints out of Camille's room, Regina William's room, and the hall. She put the vacuum away and, setting her feet on the edges of the wooden baseboard, made it to the polished wood stairs where her footprints didn't show.

Outside, she hid the keys back under the rubber rock.

Sweat prickled over Malia's body as she trotted away from the house, mentally checking over every step she'd taken to leave all as she'd found it. She hurried down the path through the vacant lots, vigilant for anyone to spot her—but as usual the Estates were deserted during the day; all were quiet but for one lone gardener doing someone's yard with a blower that sounded louder than a jet engine. The great purple cone of Haleakala volcano was a ridiculously beautiful backdrop in the distance, framed by waving palm trees and swatches of picturesque cloud.

Hiking back down the highway toward school, Malia's stomach rumbled. She'd been too keyed up to eat breakfast, and now it was noon, the Maui sun high overhead. She put her ball cap on and stuck her thumb out. If she got to school soon, she'd be able to eat a late lunch in the cafeteria. The next passing vehicle, a shiny red sports car, pulled over.

Malia glanced into the low-slung luxury vehicle. The driver had moussed-looking hair and was dressed in Hawaiian business casual—tan pants and an aloha shirt. "Where you headed, cutie?" He had very white teeth.

"Back to school. Got a late start this morning—missed the bus." Malia smiled at the guy as she got in, feeling sweaty and gross. She perched on the edge of the leather seat, setting her back-pack in front of her knees, and enjoyed the smell of buttery new leather as she shut the door with a soft, expensive sounding click.

"Which one? I'm headed to Lahaina."

Malia put the seat belt on. "You'll pass right by my school. Paradise Preparatory Academy."

"Oh, a prep school girl. I thought you were a local." He pulled back onto the road.

Malia never knew how to take comments like that. Her Mexican heritage passed for mixed Hawaiian, what they called "local" here in Hawaii. It was usually easiest not to argue with those assumptions—but inside, she always felt a little wrong about it.

The car floated like a cloud down the road. "This is a really nice car."

"That's why I drive it." The guy seemed to be looking at her breasts—but he had mirrored sunglasses on, so she couldn't be sure. "What's your name, sweet cheeks?"

"Malia." She didn't like being called "sweet cheeks," and she'd forgotten to put her concealing sweatshirt on over her tight cloth-ing. She unzipped the backpack and took the sweatshirt out, shrug-ging into it despite the awkward seatbelt.

"You look way too hot to be wearing something like that," the guy said. There was something off in the way he said it. He reached over and put his hand on her bare leg.

Malia jumped like it was a hot coal. He laughed.

Malia looked around at where they were—at least fifteen minutes from her school, driving through Wailuku. "Hey, I think I better stop and pick up something for lunch. Why don't you let me out on the corner?"

"Don't think I will." This time when he smiled, the guy's white teeth reminded her of a shark's.

Malia gathered her nerve. She narrowed her eyes at the driver. "My mom is a detective with Maui Police Department. You don't want to mess with me, Mr. License Plate Number HV22RED. I also am trained in self-defense and can gouge your eye out with my thumb."

The man chuckled, nervously this time. "Just kiddin' with you, hon. I'll drop you off right where you're going. The streets aren't safe these days."

They drove in tense silence to Paradise Prep and up the majestic, palm-lined drive. The car slid to a silent stop in the turnaround in front of the office. Malia yanked her backpack out and slammed the door overly hard; the sports car burned rubber leaving.

Malia hurried into the bathroom, splashing water on her face and combing her hair with her fingers, trying to calm her jitters. *What a creep!* She'd had her hand on the door, getting ready to jump out of the moving car if he tried anything more, but she was really glad she hadn't had to.

If she ever told her mom, Harry would say, "report the guy so he doesn't do it to someone else." But if Malia did, she'd have to tell MPD how she came to be hitchhiking, and that wasn't a conversation she wanted to have. At least she'd talked her way out of it. Harry'd told her that was the best way to handle a bully. "Don't show fear. Act confident. Get ready to fight and scream and show the perp you aren't going to be easy pickings. Most will back off."

Malia washed her leg where the man had touched it. With soap. Three times.

CHAPTER FIVE

LEI CARRIED a load of dishes to the sink as her son Kiet helped her clear the dinner table. Stevens was seated with their three-year-old daughter Rosie on the couch, a bedtime story open on his lap. The toddler lay against his side, her thumb in her mouth, her favorite blanket clutched close as she stared at the pages. On the other side of him, their Rottweiler, Conan, lay snuggled with his big square head resting on the arm of the couch.

Lei ruffled her son's glossy head as he passed by, carrying a square baking pan of leftover teriyaki beef strips into the kitchen. "Just set that on the counter, son. I'll wrap that up for leftovers. In fact, put the rice and salad up there too."

"Sure, Mom."

Kiet continued to be a joy to parent. Now eight years old, he was close to reaching Lei's shoulder in height. Forest green eyes and tan skin contrasting with black hair made the boy exceptionally good looking; they'd been approached about him trying modeling, but Kiet continued to be on the shy side, preferring to build Legos and do nerdy computer stuff.

Lei walked into the living room and peered over Stevens's shoulder. "What story are you reading tonight?"

"*'Ohana Means Family,*" Rosie said, her thumb making a pop as she removed it from her mouth. "By Ilima Loomis."

"I like how your dad reads the title and tells you the author's name, too," she said. "Good job, dad."

He reached up to pull her down for a quick kiss. "Anything to get a smile out of my girls."

"No problem there," Lei said, smiling down at the two. Rosie resembled a dark-haired angel, with her riot of curls and big brown eyes. "I have to go to the back room and make a work call," she said. "Are you okay supervising bedtime without me tonight?"

"No problem."

Lei headed back through the kitchen, pausing for a moment to watch as Kiet loaded the plates into their machine. "Do you like using the dishwasher?"

"I don't know, Mom. I still have to wash the dishes before I load them, then I have to unload them again tomorrow," Kiet said in his thoughtful way. "I'm not sure it's actually saving us any work."

Lei smiled. "I was just thinking the same thing. But sometimes we can fill it up, and it takes a few days before we need to run it. That seems like an energy saver."

"We should gather data," Kiet said. "I could measure how much time it takes and keep track on the whiteboard." He pointed to the shiny plastic laminate board magnetized to the front of the fridge where the family left messages for each other, lists, and chore reminders. Today, Kiet's day for setting and clearing the table and doing the dishes was clearly marked. Tomorrow it was Rosie's turn, which meant that Lei or Stevens would be helping their daughter learn her chore.

"That's a great idea, son."

"I'm also wondering how much water and power the dishwasher uses over manual washing," Kiet said. "I have to consider how we would measure that difference." His eyes narrowed. "Dad has a device for measuring electrical output, but I don't know how to measure the water usage."

"This sounds like a science project waiting to happen," Lei said. "Maybe one of your teachers would be interested in it as a comparison paper."

Kiet attended a Waldorf school featuring child-centered learning, and he often got to come up with his own projects. The brightness in her son's eyes showed that he was excited by challenges of turning a dishwasher versus a manual washing comparison into a combination science and composition project. "I'll let you know what Mrs. Norman says."

"You do that. I'm off to make a phone call." Lei grabbed her MPD work cell phone off its charger and headed to the far back bedroom.

She and Stevens continued to make their small house work for the family; Kiet and Rosie shared a room, leaving the back bedroom set up for guests and an office. Lei sat down at the desk in the office, opening her notebook. She hit a number in her Favorites list on the phone. A moment later, her friend's voice filled her ear. "Lei! It's been ages!"

"I know, Marcella. We gotta do better at keeping up. Did you hear from Waxman about your new case?"

"I sure did, and it's a good thing too or I might have thought you were calling me for social reasons," Marcella said, a smile in her voice.

"You know me, always looking for a twofer. I'm actually hoping that you and Ken can come over to Maui and help out with boots on the ground. This case is big and scary, and we're getting more disappearances by the day."

"I'll put in a request, but as you know we have a lot of disappearances here too," Marcella said, concern in her voice. "There seems to have been an escalation."

"Yeah. They were just nabbing runaways before, which made

the kids harder to track as far as time of disappearance. But we have two recent ones who weren't runaways." Lei filled Marcella in on two new additions to the case, the Emmitt girl and Camille William. "I'm scheduled to interview Regina William and search their house tomorrow. I've already talked to the Emmitt girl's parents and searched their house. Nothing at the Emmitt place contradicted the parents' story that she never made it home from school," Lei said. "I'm working with a new-old friend, Harry Clark. I met her sixteen years ago on a trip to Mexico."

"What? Lei had friends before me?" Lei could hear the dramatic sound of Marcella pretending to slap her forehead. "I thought Sophie and I were your only BFFs."

"Hard to believe, but yes, I did have a few friends before I joined the police force. I lost touch with them, though." Kelly, her college friend, flashed into Lei's mind with her bright blue eyes, blonde hair, and fun-loving spirit. They'd lost contact after Lei moved to the Big Island, and though Lei had thought of her over the years, never so much as now, when she'd met Harry again. "I'm going to transfer all of my notes to you, so you can add it to your file."

"That sounds good. I'll wait to receive it."

Lei said goodbye, then booted up her computer and sent documents from her case files to Marcella over a secure server. She powered down the computer and locked the office door, another security measure to prevent the kids accessing their work and the safe where she and Stevens stored their weapons. As she headed down the hall, she heard the low rumble of Stevens reading a chapter book to Kiet in the kids' bedroom.

She peeked in from the door. Rosie, her eyes closed, lay on her back in her crib, one side lowered now that she was a big girl, and she could climb in and out. She was listening to the story too, a thumb in her mouth and her favorite quilt, made by her godmother Esther, drawn up under her chin. She'd need a bigger bed soon;

they were considering bunks so the kids would have more play area.

Stevens lay on Kiet's bed with their son, his dark head pillowed on Stevens's shoulder, as Stevens read a sci-fi novel. Rosie usually fell asleep halfway through, but her vocabulary was advanced because of exposure to words like "propulsion" and "fission."

Lei smiled as she headed into the kitchen to put away the leftover food. What would their life be like without their children? Quieter and more peaceful, that's for sure, but she wouldn't trade that for the laughter and joy the kids brought.

Child-free CJ Omura and Abe Torufu would be snuggled up on their couch with their French bulldog Pepe, probably watching some gruesome detective show with the volume up. "Well, maybe that wouldn't be so bad," Lei muttered as she portioned the leftovers into Tupperware for a quick lunch at the station the next day. "Instead, we have science fiction stories and picture books."

She glanced out the back window to where her grandfather Soga's tiny house took up a corner of their large yard. Her only remaining relative on her mother's side had joined them two years ago, settling into their lives as if he had always been a part of it. Light from Grandfather's reading lamp poured out one of the windows. Lei smiled to see his face for a moment before he turned the light out; the eighty-something man's bedtime followed that of their children.

Lei entered the living room, pausing to pet Conan's head, grateful she'd had the big male Rottweiler to ease the loss of her beloved Keiki when the old girl passed of age, her resting place marked by a petroglyph carving in a private corner of the yard.

Through the front windows, light still shone around the curtains of the little cottage where her father, Wayne Texeira, lived with his wife, Stevens's mother Ellen. The two had fallen in love through shared, tumultuous life experiences and their bond as grandparents, and had settled happily in the vintage cottage surrounded by ti plants and red flowering hibiscus.

Now that Stevens's brother Jared and his wife Kathy had married, too, everyone closest to Lei was settled, and that brought her a contented feeling. Lei turned off the living room lamp and headed for bed, filled with gratitude for the loving 'ohana that surrounded them.

CHAPTER SIX

"MALIA, come help me with something in the garage," Harry said that evening, after they finished the meatloaf dinner Kylie'd made with Malia's help.

Malia followed her mom out and wasn't surprised when they went to the screen door that opened into the seldom used, weedy backyard. Harry lit a cigarette and blew the smoke outside. "I wanted to tell you that Regina called me about Camille going missing, and I took the situation to Captain Omura. She gave me the green light to pursue it, because even if Camille ran away, that puts her at risk from these kidnappers."

Malia spontaneously hugged her mom. "Thank you! I'm so glad you'll be looking for her." She met Harry's eyes. "There's something off with Regina William."

"What makes you say that? She was distraught today, a very worried mom. Everything I would be, if you ran away." Her mother's eyes were suspiciously shiny as she gazed at Malia through a curl of smoke.

"There's rat poison in Regina William's bathroom," Malia blurted. "And all sorts of pills."

A long silence as Harry studied Malia. "When did you see that?"

"Last time I was over there." Malia looked down and rubbed her toe in a chip in the cement floor. "Camille was taking a shower, and her mother was out. I was . . . curious."

"Yeah, you love poking into people's private things." Harry narrowed her eyes. "You've always been curious."

"Well, I was rocked when I saw that poison. Remember that time Camille got so sick and they found that ingredient in her stomach? Her mother said she was trying to commit suicide, but Camille swore she didn't know how she could've eaten it—but ever since, I've noticed that she won't eat at home." Malia's voice rose, her words pouring out in a rush. "I think Camille's mom fed the poison to her! She does stuff to Camille to get her sick, and then she makes a drama about it, drags her to doctors, tries to make her ex pay more . . ."

"Could be Munchausen's," Harry turned to face the backyard, frowning. "That might fit. I'd have to have a lot more information."

"I can get information for you," Malia said. "And what's Munchausen's?"

"Nothing. Too soon. But when did you start wondering about Regina and Camille's relationship?"

"From when we started being friends. I never liked how Camille's mom was always trying to get her to do things to herself —beauty things."

"No crime in that."

"I know, but it's weird, right? All that working out and tanning and waxing? And never asking Camille if she wanted to or needed any of that. Then, the rat poison thing. I thought at the time that Ms. William was just milking it, making like Camille was all disturbed to get back at Camille's dad and make him pay for all the therapy and psychologists they brought in. But now, I think she did it to Camille herself. And maybe more stuff." Malia flung up her hands in frustration. "Ms. William is a weirdo, Mom. A freak show. Botox on a sixteen-year-old? And she's got Camille so brainwashed . . . Maybe Camille finally had enough." Malia sat down on an overturned bucket as tears filled her eyes. "I think Ms. William did something to Camille." Malia felt sick. The omission of how she'd come to her knowledge about Regina William rolled around in her gut, waiting for her to trip over it and land on her ass.

Harry put a hand on Malia's shoulder and squeezed, comforting her. "Well, now that Camille's disappearance is officially a case, I can't talk about it with you anymore, honey. But thanks for this information; I'll look into it. Keep me posted on anything more you hear around the community or at school. Now let's go in and clean up the mess your sister made in the kitchen, before she thinks we're the ones who ran off."

LATER THAT NIGHT, safely ensconced in her room, Malia typed in "Munchausen's" and then its subtitle, Munchausen's by proxy, on her laptop. On a medical site she found a paragraph that chilled her: *"Munchausen by proxy syndrome (MBPS): relatively rare form of child abuse that involves the exaggeration or fabrication of illnesses or symptoms by a primary caretaker. Also known as 'medical child abuse,' MBPS was named after Baron von Munchausen, an 18th-century German dignitary known for making up stories about his travels and experiences to get attention. 'By proxy' indicates that a parent or other adult is fabricating or exaggerating symptoms in a child, not in himself or herself."*

"That's it," Malia whispered. Could Regina William have accidentally gone too far with one of her "treatments" and killed Camille? Or, decided to put her in an institution or something, and pretended she ran away so she could get attention?

How could Malia explain the photos she'd taken in the house and share them with her mom? Maybe just push her mother to get a search warrant for the house . . . but what if Regina William hid the evidence by the time Harry searched it?

Malia checked the Wallflower burner phone. Sure enough, texts had come in—but nothing new on Camille. On the Wallflower site, reactions to Malia's "missing person" post about Camille were shocked, surprised, and questioning, but there were no new leads.

Malia was too upset about Camille to do more than glance at the attention her new graphic with Blake Lee as Cupid was getting, but she needed to keep things going on the website—she had her own reputation to maintain, such as it was. She was setting up a contest for nominations to go to prom with Blake when a chat window opened in her Messenger account.

"Hello, Wallflower."

Malia, lying on her belly on her bed, blinked in disbelief and read the message again.

The Messenger account currently open was in her own name, Malia Clark. She'd been hoping Camille would find a way to contact her. She had one for Wallflower business, too, but this wasn't that account.

"Who is this?" Malia typed back.

"More importantly, I know who the Wallflower is. And I'm going to tell everyone unless we can meet."

Blood roared in Malia's head. Her whole body went rigid and hot. *"What do you want?"*

"I want to talk with you about a missing person."

Malia froze.

What she should do was go tell her mom—and she couldn't, without revealing the existence of the Wallflower. She was too deep in deception to call for help, and things were spinning out of control.

"I've got nothing to say," she typed. *"I don't know what you're talking about."* Deny, deny, deny, her lawyer father had drilled into

her head. Never admit anything. That's how criminals got off. It was horrible that she felt like one.

"I've tracked your nasty little gossip site to your computer's IP address. You're the cyberbully known as the Wallflower, Malia Clark. Meet me or I'll turn you in to the cops and your school's administration."

The frozen feeling dissolved into panic.

Malia jumped off the bed, sweat breaking out all over her body.

She wanted to slam the laptop shut, but if she did, would this person get on the phone? Call the MPD and ask for her mom? Call her principal on the emergency after-hours school hotline?

"What is this about?" She typed again.

"I know where you live. Meet me in front of your house in half an hour."

"Holy crap!" Malia exclaimed, jumping up off the bed again.

"What?" Kylie yelled from her bedroom.

"Nothing. Just saw a spider," Malia yelled back.

Lying was getting easier, but it still didn't feel any better.

WHAT DID you wear to meet a blackmailer? Malia slid her feet into socks and put on a pair of clean jeans, pulling on her invisibility sweatshirt, and lifting the hood up over her head.

She did have one thing whoever-it-was wouldn't expect—*pepper spray.* Harry had given her a thumb-sized can of it on a keychain as a stocking stuffer. She felt bad remembering the eye roll she'd given her mom, the irritated comment about being "overprotective." If only she could walk to Mom's bedroom two doors down and tell her everything—but if she did, she'd be grounded for the rest of her life. Lose her laptop, phone, and any ability to help find Camille.

Malia stopped at her mom's doorway. Harry wore her comfy

bedtime sweats and was propped against pillows with Kylie and Doodlebug. They were eating more of that bagged popcorn and watching a movie. "I need to take a walk. I'm too upset about Camille."

"Oh honey. Worrying isn't going to speed anything up. Come get in bed with us." Harry patted the duvet beside her.

"I can't. But don't worry; I won't leave the area." That was the rule. Malia could walk around outside in the overgrown yard, howl at the moon if she wanted to—but she wasn't to walk far down the narrow road in the dark.

"Okay. I'll look for you in an hour or so if you're not back," Harry said.

Malia nodded, and plugged her ears with her earbuds. She trotted down the stairs, out the front door, and down the cement steps of the aging cedar dwelling built in the 1970s.

Velvety soft darkness enfolded her as she left the lights of the house. They lived on a little cul-de-sac in Waiehu, about ten miles to the north of her school, and their road was usually empty.

Malia didn't turn on the front porch light. Instead, she stood in the shadows on the side of the house, one hand curled around the pepper spray and the other around her phone. She thumbed it to the flashlight app. Maybe she could startle the blackmailer and turn the tables on him or her.

Once her eyes had adjusted to the darkness, Malia scanned for the sight of a car, or anyone around. Their house was semi-isolated, with trees growing in vacant lots on either side of it, and a cow pasture just across the street.

She walked lightly, on the balls of her feet, to the end of the driveway. A car rolled slowly toward her, only its running lights on. *Had to be the blackmailer.*

Malia drew back, squatting in the shadows beside the scraggly hibiscus hedge. Blackmailers were bullies. She had to show she wasn't going to be intimidated from the beginning, or the blackmailer would try to keep getting her to do whatever he or she wanted.

The car cut its lights and rolled to a spooky stop right at the end of her driveway—some sort of sedan, with nice, rounded lines, but Malia couldn't see what kind or make out the license plate. She waited a moment more and was rewarded for her patience—a window rolled down. The dim outline of someone in the driver's seat was visible; the guy was staring at her house.

Her heart thundering, Malia brought her phone up and ran to the open window in a burst of speed, hitting the button for the flashlight app just as she reached the car and bringing up the pepper spray, aimed at the driver. "Put up your hands!" She hissed as loudly as she dared. "I've got pepper spray on you!"

The glare of the flashlight app had blinded the blackmailer, just as she'd hoped—but it had also blinded *her.* Malia couldn't see a thing but the bright outline of a guy's hands, raised in a classic surrender gesture.

Fortunately, her eyes adjusted faster than the blackmailer's because the full glare wasn't in her eyes—but her shock at who she recognized made her almost drop the phone.

Blake Lee, Mr. Homecoming King, blinked at her, his hands in the air.

"You," she gasped.

"Nice move. You got the drop on me," he said.

Malia flicked off the flashlight. Both were plunged into welcome darkness. "How did you figure out it was me?"

"Tracked your IP address, like I said."

"That wouldn't work. There's a host server where the blog is stored, and software to disguise my IP. That can't be how you found out the website was mine."

"Does it matter? Get in the car. I don't like sitting where your mom can see us." Blake's voice hardened. Malia couldn't agree more about her mom seeing them not being a good thing, so she trotted around to the passenger side, opened the door, and got in.

Blake started the engine but didn't turn on the lights. They rolled silently down the narrow road until they reached a shoulder pullout.

"This is far enough." Malia could still hop out and run home in just a few minutes. "I need to know how you found out about me."

"Camille told me."

Malia's breath blew out in a whoosh, the knife of betrayal and abandonment twisting in her gut. "She wouldn't."

"Yes, she would. She told me it was you, and that she'd talk to you about all those posts about me you were putting up." His scowl was lit by the low dashboard light. "Instead, your posts just got worse. First the man-slut thing about prom, then that Cupid cartoon you put up—where do you get off treating people like that? What did I ever do to you?" His voice rose.

"I'm sorry," Malia stuttered, her cloak of anonymity stripped away. She squeezed the canister of pepper spray tightly. If only she could be beamed to another planet!

"I kept messaging Camille. I thought she was believing those rumors because she didn't answer. Finally, she sent me a message telling me she believed me, that I wasn't going out with three girls —and then *you!* You put that thing up about her missing! Why would you do that? I thought she was your best friend!" Blake's voice was a low roar of fury.

"Camille really is missing. That is the God's honest truth. Mom told me there's a missing person report filed by Ms. William and everything. I'm trying to find out what happened to her."

"Camille? She'd never run away."

"That's what I said. But it looks like she did." Malia bit her lips. She didn't really believe Camille had run away, but she wasn't about to tell Blake her dark theories. He was a threat, a serious problem. He knew the Wallflower's identity, and she had no idea how to handle it. Maybe an olive branch was a good start. "I apologize for the posts about you. I'll take down the Cupid thing. And the contest."

"What contest?"

"The contest to see who should go to the prom with you now that Jodie dumped you. They're nominating people."

"You're shittin' me." Blake's angry growl made her bring the pepper spray out of her pocket, but then he laughed, a sound with a harsh edge. "I've got to hand it to you, Malia, you know how to keep people tuning in to your crap. All those little videos and captions? Brilliant." He whacked the steering wheel. "I just wish it wasn't me you've had a target on for the last year or so."

"I'm an equal opportunity slanderer," Malia said.

"No. Hell, no. You've unfairly targeted me. Count the posts— my buddies and I have, and you've featured 'the latest on Blake' way more often than anybody else."

"You're clickbait." Malia fiddled with the pepper spray. "I said I was sorry."

"Because you're supposedly Camille's best friend, and she'd be upset if I turned you in, I won't—but that site has to die. Like, now. Today."

"Can we use the site to find Camille first? Let me show you something." Malia'd brought her burner phone, and she opened the screen. "Twenty-seven new text messages since I last checked, all responding to Camille missing. Someone could know where she is."

"Why wouldn't we be the ones to know where she is, since we're her best friends?" Blake's breath was warm on Malia's cheek as he turned to her.

Friends? Blake and Camille were a couple—he was certainly acting like they were.

Blake grabbed the phone out of her hand, clicked on the closest text. "'*Nomination of Shelly Okawa to go with Blake to prom.*' I bet this is twenty-six more stupid-ass votes." And in a movement faster than Malia could track, he hurled the phone out the window into the dark trees of the overgrown vacant lot.

"No!" Malia cried. "You don't know what you just did!"

"Phase one of Operation Wallflower Shutdown complete," Blake said.

Malia jumped out of the car. "I have to find that phone! I'm using it to help find Camille!"

"Whatever you need to tell yourself," Blake said, and drove off.

Malia trudged back to the house to find a flashlight. "Why didn't you tell me you liked Blake, Camille?" she muttered. "What other secrets were you hiding from me?"

There was no answer but the sound of wind in the java plum trees and the wail of a distant siren.

CHAPTER SEVEN

LEI FOLLOWED Detective Harry Clark up the driveway to a Mediterranean style mansion in the exclusive Valley View Estates development the next morning. Regina William, a well-maintained blonde somewhere between forty and sixty, wearing an ice-blue satin robe with fuzzy white mink slippers, stood in the entranceway. "It took you long enough to come to interview me," she snapped at Harry.

Harry didn't bat an eye. "Good to see you, too, Regina. MPD is not on your payroll."

Clearly there was no love lost between these two mothers of teenaged best friends. Regina made a growling noise but stood aside, ignoring Lei. "Come sit in the living room."

Lei entered behind Harry. She glanced around at lustrous wood and terra-cotta tile in the downstairs area; a shining staircase swooped up to a second level of the house. Harry took the lead and followed Ms. William into a sunken lounge area decorated in shades of cream, overlooking a stunning view of Iao Valley's sculpted green slopes.

"I don't believe I introduced Sergeant Leilani Texeira to you; she's heading up your daughter's missing person case," Harry said.

Regina nodded to Lei, her tone warming slightly. "Nice to meet you, Sergeant. Would you two like some coffee?"

"None for me, thank you." Lei sat down on an overstuffed suede couch.

"I'll take some, thanks, Regina," Harry said. "May I smoke?"

"Yes to coffee, no to smoking in my house," Regina said, and whisked out of the room into a separate kitchen area.

Harry turned to Lei. "Fancy place she's got. This is the first time I've been inside, though Malia practically lives here. According to my daughter, Regina did well in her divorce from Leonard William."

"I wouldn't mind seeing this view every day," Lei said.

Regina returned and handed Harry a porcelain cup of plain black coffee. "What is being done to find my daughter?" She aimed her question at Lei.

"First, we have some questions for you about the timeline of Camille's disappearance," Harry said. "Tell us about her day."

Lei let Harry take charge of the interview, curious to watch her friend at work.

They established when and where Camille had last been seen— at school before she drove herself home. Regina handed Harry a note in a creamy envelope. "This is definitely my daughter's hand-writing, though I can't emphasize enough that I don't believe she ran away."

"In cases like these, we usually look at parental kidnapping first," Harry said, after scanning the note and handing it to Lei. "Is there any possibility that Camille is with her father?"

"No. I've been in touch with him. Leonard works in shipping and lives at sea. He is terribly busy, and he and Camille have fallen out of touch. She hasn't seen him in ages, nor has she expressed any interest in doing so."

"Still, we'd like his contact information," Harry said.

"No problem." Regina smiled tightly and used her phone to forward them Leonard William's information.

"This might come as something of a surprise to you, Ms. William, but our next step is to search your house for any clues that your daughter may have left," Lei said. "We'd like your permission to go through her room, to begin with."

"I don't see the point. I told you all I know, and our maid cleaned recently. There's nothing much to see," Regina said.

"I'll go upstairs if you don't mind." Lei removed a pair of plastic gloves from her waist pack, shaking them out and snapping them on. She picked up her crime kit, which she had carried in and set beside the couch. "I assume your daughter's room is there."

"How dare you!" Regina burst out. "I came to the MPD asking for help, not to be suspected!"

Harry rolled her eyes. "Come on, Regina. Surely this isn't a surprise. It's protocol anytime there is a missing child. We look through the house for anything the parents might have overlooked."

"As if I would miss anything!"

Just then, a sculptural, clear plastic phone on the sideboard rang. Regina ran over and grabbed up the receiver.

Lei was already heading up the stairs as she overheard that the caller was Harry's daughter Malia. She reached the top of the stairs and cocked her head, overhearing Harry redirect her daughter that the case was not to be discussed, and end the call with a brusque goodbye.

Good. The last thing they needed was a sixteen-year-old wannabe sleuth poking her nose in where it didn't belong.

Lei headed for the first door, which led to an immaculate bedroom dressed in girlish peach satin, so tidy that it looked as if no one had ever lived there.

Joining Lei in the doorway of Camille's room, Harry sighed. "Malia is going nuts. She's so worried about her friend."

"I can imagine. I don't envy you right now."

"The only thing that's more challenging than a teenage

daughter is having two of them—and Kylie is eleven going on sixteen."

Lei headed for the laptop and a bejeweled phone plugged in on the desk. "Let's take Camille's devices back to our tech department and see what's on them." She dropped the items into a large evidence bag, including the charge cords so that the devices wouldn't go dead before their team had a chance to unlock them. "Does it strike you as odd that Camille supposedly ran away, but left these here?"

"Sure does. Malia would rather cut off a finger than leave her phone behind." A line appeared between Harry's brows. "Maybe something *did* happen to Camille."

"We know she came home and wrote that note. Maybe she knew she could be tracked if she took her phone. She could have a burner," Lei said.

The frown on Harry's brow smoothed out. "That makes sense."

The two women searched through the desk and bureau, but there wasn't anything of interest until Harry pushed aside rows of color-coordinated designer clothing peppered with empty hangers to reveal a stash of hoodies, jeans, and Converse sneakers way in the back of the closet.

"Now I'm starting to get worried." Harry pointed to the clothing. "Every time I ever saw Camille, she was wearing these types of clothes, not the ones up front."

Regina's voice came from the front of the bedroom, making both women turn around. "What are you talking about? Camille left for school every day wearing one of her special outfits." Regina marched over to show them a laminated chart hanging from a hook on the door of the closet. "Each weekday she could choose from different sets of clothing out of her seasonal choices. See? She checked which outfit she had worn so there weren't too many repeats. She had an image to maintain."

Harry exchanged a glance with Lei—*Regina William was a control freak on steroids!* Even baby Rosie showed too much independence to allow Lei to pick out her clothing, let alone use a chart to keep track of it.

"I know this is hard, Regina, but it might go easier if you let us do our job," Harry said. "Maybe you could assemble a list of friends for us to follow up with."

The blank look on Regina's face told Lei she had no idea who, besides Malia, her daughter might be friends with. Embarrassment tightened Regina's mouth. "I'm calling my attorney."

"I would expect no less," Harry spoke to her back as the woman departed in a huff. Harry turned back to Lei. "Let's go look in Regina's room. Malia expressed some concerns about it."

Lei's brows lifted in surprise. "What do you mean?"

Harry shook her head. "My girl is a lot of good things, but she's way too interested in other people's business. Malia snooped through Regina's cabinets and was freaked out about some stuff she found. I'm hoping Regina hasn't removed the items she told me about."

Harry headed for Regina's suite with Lei in her wake.

Inside the sumptuous bathroom off the bedroom, Lei took pictures of the many kinds of medications revealed inside the cabinet and drawers.

Harry opened a cupboard beneath the sink, pointing to an empty space right in front. "Malia said there was a box of rat poison here. Some time ago, Camille was hospitalized after a poisoning incident that Regina claimed was self-inflicted. She sent Camille to all sorts of experts for treatment and evaluation, but both Camille and Malia maintain that Camille would never have made a suicidal gesture. Malia thinks that Regina, for some reason, is doing harm to her daughter, maybe to gouge her ex-husband, maybe for some other reason."

The hair rose on the back of Lei's neck as she looked around the luxurious, well-appointed bathroom with its many beautification devices, unguents, potions and concoctions. "That closet of Camille's gave me chicken skin."

"Something stinks around here," Harry agreed. Her amber-brown eyes narrowed. "I don't like Regina William. I think she knows more than she's telling us. Let's bring her in."

"Excellent idea," Lei said. "I can't wait to be bad cop." She smiled, and it wasn't a nice smile. "Let's find that rat poison."

They searched the house, garage, and grounds. The yellow box of rat poison Malia had described was gone.

⁂

REGINA WILLIAM STALLED the interview down at the station until she was able to appear with her lawyer, Keoni Chapman.

Lei heaved an internal sigh at the sight of the man, someone she had dealt with before on other cases. Chapman wore a light-weight linen suit and had sprayed down his blond combover; he was a perfect match for Regina, who wore a cream-colored sheath dress with a necklace of large, shiny gold links. She looked as out of place in the grubby, utilitarian Kahului police station as an exotic white cockatoo.

Harry gestured for Regina and her lawyer to follow them. "I've got us booked into Interview Room Number Two," she said to Lei.

Lei nodded and brought up the rear, following the pair inside the bare room with its bolted-down steel table and chairs. Regina dusted her seat before tentatively perching on the edge of it, as if the heavy steel was a branch that would break beneath her weight. She took a sanitary tissue out of a plastic envelope in her bag and wiped down the table. "I just want to register, for the record, that I am highly offended by all of these proceedings."

Harry's smile was a mere twitch of her full lips. "Well then, we better get you on the record so we can get you out of this dump." She cast her eyes to Lei. "Would you like to do the honors? Or should I?"

"Why don't you, since you and Ms. William are already acquainted?"

Harry turned back to Regina and recited the Miranda warning. "Is there anything you don't understand about what I've told you?" Chapman placed a beefy hand on Regina's arm. "I have advised Ms. William to cooperate with these proceedings, however distasteful, since she has brought you the concern about her daughter. She understands she is not a suspect in any of this, and these things are just procedure."

"Absolutely," Harry said with a plastic smile.

Lei turned on the recording gear. Often interviewees were lulled into forgetting that the equipment even existed, hidden as it was in a small unobtrusive dome above the table.

"Why don't you tell us about the time that your daughter ingested rat poison," Lei said, baring her teeth in a smile.

Regina William's mouth fell open slightly; she stuttered. "Th-that was months ago. I don't remember . . ."

"How is this relevant to Camille William's disappearance?" The lawyer asked. "Please keep the questions relevant to the investigation at hand."

"The question is relevant in that it speaks to motivation for Camille running away," Harry said.

Regina fiddled with a gold bangle on her wrist. "My daughter has been emotionally unstable since my divorce from her father over a year ago. She has often been withdrawn. She has difficulty with friendships, choosing unsavory companionship."

Harry's brows drew together. "I hope you're not inferring anything about my daughter?"

"Oh, I would never!" Regina William's laughter was as brittle as broken glass. "But you have to admit that the girls are often secretive. I believe your daughter is responsible for the clothing choices hidden in the back of Camille's closet."

"You have not answered my question," Lei said, cutting off Harry's indignant rebuttal.

"Tell us more about this relationship with your daughter, Detective Clark," Chapman demanded.

"I'll ask the questions, counselor," Lei said. She turned to Regina. "Tell us about the rat poison."

Regina scowled. "Camille's developed an eating disorder. She dosed herself with the poison, probably as a cry for help or an attempt to lose weight, according to one of the psychologists who evaluated her. Camille denies that she did it at all."

Lei let that go for the moment. "Why don't you tell us more about this emotional instability."

"Well, Camille has been secretive, as I've said. She is overeating outside the home. I have had to restrict her caloric intake when she's at home. I hired a personal trainer to work with us; of course, I wouldn't expect my daughter to do anything that I wasn't willing to do as well." Regina preened a little, tossing her hair back. "I try to give Camille every advantage. That's why it's been so worrisome that she's put on weight."

Harry, typing notes on her laptop, snorted and rolled her eyes; Lei spared a glance at her friend, warning her to rein it in, then turned back to Regina. "I've seen pictures of your daughter. She looks entirely normal. I also have her physical statistics here in her file. Her weight is below average for her height."

"Oh, that!" Once again, that jagged tinkle of sound. "We all know that those health charts are skewed to the average of this country, which is edging into obesity."

Lei frowned, leaning forward with her fingertips together. "So, your daughter had put on some weight. She was hanging out with 'unsavory companions.' What else leads you to think she has run away?"

"The note she left, of course," Regina William frowned. "Must I do your job for you?"

Harry looked up to spear Regina William with amber-brown eyes. "Malia does not believe that Camille ran away. She thinks something else has happened to her, and that you might have had a hand in it."

Regina William firmed her chin. "No one means my daughter harm, least of all myself."

"Why would she run away if she was so happy?" Lei slid the knife in deliberately. "And according to you, she poisoned herself. That is not the act of a happy child."

Regina William flushed. "Are you inferring that I'm a bad mother?"

"I'll let you draw your own conclusions," Harry drawled.

Chapman addressed Lei. "My client takes offense at this line of questioning."

Lei made eye contact with Regina William deliberately. "If you know anything more that will help us find your daughter, now is the time to share. Camille could be in danger related to another case we're investigating. We need to locate her ASAP."

Regina frowned. "What case is that?"

"The FBI will be coming out with a public announcement about the disappearance of young female runaways throughout the islands," Lei said. "Watch for it in the news. I'm giving you this information a little bit ahead of time."

Harry swiveled her laptop screen to show Regina a teen gossip site. *"Where is Camille? Stop the bickering and help find her!"* A headline screamed. Harry pointed to it. "I've been monitoring this site that shares teen gossip collected at Paradise Prep School. Even the cyberbullies who run the site are trying to find her, and that's a good thing, too, because someone seems to be disappearing our island's runaway teen girls."

Regina seized the laptop and scanned the site, entitled Wall-flower Diaries. "Who do you suspect is behind this?"

"The student gossip?"

"No, the disappearances!"

"We think it's likely human traffickers. Terrible as that is, it's better than the alternative, which would be a statewide serial killer," Lei said.

Regina gasped and covered her mouth with a hand. She turned to Chapman. "I have to tell them."

Chapman patted her arm and leaned forward to whisper in her ear.

Regina faced Lei. "I feel terrible. I have to tell you something."

"My client has been under duress," Chapman said. "She wanted to handle the situation privately, but things have escalated in the public eye."

"Tell us," Harry rapped out.

"Camille didn't really run away." Regina sniffed into a tissue.

"I knew it!" Harry exclaimed.

"Why did you lie?" Lei asked. "What happened to her?"

"My client has been confused," Chapman said. "She's been put in a difficult position by all of this."

A slow burn had begun under Lei's sternum; had this pampered woman been yanking their chain with her supposed parental concern?

"I've been stressed, it's true. I'm a single mother of a teenage daughter, and I've just been through a terrible divorce while trying to save a troubled business," Regina said. "Camille did write the note, but not for the reasons I told you."

"Cut to the chase already, Regina," Harry snapped.

Lei leaned in, trying to seem sympathetic. "Please. Tell us what's really going on."

"Well, I . . . I sent Camille to a weight loss program. I told you I was concerned about her weight gain. Her father and I decided that it would be in her best interest to go away for a while. Get therapy and a handle on her eating."

"What!" Harry shoved back from the table so violently that her chair fell over, making Regina and Chapman jump. "You've wasted our time with all of this drama! What possible reason could you have for these lies?"

Regina turned to Lei, ignoring Harry. "Here's information about the program." She reached into a designer handbag, pulling out a brochure and sliding it across the table to Lei. "I had my reasons for claiming that Camille ran away, and if you hadn't escalated the situation by dragging me down here to the station, I wouldn't have been forced into subterfuge."

"You have wasted Maui Police Department's time and resources," Lei said. "We will be issuing you a citation to that effect."

Chapman, feeling a need to earn his keep, piped up at that. "You can expect a formal repudiation of any such attempt."

Harry scanned the brochure. "We will want confirmation from the program about her attendance there."

"You are welcome to call Camp Willowslim, but with HIPAA protections they won't tell you if she's there or not . . . and you have my word that that's where Camille is." Regina William blinked imaginary tears and dabbed her eyes with a tissue. "She's on a nine-day backpacking trip with no cell phones allowed; she can't be reached except in an emergency." She balled the tissue. "You just don't understand how difficult all of this has been. Choosing to send your daughter to a program like this takes courage. Camille didn't want to go. She wrote the note herself, trying to run away before it was time to leave for the program, but her father and I are committed to doing what's best for her. In the end, she agreed."

"I'm sure that's what you tell yourselves." Harry snapped.

Lei stood up, leaning forward on her knuckles into Regina's space. "You've wasted our time today when it could have been spent searching for girls who really are missing." She tried to get eye contact with Regina, but the woman had lowered her head, sniffing noisily into a handful of tissues.

"My client is clearly distraught, and I'll appeal any fines you try to levy against her," Chapman said.

Harry sat back, glaring, as Lei turned off the recording equipment.

Lei stared thoughtfully after Regina William and Keoni

Chapman as they departed, Regina leaning heavily on the lawyer. She frowned as the door shut behind them. "Something's off there."

Harry stared down at the brochure in her hand, then crumpled it. "You're not the only one who thinks that—but we seem to have hit a dead end."

"I wish all the girls we're looking for had such problems." Lei indicated the Camp Willowslim pamphlet. "But I'm pretty sure dieting is the least of their worries."

CHAPTER EIGHT

MALIA WAS CLIPPING the hibiscus hedge late that afternoon after mowing the yard, when Harry pulled up. "Wow! To what do we owe the pleasure?" Her mom grinned, clearly impressed with the yard work Malia had done.

"Just working off my worry."

"Good way to handle that." Harry strode up the steps and into the house. "Thanks again! The yard looks great."

Malia finished, even raking up the cuttings and bagging them. Guilt over her lies was only slightly assuaged by the extra chores.

Harry was in the kitchen; her mother had arranged tonight's chicken thighs in a square glass pan and poured barbeque sauce over them. She was in the act of putting the plastic-covered pan in the microwave. "Hi, honey. Thought I'd give these a jump start in the microwave—I'm hungry. Hey, you must be hungry too. Doing the yard was a big job." Her mom's gorgeous smile had always lit up a room, transforming her face from striking to beautiful. She put her wrist on Malia's forehead, teasing. "You feeling all right?"

"Fine, Mom. Just worried about Camille, like I said." Malia poured herself a glass of water and gulped it. "Did you find out anything new?"

"You already know that Lei and I were at the William house, and searched it. I came home for dinner but I'm going back to work after this. I do have some news, but I can't tell you until I check with my superior on the case."

Malia squelched her disappointment. "I started asking around at school. Got some info." She unfolded a paper with the notes she'd made from the burner phone, which she'd been able to retrieve from where Blake had pitched it. "Someone said they saw Camille in the Lahaina area in the back of a blue car. Two guys in the car with her."

Harry grabbed the paper. "What's all this? Names, numbers?"

Malia blushed, snatching the paper back. "A little poll on who should go to prom with a popular guy. Nothing interesting." She told her mom the other tips they had, as outrageous as they were.

"Malia, please don't take this any further. We have it handled." Harry pulled Malia in for a side hug. "But man, you'd make a good detective yourself someday."

Malia's chest went tight with a potent cocktail of stress at all the lies and happiness at her mom's praise. Maybe it was time for her to come clean with her mom about Wallflower Diaries, and for the site to end—*but what if it could still be useful in finding Camille?*

Just then her sister bounced in and hugged their mother. "You're home early, Mom!"

Malia turned away and filled the rice cooker as the two went into the dining area to check Kylie's homework. Malia moved the half-done chicken to the oven, filled a pan with frozen vegetables and set it on the stove, then ran upstairs.

She turned on her laptop and while it booted up, she checked the burner phone. Sure enough, more text messages had collected, most of them wanting to know when Wallflower Diaries would be back online and who had won the Blake Lee Prom Date Contest.

She logged into the Wallflower Diaries site and put up another "missing person" bulletin with the caption: *"This site now exists to help find Camille William. It's been over 48 hours, and authorities are no closer to finding her. We've had some great intel from you so far—text your tips to Wal-flwr!"*

Sitting there, staring at the Publish button, Malia struggled with temptation to update the Cupid post with the clear winner that the student body had chosen as Blake's date to prom: Shelly Okawa, a petite, pretty girl whose elfin beauty would complement Blake's bold good looks.

But he'd hate the post, and hate Malia even more, and the site would be over for sure.

Malia exited the program and shut the laptop.

IT FELT good to stretch her legs as Lei walked rapidly down the long, paved jetty alongside the shipping transport storage area at the Kahului Harbor. Harry had joined her there after an early dinner with her daughters.

Frustration from the interview with Regina William felt like residual tightness in her muscles, and Lei swung her arms as she strode, by habit able to miss her sidearm on one hip and her radio and badge on the other.

Harry, beside her, moved just as quickly. "I've never had occasion to work with the Coast Guard before."

"Well, we don't know for sure that the girls who are disappearing are being shipped out, but it seems like the most logical way for the kidnappers to get them off the island," Lei said. "About two years ago, we had a case involving human traffickers and pirates. The pirates were opportunistic about that aspect of the case, in the sense that they sold off victims that they captured during their raids on luxury vessels. They stored the women in a modified container here at the docks. Since I don't have any other leads at the moment, I thought we could come down and take a look around. Special Agent Aina Thomas, who's meeting us, has been helpful in several cases, and the Coast Guard can open doors for us around boats and shipping that we would not be able to open by ourselves."

"Makes sense," Harry said.

Lei slanted her friend a glance as the wind off the harbor caught their hair and tossed it around. She was glad she was wearing hers in a ponytail with a ball cap. "Do you ever see Cruz? The man you trained with?"

Harry smiled. "Not in many years. As far as I know, he is still living in Mexico. He has his own training school. He lives like a king for a fraction of the cost down there."

"We should catch up on that old history sometime. I would love to hear your story. I thought of you both often after we met in Cabo San Lucas," Lei said.

"I thought of you too," Harry said. "But really, there's not much to tell. After I was done training with Cruz, I worked with his agency in private security paramilitary operations for a while. Then I met my husband . . . or, I should say, my ex-husband. He lived in Hawaii, and I felt it was time to return to my roots, so we settled on Oahu to raise Malia. I applied to the police academy there, probably just a year or two after you began on the Big Island." Harry gripped the bill of her hat against a gust of wind. "Hey—is it okay if I tell Malia about Camille being at Camp Willowslim? She's really taking Camille's disappearance hard and was asking around for clues about Camille at school today."

"Of course, you should tell her." Lei glanced at her friend. "If you really think that's where the girl is."

"I think we have to accept Regina's story, for the moment," Harry said. "Much as it gags me to do so. That woman is a piece of work."

They'd reached a small guard booth; they showed their identifications to the attendant. "We will be walking through the containers with an investigator from the Coast Guard," Lei said. "We'll let you know if we need anything opened."

The attendant was still verifying the procedural aspects with the storage area manager when Special Agent Aina Thomas rolled up in a Coast Guard truck. The women had to park their private vehicles outside the dock area, but Agent Thomas had the gate opened for his official vehicle. He grinned down at them with that flashing smile that Lei had always had a soft spot for. "I see you have someone new for me to meet today," Agent Thomas said, getting out of his ride.

Lei grinned as Harry checked out the handsome Guardsman from stem to stern in his sharply pressed uniform while she made the introductions. "As I told you on the phone, we want to walk through the container storage area and look for any shipping cartons here that might have any of the same kind of adaptations that were made to a container to hold the women in the pirate case."

"We're on the same page," Agent Thomas agreed. "Let's do it."

After the attendant unlocked the gate, the trio walked between the high steel stacks of shipping containers. They scanned for ventilation square irregularities, an air conditioning unit, ducting, or any other modifications that could indicate that the container was being used for human transport.

Agent Thomas and Harry walked ahead of her, chatting, and getting to know each other as Lei brought up the rear, traversing the aisles of huge metal boxes. The evening wind that cooled the harbor area was stifled by the tall metal walls. As Lei scanned them, she mulled over the pirate case and the rapidly escalating hostage situation that had culminated into a standoff between the human traffickers and rescue operatives, including her husband Stevens. That confrontation had been dangerous, most of all for the women and girls held hostage in a stifling steel box on a hot day.

Lei wasn't sure if she felt relieved or frustrated when the three of them finished searching the entire area but found no sign of any modified containers.

Agent Thomas turned to face Lei, standing in the shadow of

one of the stacks. "Might this situation be the same operation that was never completely shut down after the pirate attacks?" He had played a key role in the resolution of that case.

"We don't know. The FBI is working with us on disappearances of runaway teen girls throughout the islands. Our best speculation is that they are being held somewhere, then periodically moved out to other destinations. Perhaps that case spooked this ring of operators, because things went really quiet for a while," Lei said. "But I thought it was worth a walk-through and getting you on board to keep an eye out for anything odd going out of the docks. It seems like it would be easier to ship live cargo than fly them out."

Agent Thomas cocked a brow. "Are you sure about that? There's a very busy private airstrip operating right alongside the commercial one in Kahului. They could as easily be moved off this island in a plane. Maybe the operators changed it up after that case brought so much scrutiny."

"You have a point." Lei moved out of the shade of the container with Harry in her wake. "We'll check out the airport and see if we can get a handle on that. In the meantime, give us both your cell number in case we need to make contact."

Lei already had his number but stifled a smirk as Agent Thomas eagerly texted Harry his contact info.

Lei wasn't above playing matchmaker; happily married herself, it was nice to see good friends fall in love too.

CHAPTER NINE

MALIA HEARD her mom opening the front door, then Harry's voice called, "Girls! I'm home!" Harry came upstairs as she usually did first thing, to lock up her gun and badge. "Malia! I've got news for you!"

Malia's pulse quickened as she hurried out of her room. She banged into Kylie in the hall outside Harry's bedroom door, and they both went inside.

"If it's about Camille, I'd like to speak to you without Elephant Ears here," Malia said, indicating her little sister with her chin.

"I have a right to hear what's going on," Kylie pouted. "I care about Camille too."

"Girls. Bickering already?" Harry was bent over, spinning the dial on her safe.

"We seem to bicker less when you aren't here," Kylie observed, as Harry put the police issue Glock .40 and her creds wallet into the safe and spun the dial.

"Well, I guess there's an upshot to me being gone a lot, then." Harry's smile was a little sad as she turned to face them. "Sit a minute while I tell you the latest."

Kylie threw herself onto the bedspread, kicking her feet, and Malia sat cross-legged beside her.

Harry gazed directly at Malia. "Camille's been found."

"What!" Malia clapped her hands to her cheeks. "Where?"

"We brought Regina in for questioning. Really got into it with her, and finally she broke and admitted she sent Camille to a weight loss camp."

"No!" Malia bounced up off the bed. "That doesn't make sense! Why would her mom pretend she ran away?"

"Regina says she thought it was better than saying she basically kidnapped her own daughter and sent her to a fat farm by force." Harry massaged the bridge of her nose, frowning. "Regina says she hadn't realized how seriously people would take it, how resources would be allocated to find Camille, and that so many in the community would be looking for her. The principal of your school even called me today with a link to a school gossip website that's dedicated just to finding Camille."

Malia gasped involuntarily. "Wow," she said faintly.

"Yeah. Regina finally cracked when I showed her a post on the Wallflower Diaries site. The blogger was passionate about putting aside student pettiness and finding Camille. Regina finally told us how she'd sent Camille away to get in shape and 'away from negative influences.'" Her mom gazed at Malia. "I knew she was talking about you when she said that, though she didn't come right out and admit it."

"Ms. William has never liked me." Malia's cheeks burned with hurt and anger as she paced. "I want to speak to Camille myself! I can't imagine what Camille's mom did to get her to agree to go, and not even say goodbye!"

"Apparently, Camille's on a nine-day backpacking and workout hike in the wilderness with no cell phone. There's no way to communicate with her, unless the staff person initiates it in an emergency. Regina wouldn't say what she did to get Camille to go."

Malia frowned, folding her arms. "Do you believe her? Is the case over?"

"Well, honey, thankfully Camille's case is over. Regina showed us a pamphlet for the camp." Harry dug in her purse, set down beside the safe. "I made a copy of it for you."

Malia snatched the photocopied brochure out of her mother's hand.

A snow-capped peak and pine trees overlooked a lake with a canoe filled with girls paddling on the front. '*Camp Willowslim: Where Young Women Go to Pare Down to the Essentials,*' declared the brochure.

"Is there any proof Camille is really there?" Malia asked.

"Malia." Harry reached out to tip Malia's chin up until she was forced to meet her mother's penetrating brown eyes. "Regina William came in with her lawyer. She faced major humiliation recanting her story. We fined her, too, for filing a false missing person report. She's Camille's mother, and she's the one who's responsible for her. Not you."

Malia tightened her jaw and jerked her chin away, setting her mouth mutinously.

"I know you are having trouble accepting this, honey, but consider the alternative. The other girls who are missing are facing a much more terrible experience than a diet camp," Harry said.

"I just don't believe anything Ms. William says, Mom!" Malia hurried out and went into her room, slamming the door.

She threw herself on her bed, holding the brochure, and flipped it over. What would have been the back of the brochure was a second photocopied sheet, describing the various programs the camp offered, including 'Wilderness Extreme,' with its nine-day backpacking hell.

They probably hiked all day and ate nothing but chia seeds and prunes the whole time. Malia could imagine herself trudging along a forest trail carrying forty pounds of rocks to lose weight, but Camille would totally hate it. *"All campers are provided with nutritional education and behavioral counseling to develop new habits,"* trumpeted the brochure. *"Social skills and etiquette are also taught. Your daughter will never be the same!"*

"Oh Camille. How could she do that to you?" Malia whispered. She reached over and booted up her laptop's search engine and typed in the camp's title, locating it in southern Idaho.

Her mind ticked over the steps that had to happen: Regina William must have ambushed Camille after school, and then hustled her off on a plane, leaving even her phone behind. But how could she have forced her to go all that way alone?

Malia clicked around on the site and found a drop-down menu: 'Special Circumstances: *"If your daughter is unwilling to attend, a chaperone can be provided to accompany her to camp and ensure compliance with the program."*

Regina William probably had one of these "chaperones" frog-march Camille to the camp!

At least, Malia could call the camp and check if Camille was really there.

Malia found the *Contact Us* information and dialed, but of course with the time zone differences, it was much later in Idaho. A recording came on telling her to call back during business hours.

Malia hopped up and ran down the stairs to where her mom and Kylie were in the kitchen, prepping food for the next day. "I know you want this case to be over, Mom, but I just don't believe that's where Camille is. Isn't that camp a form of child abuse? It seems abusive."

"I personally think it's wrong, and girls, obviously I'd never do something like that to you—but Regina is legally able to put her daughter in a program that she thinks will benefit her, even if Camille isn't willing."

Malia drooped against the kitchen counter. "It's just so wrong that Ms. William did this—and I know she has been abusing Camille. What about the rat poison?"

"Malia." Harry turned fully toward her; the knife raised. The full brunt of her mother's level, searing eye gaze made Malia want to look away, even step backwards. *This must be how perps felt when Harry had them in her sights.* "I looked into all your concerns. There's no proof of abuse. I even tried to subpoena Camille's medical records, but the judge wouldn't sign off on it without more probable cause. If it's any consolation, I did pass your concerns on to Child Welfare Services. They may do their own investigation on Regina, but I doubt it. Without bruises and blood, there's no case." Harry brought the butcher knife down so hard that celery flew through the air. Malia and Kylie jumped.

Clearly, Harry was frustrated too.

Malia headed back upstairs. She wouldn't give up on finding her friend until she heard from Camille herself that she was okay.

Her mom's Maui Police Department laptop sat outside the bedroom door in its black case—Harry usually took the laptop out of the case and locked it up with the gun, but she must have been distracted and had forgotten to do so.

Malia grabbed the laptop and slipped into her own room, closing and locking the door. Removing the slim silver laptop, Malia's pulse beat in her temples in heavy thumps. It was one thing to cut school and sneak into her friend's house snooping—but getting into her mom's work laptop was probably an actual jail time offense.

Well, Harry had accepted Regina William's lies because she had to. Malia couldn't. *Wouldn't.* And to hell with what came after. Looking at the police file, she'd be able to see where Camille's dad was, and maybe even contact him. If anyone could get Camille out of purgatory in Idaho, it was Camille's scary dad, Leonard William.

Malia could picture Mr. William clearly. She'd seen photos of him at the helm of his yacht, every inch the intimidating tycoon captain: a square-jawed, dark-haired older man with wings of silver above his ears, a cigar clenched in his teeth, and eyes squinted into the wind.

Leonard William wouldn't put up with his daughter being anywhere she didn't want to be.

The MPD logo filled the laptop's screen with its little security code login. Malia knew most of Harry's favorite codes and systematically entered each of them: birthdates and pet dogs' names from the past. The cursor turned red, repulsing her efforts over and over.

Sweat gathered under her arms as Malia listened to the muffled conversation and a burst of giggles from the kitchen below—there was no telling how long she'd have before they called her down to dinner.

Malia put her head down and considered. What was something her mother knew by heart, something she'd never forget, something obscure, not well known?

The wedding anniversary date of when she'd married the man who'd left her.

Her parents had been married on June 9, fifteen years ago. Malia counted back and entered the date in two-digit combinations and pressed Enter.

She froze as the computer spiraled open to an unfamiliar desktop arrangement.

Even in the "Open Sesame" moment of overwhelm as the computer gave up its secrets, a sliver of sorrow pierced Malia's heart: that anniversary date still meant something to Harry—enough to type it over and over throughout the day.

Malia forced herself to focus, finding an icon in the corner of the welcome screen marked *My Cases*.

She clicked on it.

The icon opened into a window with file folders in neat rows of numbers and initials.

Nervous sweat spread from under her arms to along her spine as she scrolled through the folders, finally clicking on the one with the initials "R & CW."

The file opened into a form, completed by Regina William, and then pictures of the note, the pill bottles, and something else Malia hadn't found on her trip through the house, or any of the other times she'd been there—a secret "safe room." She frowned at the sight of screwed-in metal loops in the wall, then saw the caption her mother had labeled it with: *"Soundproof hidden safe room. Metal restraints used for S&M sex, per Regina William."*

"Gross!" Malia exclaimed, and clapped her hand over her mouth. "I could have happily lived my whole life without knowing that," she murmured as she went back to the original missing person report. She scrolled through the "Contacts" section until she found Leonard William's cell phone number and e-mail address and hastily forwarded the info into her own contacts. She closed the files, getting up to scramble toward the door as she powered down the laptop, stopping to grab a tissue and polish her fingerprints off the keyboard before slipping the laptop back into its case.

"We made some dessert!" Kylie hollered up the stairs.

"Coming!" Malia took a moment in the bathroom, splashing water on her face and washing her hands. Her wide brown eyes stared at her from the mirror: curving brows that made her look surprised all the time, olive-brown skin, a mouth too full and dark for lipstick, chocolate-brown hair springing up from her forehead and tangling down her back.

She didn't look like the kind of girl who'd break into a house and hack a police officer's computer.

A wave of fright washed over her; Malia felt the urge to puke, the toilet so handy nearby—but she'd at least found Leonard William's contact information.

Now she had to call Blake to talk over next steps. That thought was enough to make her slap more water on her cheeks. "You sick bitch," Malia said aloud. "He's Camille's boyfriend. He's totally not into you."

"Malia!" Harry called. Malia turned away from her schizophrenic moment to trot downstairs.

"Just so you know, I called the fat camp," Malia said at one point during dessert, forking up a bite of pie. "They were closed."

"I did, too." Harry said. "They have a confidentiality policy. Without a subpoena, they can neither confirm nor deny that Camille's a client there. And again, I didn't have enough proof of wrongdoing to get one issued. Believe me, Malia, I took this seriously."

"I know, Mom." Guilt twisted her stomach. "I'm sorry. I'm not hungry." She got up and carried her plate to the sink, and Harry didn't stop her.

Malia glanced at the wall clock in her room; it was 8:00 p.m., still early enough to call Leonard William.

CAMILLE'S FATHER had a deep voice with sandpaper in it. "Yes? Who is this?"

"Hi, Mr. William. This is Malia Clark, your daughter's best friend." Malia imagined the man shifting the cigar to the other side of his mouth, squinting keen blue eyes in annoyance as he dealt with this intrusion.

"How did you get this number?"

"Camille gave it to me." Malia crossed her fingers behind her back. "Before she was sent to an abusive fat farm to lose weight. Her mother sent her there, and I'm hoping you can help me get her out."

A short, charged silence. "Who is this, again? Malia who?"

"Malia Clark. I'm calling about Camille. I think she's been sent to a fat camp against her will by your ex-wife. Maybe you can help her." Malia's voice trembled. "I know she'd want to come home if she could."

A sudden bark of laughter, so harsh that Malia moved the phone away from her ear. "I know all about that camp. Won't hurt Camille a bit to toughen up, lose a few pounds."

Malia's stomach hollowed with disappointment. This had been her last hope to bring Camille home. "I don't agree, Mr. William."

"We're her parents, young lady." Mr. William's voice warmed slightly. "But I'm impressed that you care that much about Camille. She's lucky to have a friend like you."

"Yeah, well. I just thought it was worth a try, because I know how miserable she would be there." Malia shut her eyes against the prickle of tears.

"Camp Willow-something, right? Regina's having me foot the bill. We'll see her soon enough, and I'm sure she'll be fine until then," Mr. William said heartily.

"Thanks, Mr. William, for not being offended that I called you."

"No problem. You're a very enterprising young lady," he boomed.

Malia ended the call. She was so depressed that she got out of bed and went to her mother's room. "I came for a snuggle."

Harry opened her arms with a welcoming smile. Kylie joined them. Malia fell asleep, squished in the middle, as the three of them watched TV.

⁂

HARRY SHOOK HER SHOULDER. "Time to get up, Malia." Somehow, she'd migrated down near the foot of her mom's king-sized bed.

"Sorry, I didn't mean to camp out here." She sat up groggily.

"It's fine. Reminds me of when you were little girls. Remember the puppy pile?" Harry's mouth pulled down with old sorrow. Deep creases Malia hadn't noticed before had gathered around her mom's eyes. *Damn Dad.* Mom was still not over him.

'Puppy pile' was a game they'd played on Mom's day off. The girls would run and jump on their parents' bed for hugging and tickles in the mornings. As they got older, Malia would sneak down and start coffee and bring Mom and Dad each a mug after Kylie woke them up by cannonballing into the middle of the bed.

"Thanks for letting me sleep." Malia patted her mom's shoulder. She got out of bed and went straight to the bathroom, hopping in the shower to wash her hair and get a few extra minutes to blow dry it halfway—fully dry took so long it was out of the question. She braided it in two tails that hung over her shoulders, dampening the turquoise-colored scoop neck shirt she chose. She wriggled into flattering jeans Camille had bought her for her birthday.

"I'm gonna wear these jeans until you come home, Camille," Malia said aloud. She pulled her camouflage sweatshirt on over the whole ensemble and snatched up her trademark ball cap.

Today was Friday, and the weekend loomed without a plan to find her friend or the blog to update. Nothing to do but get through the day.

Mom had gotten Kylie moving too, so her little sister was ready at the front door on time as Malia unhooked their backpacks and handed her sister hers. "Bye, Mom!" she called up the stairs, but Harry was already in the shower.

Stepping outside into a cool morning filled with the chatter of mynah birds and the cooing of doves on the roof, Malia stiffened with shock. Blake's Mercedes was parked in their driveway, and he opened the passenger door and stood out from it.

"Your chariot awaits, milady," he said, with a flourish.

Kylie giggled. "Thanks." Her little sister scampered to the car. "Don't mind if I do. You can take that smelly old school bus, Malia."

"Someone has to call the bus not to come by," Malia protested.

"So, call," Blake said. Just then the bus pulled up at the end of the driveway, and Malia waved it away. Yeah, they would send a complaint note later, but she'd probably be able to intercept it. The bus pulled away, and Malia advanced. "Kylie. In back."

"I got here first."

"Seriously? Airbags. Back seat."

"I'm eleven, and you're the same height as me," Kylie sulked, but slithered into the back.

Malia slid into the buttery leather passenger seat, and Blake glanced down at her. "Guess she's right. You are short."

"Shut up."

"No good deed goes unpunished." He shut the door, then trotted around to the driver's side and started the car. "I see you're back in stealth mode." He gave a nod toward her braids, hat, and big sweatshirt.

Malia ignored that. "Big news, Blake. I have to put an announcement on the blog about Camille. She's been sent to Camp Willowslim in Idaho by her parents, supposedly."

"What?" Blake hit the brakes. "You found Camille?"

"I just found out the story her mom told the police." Malia filled him in on what Harry had told her as he got the car moving again. "And I called her dad to check."

"What did Mr. William say?"

"He confirmed she was at the camp and shut me down."

Blake cursed, then shot Kylie a glance in the rearview mirror. "Sorry, Kylie."

"I've heard worse," Kylie said, clearly enjoying her position leaning in between their seats. "Why don't you believe Mom and Ms. William, Malia?"

"I'm having a hard time believing that Camille could be taken so far away, legally, by force—and not find some way to communicate. I've left my chat window open constantly; I'm always checking for text messages . . . I'll let it go once I know she's really there, and that she's okay."

Blake reached over to give her leg a pat and stopped, his hand doing an awkward movement back onto the steering wheel.

"You guys going out? Cuz that would be something to post on the blog," Kylie said. Clearly, she'd seen his gesture.

"No," they both said, and Malia glanced at Blake. "Glad we're in agreement on that."

Blake flicked his gaze to Kylie via the rearview mirror, and

Malia thought he might have winked. Kylie removed herself to the back seat, smirking.

At school, they parked in the upperclassmen student lot. Kylie made a big production of leaving, pretending to lose something, digging under the seat and procrastinating. Finally, Malia barked, "Get lost! We're talking here!"

"Well. Maybe you're going out after all." Kylie gave a sassy grin and trotted off.

"What did Leonard William say, exactly?" Blake asked. He seemed to have inched a bit closer toward her; in fact, he was definitely closer. His eyes were so dark, and those eyelashes were totally wasted on a guy . . .

Malia jerked back and turned away. "Oh. Mr. William. Yeah. He said Camille was at the camp with his permission. Said he was footing the bill, and that it wouldn't hurt her to, quote, 'toughen up and lose a few pounds.' A mean old man. I was glad he wasn't pissed at me for calling."

"Too bad." Blake was back in his own seat; it must have been her imagination that he'd been halfway into hers. He flexed his hands on the steering wheel. "That's it then."

"I guess it is. I'm out of ideas."

"Never thought I'd hear you say that."

"Yeah, well." Malia tugged the handle on the door. "Thanks for the ride. We should probably go onto campus separately."

"Why? Ashamed to be seen with me?"

And that's how she came to be walking through the quad of Paradise Prep with the most popular, best-looking guy on campus at her side, and when she tried to hide, Blake snatched the ball cap off her head and made her chase him to get it back.

CHAPTER TEN

LEI HELD out a thick case file to Harry the next morning at the station. "This is what we gathered from the last time we had a clear case involving human trafficking. I've already duplicated these records and sent them to the FBI; my partners there suggested we contact the suspects who were involved back then and see if we can find anything new."

Harry took the folder. "On it."

Lei liked Harry's can-do attitude as she sat down in Pono's chair and flipped the folder open, but on closer inspection, her friend had circles under her eyes and her thick hair was piled on her head in a messy bun speared by a pencil. "You look tired. How did Malia take the news about Camille?"

Harry shook her head, dislodging the pencil. She grabbed it and twisted her hair back up. "Malia is still upset. She tried to call the fat camp; she doesn't believe Camille could be there and wouldn't have contacted her."

"There does seem to be something off about Regina William and the whole way that scenario played out, but we have to focus on the other girls right now." Lei pointed to a couple of bios near the top of the file. "I've set up a meeting at the airport with one of my confidential informants, a guy named Nisake. Nisake was involved in coordinating the storage of the women captured by pirates on our last case; he did six months as an accessory but is still here on the island. There might be a connection through him to the Chang crime family and their statewide prostitution ring."

"Whoa. We dealt with the Chang empire a lot on Oahu. They have ties to the Boyz," Harry said, naming the notorious Hawaii gang. "That group controls a lot of the construction and transportation unions related to development."

"I know. The Changs have fingers in a lot of pies. I've had plenty of dealings with them in the past." Lei said. "I've also asked Stevens to contact one of his confidential informants, Freddie, to see if that little weasel has heard anything—Freddie has his ear to the ground for anything nasty around transportation."

Pono arrived, carrying two mugs of inky station coffee. "Ho, sistah, you like my chair or what?" he exclaimed at the sight of Harry sitting in his seat.

"*Bruddah*, you broke this one in so nice." Harry grinned as she stood up. "I'm out of here. When is the meeting with Nisake?"

Lei told her the time. "That should give you a few hours to get through that file. We can talk about it on the way to the meet."

Harry nodded. "Rendezvous in the parking lot." She left with the file under her arm.

Pono handed Lei one of the cups. "Just how you like it."

"You da bomb." Lei stirred dissolving chunks of creamer into the black brew with a red swizzle stick. "I like Harry."

"I noticed." He cocked his head. "Angling for a new partner, Sweets?"

"Never." The two of them banged their mugs together lightly in toast. "But I don't have many friends, in case you haven't noticed, and she might become one. At least, I'm hoping so."

"I like her too. Sharp lady and a hard worker," Pono said, high praise. "I saw your notes—looks like we can cross one victim, Camille William, off the list."

"Looks that way." Lei took a sip of her coffee, swallowing her doubts about Regina William along with the harsh coffee. "I didn't get a chance to write up the visit we made to the docks looking for any adapted containers yesterday. Just so you know, that's a dead end too, for the moment." She filled Pono in on the meet with Agent Aina Thomas and their tour of the shipping containers. "How about you? What are you following up on?"

"Remember that kid Owen Mancuso that you interviewed at that house in Lahaina where runaways were being groomed? The boy's nineteen now. I've been keeping him on my CI list the last couple of years and coaching him at the gym and such." Pono flexed his considerable bicep, making the scarred tribal tattoo on it ripple. "The kid was kinda stunted when we started, but he's starting to bulk up. Anyway, he's got ties into the Filipino community and the cockfighting scene, so I thought I'd touch base with him about the girls, too, check to see if he's heard anything since he was caught up in that other ring." He sat in his chair at last. "But first, coffee and departmental e-mail."

"You read my mind," Lei said, and began the process of booting up her aging computer.

Lei and Harry got out of Lei's silver Tacoma where she'd parked at the windswept private terminal of the Maui airport. The area was reached via a narrow, two-lane road off busy Hana highway, and Harry gazed around the small, unpretentious runway with its simple passenger waiting building. "I've never been back here before and I thought it would be glamorous. I know a lot of celebrities fly into Maui on their own jets. This is not very fancy."

"They also do helicopter tours out of this terminal." Lei indicated an area where choppers were parked in neat rows. "There's a bill in front of the Maui County Council to expand this area to accommodate more personal aircraft, but the council wants more private funding to go to the pot so that the local islanders are not paying for it."

"That makes sense."

They headed for the terminal building, where Lei had arranged to meet Keone Nisake. Nisake had been caught up in assisting to procure a system of transport for the women captured on Lei's pirate case a few years ago, and she had kept Nisake as a CI, checking in with his parole officer and Nisake himself as she built a relationship with him over the past two years.

Lei had come to like the young mixed Japanese man. According to Nisake, he had been recruited into the trafficking by a charismatic criminal. He'd not realized that the workers he had arranged to modify a steel shipping container (including Stevens's informant Freddie) were preparing it for women who'd been taken captive.

Lei raised a hand in greeting now as Nisake, a slender man dressed in board shorts and a surfer tee, came out of the terminal building with a Caucasian man in tow. "Hey, Lei. I brought a friend for you to speak with as you asked."

The man looked to be in his late twenties, with thinning blond hair, pale blue eyes, and the kind of tan and muscles that came from spending his days outdoors in the ocean. "I'm not sure what this is all about," the man said, extending a hand to Lei. "I'm Chuck Beemer."

Lei smiled big, and so did Harry. He seemed a bit dazzled and blinked at their combined effect. "Is there anywhere private inside the terminal building where we can talk?" Lei asked.

"I can take you to the pilot's lounge," Beemer said. "It's currently empty."

"So you're a pilot then?" Harry flirted. "I *love* pilots."

"Yep. Been flying since I was legal to do so."

Beemer led them into the corrugated metal building via a side door marked *Pilots' Lounge: Authorized Personnel Only.*

Inside, a battered Formica table with folding metal chairs, a refrigerator, a hot plate, a couch, and a coffee pot made up unpretentious furnishings.

Beemer pulled out a chair for Harry, and she seated herself with a smile. "A gentleman too. This is my lucky day."

Lei noticed Beemer checking out the lack of a wedding ring on Harry's slim hand. She almost hated bursting the bubble of his interest as she sat down across from him and Nisake. "Full disclosure. We're police officers."

The high color in Chuck Beemer's face faded. He glanced accusingly at Nisake, who shrugged.

"That doesn't mean I don't still enjoy a gentleman pilot on occasion," Harry purred. She reached for the ashtray in the center of the table. "I hope you don't mind if I smoke."

She lit up in a rehearsed and sexy way. Lei smirked as the men watched. There was no doubt that smoking, while a terrible habit, could also be a nice performance enhancer.

Lei cleared her throat to get things started. "I'm sure you're wondering what this is about, Chuck. Keone has helped Maui Police Department several times in the past with information related to the trafficking of women here on Maui."

Beemer frowned. "I don't know how I could help you with something like that."

"I asked Keone if he knew anyone who was a pilot who might be able to help us figure out how a victim could be smuggled off the island. We would be grateful for any way that you could help. We're concerned about a number of missing teen girls." Lei outlined what she could tell him about the case.

Beemer shook his head violently, but he was still watching Harry's lips, wrapped around her cigarette. "I don't know anything. I've only been on the island for six months. I fly for a company called Hawaii VIP Charters. We cater to celebrities, musicians, athletes. We shuttle them to and from the airport in limos and island-hop them within the state. We don't do long mainland runs."

"Perhaps you know something you don't realize you know,"

Lei said. "Have you observed any suspicious or odd activity at the airport? Cargoes that looked strange, comings and goings late at night . . . I'm not sure what this would look like, so that's why we're talking to you."

"Are you sure the girls are being trafficked? Maybe . . . there's something worse happening." Beemer's changeable complexion flushed. "I hate to suggest this, but maybe somebody is doing away with them."

"We haven't ruled out that possibility," Lei said. "But we suspect the trafficking because we found a victim who looked as if she'd tried to escape. She was in the water."

"So why aren't you focusing on ships?" Nisake asked.

"We are," Lei said, suppressing irritation. "Keone, maybe you can give me a few minutes to talk privately outside while Harry and Chuck get to know each other better."

Nisake nodded. "Sure."

The two of them got up and went outside of the lounge. The wall of the terminal building reduced the gusty wind that usually cut across the airport, and Lei turned to the young man. "Thanks for bringing Beemer on board. It's good for us to have a contact with someone inside the industry. Maybe Harry can motivate him to dig more deeply into what he's seen over the past six months of movement in this terminal."

"Chuck's going to know I snitch for you now." Nisake cast down his eyes. "I don't know who he might tell. I'm walking a fine line ever since I got out and have been giving you information."

"If it's the Changs you're worried about, I have a contact within the family. I'll let him know to keep an eye out for you." Over Lei's years of dealing with the Chang crime syndicate, she had found an unexpected asset in Terence Chang, the young heir apparent on the Big Island of Hawaii who had decided to go straight. "My source can tell me if there's any Chang activity going on related to your involvement and manage any threats."

Keone looked up, relief evident in his sallow face. "Good. I'm trying to keep my nose clean. I've got a new job detailing cars at one of the rental companies. It's hard work, but the pay isn't bad."

Lei unslung her backpack, reaching in for her wallet. She pulled out a crisp hundred-dollar bill. "Just a little token of my appreciation and thanks for your help."

Her CI nodded his head. "Thanks, I need all I can get."

"Now, let's go rescue your friend Chuck from my friend Harry," Lei said.

Nisake smiled for the first time. "I think it might already be too late."

CHAPTER ELEVEN

By LUNCHTIME, Malia had figured out a plan to deal with the new information about Camille. Instead of going to the cafeteria, she toted her backpack to the library and found her special spot between the rows of books—a study carrel that faced the wall with good Wi-Fi strength.

She put her hood up and earbuds in, and with music going, she developed an update for the blog: *"MPD says Camille is at a fat farm! Regina William received a citation for filing a false claim that Camille was a missing person, and tycoon father Leonard William confirms that he's paying for Camille's forced-march starvation program in Idaho, where she supposedly can't communicate due to no cell service.*

Vote here if you believe this is what really happened to Camille!

YES/NO

Even as Malia posted the update, seeing the facts of what she'd written began to erode her conviction that something more was going on with Camille's disappearance.

Wouldn't the camp people have to let her speak to Camille after the nine days were over?

Unless her parents kept things going with "Camille's grounded with no phone. Camille's trekking in Alaska. Camille's at a military school training in the Outback . . ."

Camille's parents could keep her friend incommunicado as long as they wanted.

Malia put her head down on the desk, feeling defeated, as the site's ticker registered votes overwhelmingly in favor that Camille had, indeed, gone to fat camp.

"Hey. You hiding?" Blake's voice, directly behind her.

Malia didn't lift her head. "This is where I hang out," she said. "You just never noticed before."

"Well, I'm here now." Blake grabbed a chair and scraped it across the short hard carpet. He forced his way into her space in the carrel and squished in beside her.

"What?" she sat up, tweaking out her earbuds, and glared at him. "Quit pretending we have something to talk about anymore. Everyone believes the fat camp thing. See?" She pointed to the vote counter, already registering fifty-three votes YES and two votes NO. "I have to give up on this. It's driving me crazy. And you hanging out with me—it's starting rumors neither of us need."

"I believe you about Camille. And I like hanging out with you."

"Yeah, right." Malia put her hands on the keys of the laptop. "Camille's your girl and I'm loyal to our friendship. I'd never go behind her back with a guy she liked. So there, you made me say it. God!" The stress made Malia bury her face in her hands.

"Things change," Blake said. "I like you. You're smart. Gutsy and pretty, too, when you let yourself be. But hey—if you don't like being with me, I'll go."

"I do like you. That's the problem." Malia gazed into his dark brown eyes a little too long. "This is so embarrassing," she whispered. A student headed down their row, spotted the situation, and wheeled to go another way. "I know how I'd cartoon this if I was still the Wallflower. I'd make a funny cartoon about us: you on Mount Olympus holding your trident down to fat, ugly, 'emo' me."

"That's plain wrong, and just shitty." Blake stood up, offense in every line of his body. "I liked Camille because she was sweet and a good friend. But I was never . . ." He rolled his shoulders, obviously trying to find words. "I was never challenged by her, like you challenge me. Now I remember what a snake you are. Lani Benito left our school because of that photo you posted. You're a little bit evil, Malia, and I've just been reminded of it."

Malia held up a hand, palm out. "Whoa. What's this about Lani Benito?"

"She's in an eating disorder clinic now, but only after she cut her wrists and was in the hospital first, all because you put up a Wallflower post of her puking up her lunch on your damn website. I thought you were changing because of this search for Camille, because you care about someone so much. But what you just said —hell no. If I'm on Mount Olympus, it's only because you put me there, and I resent the hell out of it." Blake walked off.

Poor Lani.

Malia collapsed, shutting the lid of the laptop. "I'm a snake. An evil cyberbully."

When Malia thought back on posting Lani's picture in the bathroom, all she remembered was being excited that she had something so great to put up that day. She'd even thought she might help Lani by making her ashamed of barfing up her food; instead, she'd almost driven Lani to suicide.

Malia felt sick with self-loathing.

She pushed up her sleeves and pinched her arms viciously, digging her nails into the meat of her forearms and twisting until she'd broken the skin's surface, until blood ran and the pain inside was matched by the pain outside.

Malia deserved punishment, and no one knew it better than she did.

THE FUN WASN'T over for the day.

When she got home, Harry was waiting at the door with that cop look on her face that promised nothing good. "Kylie, get started on your homework," their mom barked. "Malia, come upstairs. We're going to get a few things straight."

A breathless sensation in Malia's chest made her nauseous. Had her mom figured out Malia had gotten into her laptop? Cut school? Was the Wallflower?

Harry shut the door once the two were in her bedroom. "I had a call from the headmaster of your school today. He put me onto that gossip blog he'd told me about. I want to know everything you know about it."

"What blog?" Malia said. *Deny, deny, deny*—she'd learned that from Dad. "Geez, Mom. What's up with the third degree? I can't even take a pee? Put down my backpack?"

"This website right here." Harry punched a few buttons on her open laptop and swiveled it to show Malia's "update" with the voting buttons enabled. "As far as I know, the only person to have this kind of information about Camille, is *you*. Who have you been talking to?"

Malia's chest loosened a fraction—it didn't seem like her mom had realized Malia was the blogger. "I don't know what you mean."

"As soon as I read this, I called Leonard William. When I asked if anyone had called him about Camille, he said *you* had. Seemed surprised I didn't know about it. Thanks a lot, Malia, for going behind my back. You had no business contacting that man about this case!" Harry's voice had risen, her hands were on her hips, and her cheeks were flushed with the scarlet of betrayal.

Mom didn't know the half of it, but the best defense was a good offense—another Dad-ism. Malia imitated her mother's posture. "I can't believe you didn't talk to me first, before you called Leonard William!"

"And what would you have said?"

"I would have said that I wanted Mr. William to get off his rich fat ass and rescue Camille out of that concentration camp in Idaho! I hoped that he cared about her, but obviously, just like *my* dad, he thought paying for school was all she needed!" Malia's eyes filled.

Harry's gaze narrowed. "I'm not responsible for how your father has behaved."

"Dads who run away and throw money over their shoulders suck! And that's the kind of dad Camille and I both have."

"You're trying to distract me." Harry shook her head, her eyes still narrowed. "How did the website get this information? Only you knew those specifics!"

"How do you know that? Without Camille, I don't have any friends to even talk to!"

"What about that boy who's been sneaking around and picking you up in the gray Mercedes? Feel free to tell me any time you're getting a ride to school with someone else and not taking the bus like you're supposed to!"

Malia scrambled for a response. "It's not what you think. Blake's been helping me find Camille. He's Camille's boyfriend. He hates me now, anyway."

"Oh, for crap's sake." Harry sat down on the bed, her tone suddenly defeated. "Come here." She patted the spread. "Sit down. Tell me what the hell's going on with my daughter in my own house."

Malia sagged onto the bed, feeling terrible—she was hurting her mother. She reached into her loose sleeve, sliding her fingers up inside of her elbow. She pinched the skin, digging her nails into it until fresh tears filled her eyes and she gasped at the pain.

"What are you doing?" Harry grabbed Malia's hand and yanked it out of her sleeve. "Show me your arms."

Tears streamed down Malia's cheeks. "It's nothing, Mom! It's nothing. I'm just upset, that's all."

"I said, show me your arms! Take off that sweatshirt!"

Malia unzipped the hoodie and shrugged out of it. She held out the pale interiors of her arms, gouged with scratches and blue with bruises. Fresh tears of shame welled, and Malia bit her lips to keep from weeping aloud.

Her beautiful mom, Harry, the strong detective who knew all the answers to everything, threw back her head and wailed. *"Nooooo!"* She sounded as awful as if she'd been stabbed, as if her heart was utterly broken. "Oh, honey. This has to stop! All this has to stop!"

Harry reached out and pulled Malia in close. Their tears mingled as they cried together.

CHAPTER TWELVE

AFTER LEI and Harry's visit to the airport, Harry had gotten a phone call. She'd seemed upset, and excused herself from the next meeting, claiming a problem at her daughter's school.

Hungry, Lei walked into Ichiban, her favorite restaurant for lunch in Kahului. Stevens and his CI, Freddie, were already seated at one of the slightly greasy Formica tables. A lighted paper lantern swayed in a breeze from one of the fans rotating back and forth from the corner of the room.

Stevens stood up to give Lei a brief hug. "How's your day going?"

Lei shrugged, but turned to smile at Freddie. "Better, now that I get to eat lunch and see my husband and one of our best confidential informants."

Freddie fiddled with his laminated menu, chewing something rapidly. "Anything I can do for Mike, here."

"Thanks, Freddie," Stevens said. Her husband didn't always like the wiry little man's choices, but they'd somehow kept their relationship going over the years.

The waitress came by and took their drink orders. Lei made a little pyramid of her fingers and leaned over it toward Freddie.

"We really appreciated your help on that pirate case—and now I need any information you can give me on something similar."

The waitress came back, delivering two glasses of iced tea and a Kirin beer for Freddie. Lei ordered a combo plate of teriyaki beef and tempura vegetables and the men placed their orders as well. Once the waitress had left, Lei made eye contact with the 50-ish veteran, his thinning hair concealed beneath a grubby ball cap.

"We're having a problem on Maui with missing girls, and we need any information we can get about where they might be ending up," Lei said. "Have you heard any rumors about this?"

"Yep, I've heard some things," Freddie said, puffing his chest with self-importance. "Remember that young guy from Lahaina? Keo Avila? The dude got out early for good behavior, and rumor has it he's back to his old tricks."

Lei frowned as her belly tightened with frustration. "How is that possible?" She addressed her question to Stevens. He shrugged, opening his hands in a helpless gesture.

"We just bust them. We can't do anything about what happens after that, and the guy was working for the Changs." He turned back to Freddie. "Where did you hear this?"

"I have my ways." Freddie chewed rapidly and swigged his beer. "I've given up smoking, and nicotine gum isn't cheap."

Lei pulled out her wallet and extracted a bill, pushing it across the table. "We're also picking up your meal and your beer. I hope you have something real for us."

"Rumor has it Avila is operating a shelter for runaway teens," Freddie said. "They call it the 'underground railroad for runaways.' I imagine some of those kids, the cute female ones, aren't making it to where they want to go."

"Where are you getting this?" Stevens asked sharply.

"I have my sources, just like you do," Freddie shot back.

"We need more. An address. A contact. Something hard to follow up on," Lei said.

"All I've got for real is a website on the dark net," Freddie said. "From what I heard, a kid can find a place to crash by getting in touch through that portal."

Lei's eyes widened slightly; she'd not taken Freddie for someone that computer savvy.

Freddie looked down at his plate as the waitress delivered their food. Once again, they waited until she'd left, then Lei leaned forward. "I need to know how you found out about this."

Freddie spread his napkin open on his lap and took a sip of beer, settling back in his chair now that he'd decided to share his gem of intel. "My nephew's sixteen and has been in trouble a lot. My brother's strict, and my nephew has threatened to run away a time or two. I dropped by to take the boy fishing and caught him looking at that site on his computer. He told me he'd heard about it from some other kids at school." Freddie dug into his lunch.

Lei couldn't get anything else out of him until most of his meal was eaten, but eventually he told her the name of the website. She looked it up immediately. Sure enough, the handle Runaway Railroad led to an entry portal page. "Pretty cheesy name." Lei forwarded the site to her friend Sophie Smithson on Oahu to be followed up on.

"Whatever gets the idea across and is easy to remember." Freddie wiped his mouth with his napkin and drained the last of his beer. He stood up. "If that's all then?"

"Thanks, Freddie, I hope this lead pans out. A lot of young people are in danger right now, and you could be a part of saving them." Lei smiled.

"I do what I can." Freddie glanced out the window nervously. He flapped a hand to say goodbye, tossed his napkin down, and left.

Lei turned to her husband. "What was that all about?"

Stevens tilted his head, indicating a dark SUV trolling through the parking lot outside the restaurant. "Freddie doesn't want to be seen with us."

"I don't blame him for that." Just then, Lei's phone dinged with a message from Sophie.

-What do you want me to do with this website link?

-I need you to find out anything and everything you can about this site, mainly who's running it and from where. It might be linked to a missing teens case that MPD is sharing with the FBI.

-On it. No problem.

Lei immediately felt better. She dug into her meal with appetite. "It's been a frustrating day so far, but it just might be getting better."

"Eat up while I reach out to Keo Avila's parole officer." Stevens took out his phone. "Maybe we can pay that slimeball a visit."

"I love you," Lei said, around a mouthful of teriyaki beef.

"Good. I'm holding you to it." Stevens's blue eyes gleamed with pleasure.

THE NEXT MORNING, Harry and Malia headed straight into the headmaster's office after seeing Kylie off to her classes.

Paradise Preparatory Academy's headmaster, Dr. Mercado, had a fringe of tailored gray hair around a shiny bald pate, and he always wore bow ties. "It's my signature look," he'd often said. Today's bow tie had tiny, bright green palm trees on it.

Until today, Dr. Mercado had been a benign and distant presence in Malia's life at school, though she'd heard he could be a hard-ass, and that one of his pet peeves was cyberbullying.

Malia and Harry sat in armchairs in front of his shiny black desk. The window behind him framed a gorgeous view of the West Maui Mountains, sun-kissed by late afternoon.

Malia's eyes felt heavy and gritty from crying, and under the long-sleeved black tee she wore, her arms crinkled—Harry had covered the gouge marks of her self-mutilation with fresh bandages.

Her mom wasn't speaking to Malia; her face looked older, the skin so tight on her cheekbones that it seemed to gleam with the bone beneath. "I understand you have some concerns about the website you told me about," Harry said, when the adults were done with pleasantries. Malia hadn't said a word.

"Yes. We discovered this extremely toxic student gossip site some time ago when the parents of one of our students complained to the administration and brought it to our attention. We've been trying to find out the identity of the "Wallflower" cyberbully ever since, and from our conversation, it seems your daughter knows something about who that might be."

Both pairs of eyes swiveled to fix on Malia. She stared at the tiny palm trees on Dr. Mercado's bow tie. They jiggled whenever he spoke.

"Malia. Tell Dr. Mercado who the Wallflower is." Harry's voice cracked like a whip. "Now."

Deny, deny, deny. "There's a number you can use to communicate with the Wallflower. People send stuff to the guy on text message. I don't know who the Wallflower is." Her mother's eyes seemed to be drilling hot holes in Malia so she kept her gaze on Dr. Mercado. "I texted the Wallflower number the info you told me about Camille. I was trying to help." Malia bit the inside of her cheek until she tasted blood.

Harry turned to Dr. Mercado. "We've been going through a rough time in the Clark house. I'm not sure if you're aware, but Malia's dad left us a year ago and we're recently divorced."

Dr. Mercado grimaced. "I'm sorry. No wonder Malia has been a little out of sorts."

"I'm just discovering the extent of the problems," Harry said. "I've called her father and he's coming in tomorrow to help deal with the situation."

"What?" Malia turned to her mom. Her mouth felt gummy, her

vocal cords sore from crying. "Why are you telling Dr. Mercado our private business?"

"So that the headmaster understands you aren't yourself." Harry pinned Malia with her gaze. "So that he understands why you've been cooperating with this cyberbully." Her mom's dark eyes promised to root out further secrets.

Malia looked down, fighting the urge to rip at her arms with her nails.

She was tempted to tell all.

This was her mom's hypnosis magic, how she got perps to talk.

But Malia couldn't tell, or the consequences would be dire. She could be expelled, or worse! She was going to find a way to turn Wallflower Diaries around for good; it was the only way she could live with continuing to lie about it. "I may have passed on a few things to the Wallflower here and there, but I don't know who's behind the site."

"Are you sure you don't know who the Wallflower is?" Dr. Mercado's tone was steely. "Cyberbullying is an expulsion offense."

"I provided the stuff about Camille William because I'm worried about her, and I'm glad the Wallflower made the site about finding her," Malia said.

"Well, we have another student we're interviewing," Dr. Mercado told Harry. "A young man. Hopefully, we'll get some answers today."

Was it Blake they were pointing a finger at? Would he tell on her? "Who's that?"

"I can't say, Malia. I'm sure you understand. But anything you can tell me about the Wallflower, please let me know. Do the right thing and help us shut this site down. It's hurt a lot of people."

"It was mostly funny." Malia's voice was small. "Not all of it was mean."

"That's true. But the meanness outweighed the good by a long shot. If you do communicate with the kid who's behind it, tell him or her that, will you?" Dr. Mercado's tie was aquiver with sincerity.

Malia nodded and stared down at the toes of black athletic shoes that showed beneath the hems of her 'Camille jeans.'

Outside the office, in the deserted hallway, Harry pulled Malia into her arms. "No more hurting yourself. Your dad will be here tomorrow, like I said, and we're having a family meeting first thing. I'd like you to go to counseling."

"Oh, Mom. It's okay. Really. I was just so upset about Camille. I won't do that thing again." She patted her arm.

"Too late, my girl. I know a cry for help when I see one, and I've got both eyes on you." She made a V with her fingers from her eyes to Malia's, back again. "Now give me your phone. You're grounded from it."

"Great. I love having a mama cop," Malia said, the old joke that had ended up on Harry's license plate. She reluctantly handed over her phone, conscious of the Wallflower one weighing down the pocket of her hoodie.

"Get to class. And tell the bus company next time if that boy gives you a ride." Harry slid Malia's phone into her purse.

"Don't worry. He won't." Malia turned and walked down the hall; her shoulders hunched under the burden of her backpack.

CHAPTER THIRTEEN

L<small>EI AND</small> S<small>TEVENS</small> entered the parole officer's small, dingy office on the fourth floor of the Maui County Building in downtown Wailuku the next morning. A worn-looking woman whose desk plaque identified her as Peg Roberts pushed up from behind a battered metal desk to greet them.

Peg had told Stevens on the phone that she would bring Keo Avila in for them to interview, since she needed to do his monthly check-in anyway, and the man was due at any moment.

Roberts came around the corner of the desk, her hand extended toward Lei. "Great to meet you, Sergeant. I've heard good things about you over the years. And Stevens, it's always a treat to lay eyes on you." The older woman bounced her brows in a teasing way.

Stevens laughed. "I knew I could count on you, Peg. What we're both surprised by is how quickly this piece of shit psychopath got out of jail. Can you tell us more about that before he gets here?"

"I'm given to understand it was a combination of overcrowding and good behavior on the part of my client." Roberts returned to her desk to check a thick manila file folder. "Avila has complied with all of his check-ins, and his drug tests have been clean. I haven't heard any negative reports about him since he got out six months ago."

Lei sat down in one of three cheap plastic chairs. "Avila was instrumental in luring in runaways for human traffickers. We hear he might be up to his old tricks."

Roberts's eyes had a rim of white beneath them like a sad basset hound; her brows rose, increasing the impression. "I'm aware of his record. We will have to have some evidence of wrong-doing before tossing him back into jail."

"Is there somewhere private where we can interview him?" Stevens asked.

Roberts shook her head. The jowly skin around her neck flapped. "Unfortunately, no. Space is at a premium in this office. I'll have to sit in on your interview."

Just then the door opened, and Keo Avila walked in with a wide grin on his face and a bouquet of tropical flowers in his arms. Lei often saw these beautiful homegrown bouquets near her home in Haiku, available in buckets on the side of the roads next to small honor system payment kiosks.

The charming smile died on the young man's lips as he took in Lei and Stevens. "Oh, excuse me. I'll come back, Peg, if this is a bad time."

Roberts made a welcoming gesture and took the flowers, large heliconias, proteas, and torch ginger rubber-banded with a plastic bag around their stems. "Thank you, Keo. These two detectives are here to speak with you. You can have a seat right here."

"Anything I can do to help the Maui Police Department." Avila kept his face expressionless, but a slight tightness around his mouth revealed tension as he took a seat between the two.

"I'm Lieutenant Stevens. This is Sergeant Texeira." Stevens, leaning his long body against the wall, turned languidly. If Lei didn't know him so well, she'd have sworn her husband was completely relaxed as he chewed a toothpick, looking down his broad chest at the young man seated in the chair.

"We've met," Lei said. "A few years ago." Lei distinctly remembered meeting Keo Avila's mother, too; that sweet lady hadn't a clue how or why her handsome, charismatic son had gone bad.

Avila stayed silent.

Stevens took his chair and spun it around, straddling it. He crossed his arms over the back, gazing at Avila. "We hear you've gotten out on good behavior. What have you been up to for work in the last six months?"

"A little of this, a little of that." Avila leaned back and crossed his arms on his chest; he must have been working out because his arms were ridged with muscle and his pecs were pumped. Lei continued her perusal: the young man's jeans were new, his shirt was silk, and his pristine white athletic shoes were top-of-the-line.

"Now, Keo. You need to do better than that. Tell them about the job program I got you into." Roberts tapped the top of Avila's file.

"About that, Peg." Avila ducked his head deprecatingly. "I'd been meaning to tell you that it didn't work out."

Roberts picked up a pair of reading glasses from her desk and opened the file. She surveyed him through the lenses. "For a young man with no visible means of support, your threads are pretty fancy." Roberts had a slight southern drawl, and she emphasized that as she looked him over. "If I don't miss my guess, your tennis shoes alone are worth several hundred dollars."

"They were a gift. I've been working for my uncle," Avila said. "He has an import/export business."

"Let me guess." Lei leaned into Keo's personal space with a suddenness that made him recoil. "Your uncle's last name is Chang, and his import/export business deals in human flesh."

Avila shook his head. "Of course not. I've paid my debt to society and I've gone straight. My uncle deals in home furnishings, and if you've ever tried to buy anything for your house on Maui, you know we don't have enough furniture or interior design stores on this island."

"Give us a name." Stevens took a small spiral notebook with its tied-on stub of pencil out of his back pocket. "We're going to want to follow up on his business, and this job of yours."

Avila reluctantly gave the name of the business, Hawaii Interiors, and that of his uncle, a Keith Evenson. "He's related by marriage on my mother's side," the young man said when Roberts asked about the connection.

Roberts tapped the manila folder containing Avila's records again. "As you know, one of the conditions of your parole is that you submit to monitoring, should anything you're doing come under investigation. Put your foot up here on my desk. I just happen to have an ankle bracelet on hand."

White tension brackets appeared around Avila's nose and mouth, but he lifted a designer sneaker and set it on the corner of Roberts's desk. "Snap away, boss lady."

Roberts put on the heavy-looking ankle monitoring device, activating it with an app on her phone. She smiled, a brief switch of thin lips. "Give me your phone. Now we won't have any trouble finding you the next time we need to ask you a few questions. Thanks for the flowers, Keo. We'll be in touch."

The young man surrendered his phone and left, shutting the door a little harder than necessary. Peg's hound-dog eyes gleamed. "Tell me what you find in that furniture warehouse, will you?"

CHAPTER FOURTEEN

M ALIA HAD to warn Blake about Dr. Mercado's investigation. Fortunately, she remembered his number, and safe from her mother's view, hidden behind one of the school's fancy pillars, she phoned him on the Wallflower burner. As expected with a strange number, he didn't pick up.

"Hi Blake, it's Malia," she said into the voice mail. "I'm grounded from my phone so this is the Wallflower one. Listen, the shit's hit the fan with the website, and I was just in the Headmaster's office getting grilled. I wanted to give you a heads-up that he might be pulling you in to try to find out about the owner of the site. Please don't tell him it's me. I have a plan to make everything better—to use Wallflower for good. Meet me at that place in the library at recess so I can tell you about it." Malia hung up before she could lose her nerve, and then broke into a trot for class.

At recess, which was just a twenty-minute respite in the academically rigorous day, Malia went to the study carrel and drew two chairs into the space. She took out her books and opened them but couldn't focus. She put her head down on her folded arms and shut her gritty eyes.

"Good thing you left me a message." Blake's voice, harsh with emotion, brought Malia bolt upright.

She gestured to the chair next to her. "Did he call you in?"

"Yeah. I listened to your message on the way to the office. Good thing, or I'd have told him who the Wallflower is." Blake's mouth was set in a hard line, and there were dark shadows under his eyes. Somehow, he was still the best-looking guy she'd ever seen, but as he glanced at her, one side of his mouth quirked up. "You look like hell, Malia."

She sighed gustily. "It's been a hellish twenty-four hours." She ground the heels of her hands into her eyes.

Blake grabbed one of her wrists where the sleeve had fallen back. "What are all these bandages?"

"Nothing. Burned myself on the stove." She tried to pry her wrist out of his hand. Embarrassment made her face hot.

Thankfully, he let go. "I bet the Wallflower could make an interesting post about those injuries."

Malia took a deep breath, let it out. "Please, sit down."

He sat.

She raised her eyes to his. "I feel terrible about what you told me yesterday about Lani, and how the website affected you, too. I truly didn't realize how ugly it was, or how it hurt people. It was a game to me; it made me feel good to know things, to dress up stories about people and make them entertaining." She blinked as tears rose up. "I'm truly sorry about all this. The only way I can live with myself and justify not turning myself in . . . is to make the website into something good. I already started that with the search for Camille, but now I'd like to change the whole focus of the Wallflower Diaries to reporting interesting, good news on campus, like solving problems for people and the school."

"You'll lose half the readership," Blake said. "Nobody wants to read good stuff." He leaned in closer so as not to be overheard by a passing student, and took her hand, idly playing with her fingers, his gaze on the bandage decorating her arm. The study carrel seemed to wrap around them, creating intimacy. "It's dirt they love." His fingers stroked the tape at the edge of her bandage.

"I don't care. I just don't want to hurt one more person." Malia shut her eyes. Two fat tears escaped from under her swollen lids and slipped down her face, catching on her lips.

Before she could dash the tears away, Blake's warm mouth touched hers. She opened her eyes in surprise, and he kissed her more deeply, sipping at her lips, drawing in her tears. One of his hands came up to cup her wet cheek and the other wrapped around her nape, tangling in her hair as he drew her closer.

This can't really be happening was what came to Malia's mind before all words fled, and there was nothing but a kiss that awakened every nerve ending in her body, taking her to an entirely new place and lighting her on fire.

"Get a room," she heard from somewhere back in the stacks, followed by a burst of male laughter. Blake's posse of jock dudes had found them.

Malia wrenched away and hid her face in her arms as Blake turned and barked, "Get lost, assholes!"

The guys must have gone because things went quiet, and Blake's hand found her cheek again. He tipped up her face; Malia's was hot with humiliation, so she kept her eyes closed.

"Where were we?" was all he said.

A giggle of pure joy tried to escape and was captured between their mouths.

The bell rang, and by then they were deep in the carrel. Malia's head rested on Blake's arm and their faces were inches apart as they breathed each other's air. Malia hadn't opened her eyes or said a word the whole time; to do so would break the spell.

Blake kissed her one more time on the tip of her nose, and on each of her closed eyelids, and left.

Malia rested there, in a fog of bliss, until the tardy bell rang.

"How do people function?" Malia said aloud. The experience had set a high standard for her first kiss. She gathered her crumpled papers and books, then pulled her hood up over her head and slid her sunglasses on to dim her own glow—but as she headed for class, she remembered Camille, and that doused her like cold water.

She'd fallen down on her best intentions. She'd betrayed her friend by kissing the guy Camille liked. So many things seemed crystal clear to her; all the stupid shit couples in love did made total sense now.

Malia wouldn't think about Camille anymore because heartbreak lay in that direction—she needed so badly to feel something good, and there wasn't anything better in the world than the kiss she'd just had, whatever its cost.

Malia managed to get through her studies, and was able to log on a computer in the library at lunch to delete most of the Wallflower's entries and suspend the blog's activity. The relief she felt when she did so, told her it was the right decision.

Blake met her outside her last class at the end of the day.

"We need to talk," he said. "I'll drive you home."

Malia stopped at the bus to tell the driver she had a ride home, avoiding Kylie's accusing glare from one of the windows. On the drive back to her house, Malia took a brush out of her backpack and worked the bristles through thick ripples left by her braids.

Blake reached over, tangling his fingers in it. "So soft. This hair has got a life of its own."

"That's it exactly. Wild Latina hair."

"I thought you were Hawaiian or something."

"Or something. I'm Mexican. Adopted."

"Interesting. You pass for local."

"I know. Awkward. Not usually worth trying to explain to people, so I let them think whatever, but I end up feeling kind of —I don't know. Like I'm a traitor to my heritage. Not that anybody knows what my bio parents were. Mom thinks maybe Mexican Indian. It's Kylie with her hazel eyes that has Hawaiian blood."

"I'm white and Korean. Little bit of both, a whole lot of neither."

They exchanged a glance, a smile.

They shared this, a sense of being different, not really fitting in. Malia never would have imagined that, with his popularity.

She reached for his hand. "Tell me more about your family."

"Well, Mama and Father aren't doing too well. Mama misses her modeling days and hasn't found enough to do since we moved here full-time, and Father is a workaholic. I'm an only child, which kind of sucks. It means they're both on me like white on rice, and there's no one else to distract them. When you get mad at your little sister, remember that."

"I will. And talk about weird, my dad's coming home. We have a family meeting scheduled and Mom wants me to go to counseling. Fun times."

"But it's good that Camille's disappearance is solved. You can focus on dealing with your personal stuff." He lifted her wrist and touched the bandage lightly.

He knew.

Malia wasn't about to discuss her self-injury. "That's the thing. I'm trying to let it go, but there's still something weird about what happened with Camille."

"The dad said he was paying for the camp, though, didn't he?"

"Yeah, but there was something off about our conversation. I want to find out more about him."

"Well, it's a good thing that I sent Leonard William an e-mail asking how Camille was doing, with a little Trojan tracker in it. I was able to find his IP address, and his computer's somewhere on the island."

"What? Really?" Malia bounced with excitement. "I thought the guy was on a yacht, somewhere faraway."

"Or maybe the yacht is parked in a Maui marina. I've started putting together a file on him—the businesses I could find, the articles on him and the family in the news, etcetera."

"Tell me more." Malia was impressed. "And I thought I was the nosy one!"

"Well, let's see." Blake navigated the car around a truck piled high with windsurf equipment. "William's from money. He has an import/export business in Southeast Asia and the USA. Furniture, art, even some fancy spices that are packaged and sold wholesale to food companies. He basically gets stuff made for other companies. A middleman. He also has income from his family money. All of that, and his mobile office on the yacht, make for a handy way to smuggle arms, which he's rumored to do, but has never been caught."

"How'd you have time to do all this?" They'd already turned onto her street; time certainly seemed to speed by when she was with Blake.

He shrugged. "Been having trouble sleeping."

"Don't take me home yet. Just a little while longer," she begged as they approached her driveway. Blake drove on past and pulled out on the shoulder at what Malia had begun to think of as 'their spot.'

"I'd like for us to try to find William's yacht," Malia said. "Do you have phone signal out here?"

"Sure."

"Let's see if we can locate it. Camille told me the name. It was something with 'mermaid' in it."

"I don't know if that's much to go on."

"Well, wouldn't he have to register the boat on Maui since he's from here? Let's look up the county records first."

They ended up having to phone as the Maui County Division of Boating and Ocean Recreation had no database available for viewing. Malia cleared her throat, deepened her voice, and asked for the Coordinator of Recreational Boating. She used the star-six-seven block code when she dialed, using Blake's phone. He fiddled with the radio, watching her.

"Department of Land and Natural Resources. How can I help you?"

"Is this the Recreational Boating Division?" Malia asked.

"It is. This is Stewart Uyetake, Recreational Boating Coordinator."

"Hi, Mr. Uyetake. This is kind of personal, but I am looking for my dad. My name is Camille William, and my dad, Leonard William, has a boat he lives on. I just need to know what harbor he's at so I can go see him."

"Young lady, I can't help you. That's confidential information."

Malia let her voice wobble, nervousness translating into traumatized hurt. "Dad's supposed to take me out on the boat, but my parents are divorced and he's been dodging his child support payments. I don't think he'll contact me while he's on Maui because of it—but I just want to see him."

Blake's brows rose and he gave her a thumbs-up; Malia sounded just like a hurt and abandoned teenager with an irresponsible father.

"What's the name of the boat?" Malia heard the rattling of computer keys.

"I can't remember, exactly. It has Mermaid in it."

"The Moonlit Mermaid? It's in Lahaina Harbor."

"Oh, thank you Mr. Uyetake! You practically saved my life!" Malia gushed.

"I don't care for deadbeat dads." The man hung up briskly.

Malia handed Blake his phone. "What do you think of driving out there tonight and spying on Leonard William?"

Blake narrowed his eyes. "What do you expect to find?"

"I don't know. Drug running? Gun smuggling? Maybe he's even got Camille on board?" Malia threw her hands up. "The man's a sleazebag."

"Let's slow down and think about this for a minute." Blake played with her fingers. "Why would Leonard and Regina lie? Seriously. Regina's getting cited, there's a ton of gossip about them as it is with Camille at the fat farm. I just don't see how pursuing this further is going to find out anything."

Malia shook her head. "Something is still off to me. I just don't believe the fat farm thing. I want to see what Leonard William is up to. Are you in or not?"

Blake smiled. "I want to know how you're going to do any of this without my help—no phone, no laptop, no wheels. The Wall-flower is stuck to the wall without me."

Malia folded her arms, thrust out her lip. "I'll find a way."

"Sure you will. For starters, how will you sneak past your mom and sister?"

"Leave that to me. Pick me up at eleven p.m. right here. We'll all supposedly be sleeping by then."

"Good thing there's no school tomorrow." Blake restarted the engine. He drove her back into the driveway.

Malia glimpsed the movement of a curtain and sighed; Kylie had been watching for her return. "I'll see you later."

"Wait. I need a goodbye kiss." Blake had a hank of her hair in his hand, and, his eyes on hers, he began winding the wavy, rich brown skein around his finger, drawing her toward him.

"It's wrong," Malia whispered. "I'm going to hate myself later."

"I promise there was nothing going on between me and Camille," Blake said, inches from her mouth. "We never even kissed. We never went on a date. We liked each other; I care about her. That's all. But not like this."

Malia melted like butter in the sun as he kissed her. If only she could freeze time, hold this breathless feeling close, and make it last . . .

"I'll see you later." Malia gathered her backpack and opened the door. "But no more— you know. Seriously. We have to clear things up with Camille before . . . anything else."

"I'll be a perfect gentleman on our midnight raid. But if you end up kissing me, well." He shrugged. "I've been called a man-slut before by a certain Wallflower."

"I mean it."

"Of course. No means no." He started the car and backed out of the driveway.

MALIA MADE sure her door was locked before she plugged in the burner phone to recharge it, then lay down on her bed with her spiral notebook and a pencil.

She scrolled through texts, wincing at comments about her and Blake: *"What does he see in that emo chick?" "Apparently Blake's slumming now that Jodie dumped him for the prom . . ."* and more in that humiliating vein. Well, Malia deserved it, had been thinking the same herself.

More comments had come in about the post on Camille, including some "sightings" everywhere on the island from Upcountry to Hana, but nothing seemed solid enough to pursue.

Then, as suddenly as if surrounded by neon, a text: *"This is Camille! Help me! Tell MPD I'm being held prisoner. I was kidnapped out of my house by two guys with hoods on. They made me write a note about running away. I don't know what's going on, but I'm in a small storage shed. I stole this phone off the guard's belt, so don't call this number. Please just get someone to find me, I'm somewhere about an hour away from home by car. This is Camille, and my favorite shoes are my glitter Converse. Believe me! Please get help!!!!"*

Malia shot upright, her stomach churning.

Her instincts had been correct. Someone had taken Camille!

If her friend was kidnapped and her parents were being threatened, that explained why Regina William had recanted her story about Camille running away. It also explained the oddities in Malia's conversation with Leonard William. He must be the one being hit up for kidnap money—though Regina William was wealthy too.

Malia had to get this information to her mom.

But how? If she told Harry she'd got a text from Camille, she'd have to disclose the burner phone and admit she was the Wallflower.

She would call in to MPD, disguise her voice, and pretend she was Camille. She'd have to keep it short. Her mom had said at least a minute was needed to get a trace on a cell phone and triangulate its location—that's why emergency calls were better done from a land line.

Malia held an old T-shirt over her mouth and dialed. "911. What's your emergency?"

"My name is Camille William, and I've been kidnapped! I'm being held somewhere about an hour by car from my home near Wailuku. I've taken this phone from a guard, so don't call this number back. Please help me! Don't believe what they say about me running away or being at a fat camp!"

Malia ended the call. Her message had sounded realistically terrified, because she felt totally hysterical.

She turned the phone off and took the battery out, though she was fairly sure they couldn't have traced her location during the brief call.

She heard her mother come home, her shouted greeting, and the sound of her putting away her weapons, computer and ID. The shower turned on in the bathroom across the hall.

Harry was washing off her tiring day, and all Malia could think about was telling her this news.

She'd passed on the call for help from Camille to the MPD. Wasn't that enough? Wouldn't they call Harry's work cell, as she was a detective on the case? But what if they thought it was a crank call?

Malia found herself biting a nail, and stopped, grossed out— she'd never done that before. She got up, paced back and forth.

She checked the number of minutes on the burner: only thirty-five left.

She called Blake. "Camille texted me that she was kidnapped!"

"Oh shit! What did she say?"

"I'll read it to you." She read the text message aloud. "I just called 911 and left a message that I was her. Is there something more I should do, do you think?"

"Give that phone to your mom," Blake said.

"I can't. Then she'll know I'm the Wallflower! And she'll turn me in for sure, and I'll get expelled!"

"Camille's life might be at stake!" Blake's voice rose. "You can worry about getting in trouble later."

"I know—and I feel terrible—but there has to be some other way!"

"Wait—are you sure that message was her? Why would she send it to the Wallflower phone, not your cell phone?"

"Maybe Camille sent it to both, but my phone is in the safe. She told me her favorite shoes—glitter Converse."

"Everyone has seen her wear those shoes. A lot of people, including me, knew those Converse were her favorite," Blake said.

A long pause as they both digested this.

"Is there anybody who doesn't like Camille? Who would pull a prank like this against her? I can't think of anyone." Malia rubbed her aching forehead.

"Everyone liked her, as far as I know. But she was rich, and pretty. Maybe she had a hater, or even someone who saw something real and can't think of another way to get attention. Did the text ever identify you as the Wallflower? Because only Camille would have known that."

Malia read the text again. "No. It just said, 'I'm Camille.' But what if she was panicking? And only had a few minutes?"

"What's the time stamp on the text?"

"This morning, eight a.m." Malia had been sitting in Mercado's office right about then. More importantly, class was in session.

"Most kids who might have done this prank would have had a hard time texting this kind of message in the middle of class, don't you think?"

"I want us to be careful this wasn't a hoax. Is there some way you can check your normal phone for communication from Camille? Ask your mom to let you see if she texted you there? Because not too many people have your cell phone number, I imagine—but anyone who wants it has the Wal-Flwr number."

The cursor began flashing on the burner. "I'm running out of minutes. I have to go. See you later." Malia hung up, feeling queasy from the stress. She returned the burner to its hiding place. She had to get Harry to open the safe and let her check her phone for a confirming message from Camille.

CHAPTER FIFTEEN

AFTERNOON HAD DROPPED LONG, cool blue shadows over the Kahului harbor area. Lei, Stevens, Gerry Bunuelos, and Abe Torufu moved toward Keith Evenson's warehouse at the docks in full raid gear, their weapons at the ready.

Lei's heart hammered inside the tight carapace of her bullet-proof vest. A helmet cut her visibility; she hated that. She'd argued that the SWAT outfits were a bit much for this mission, but Stevens had insisted that they be properly geared up, not knowing what they would face at the huge metal building outside the storage area where the containers used for shipping were kept.

Keo Avila had surrendered his phone to Roberts so that he couldn't warn anyone about their approach; but, even with all the good reasons that they had to search the warehouse, it had still taken too many hours to get the warrant that Lei now carried tucked inside her Kevlar vest.

"Convenient location," Lei said in an aside to Stevens. Her comment crackled through all their comm units.

"I'll say it is," Bunuelos replied.

Stevens made a throat-cutting gesture for silence.

They moved to the nearest opening of the warehouse. The main doors were two large barn style sliders held shut with a heavy chain and padlock; they looked corroded and firmly shut, as if seldom used. The team continued along one wall to a smaller side door halfway around the building. A sensor light overhead flicked on at their movement.

Stevens pounded on the door with a closed fist. "Open up! This is the Maui Police Department!"

The banging caused sleeping birds in the eaves of the building to take flight with a rush of wings. Lei ducked instinctively, the smell of rust and seaweed from the nearby harbor strong in her nostrils. She kept her breathing calm by staying focused on the door, standing to one side as they all did in case of a gunshot blast, an occurrence that had stolen more than one officer's life.

No one answered Stevens's vigorous hail, so he pounded and called out again. Still no response.

Stevens gave a jerk of his head, and Abe Torufu came forward with the door cannon. The heavy metal ramming device was equipped with a pair of handles on top, and Torufu and Bunuelos each held a handle. They swung the cannon back and rammed it forward right next to the door handle. The steel-lined portal flew inward with an unholy screech of noise.

The interior was dark but for a crack of light coming from beneath a door to the back. Lei reached inside the doorjamb and touched a switch on the wall. The warehouse lit up, blooming into brightness from several long, dangling bulbs that ran down the spine of the huge steel structure.

A series of corrugated metal rooms with open ceilings divided the area; their walls were lined with stacks of heavy metal shipping crates. The boxes were approximately four feet high by eight feet long, with slots built into them for forklift moving. At one end of the barnlike space, the ray of brighter light coming from beneath one of the doors was still on. Lei pointed to it, and the three men fell in behind her as she trotted quickly towards the door.

She pounded on the portal. "Open up! Maui Police Department!"

Bunuelos and Torufu were readying the door cannon again when they heard a shout from inside. "I'm coming!"

They fell back, weapons drawn, as the door opened.

A short man with a shiny bald head wearing baggy gray sweatpants and a threadbare flannel shirt stood facing them. He peered at them through thick glasses, a pair of soundproof headphones around his neck. "Who the hell are you?"

Lei fished the badge hanging around her neck on a beaded chain out of the vest and held it up. "Sergeant Lei Texeira, Maui Police Department." She dug out the folded warrant as well and handed it to the man. "We're here to search these premises."

"Are you Keith Evenson?" Stevens stepped up to crowd the little man with his tall form.

"Yes, I am, and I demand to know what this is about!" Evenson blustered, hands on his hips.

Lei tipped her head for Torufu and Bunuelos to begin searching.

"I'm calling my attorney!" Evenson yelled. "I run a legitimate import/export business; you're not going to find any drugs here!"

Lei bared her teeth in a smile. "We'd have dogs if we were looking for drugs."

Stevens leaned against the doorframe, his elbow above the short man's head. "What relation are you to the Chang family?"

"Cousin by marriage," the man said automatically, then slapped his forehead as if realizing his mistake. "I'm calling my attorney."

"You already said that. Meanwhile, I'll search your office once I make sure you're clean." Lei said. "Turn to face the wall and put your hands on it. Spread your legs." Lei frisked Evenson briskly, then brushed past him to enter the office.

Evenson fumbled his phone out of his pocket as Stevens moved from the doorway to join the other two men in their search of the larger area.

Lei kept a wary eye on Evenson but headed straight to his desk, removing her helmet and setting it down. She pulled open the drawers, rifling through, looking for . . . she didn't know what at this point, but anything that might tie the victims to this location given by Keo Avila.

Nothing in the desk except the usual office crap, including pens, pencils, stapler, tape, and paper clips along with stacks of Post-its decorated with Hawaiian T-shirts and rubber slippers.

The lower right-hand drawer was locked. "Open this," she told Evenson tersely.

The man scowled; he was still talking on the phone as he fumbled a bunch of keys out of his pocket, bent over and unlocked the drawer.

Lei leaned down to look inside. The drawer was empty except for a small bottle of Jim Beam and an old cigar box behind it. Lei took the box out, flipped it open, and stifled a gasp at the sight of a collection of girls' rubber hairbands, each neatly wrapped around a cut piece of hair. There were nine swatches in the box, in an array of colors from blonde to black.

Lei's stomach clenched with an unpleasant memory from a case early in her career—a serial killer who'd taken hair cuttings as trophies.

She breathed through nausea—could they have been wrong about these disappearances? Was someone killing these girls? Did kidnappers keep trophies, too?

Lei pointed to the cigar box's contents. "Get off that phone and tell me about these."

Brought up short by Lei's tone, Evenson ended his call. He leaned over to look, and backed up, sputtering. "I don't know anything about that. Never seen that box before. I just locked the drawer because I keep a bottle in there—in case I need a nip now and again."

"We'll be talking further about this downtown," Lei said. "It's probably a good thing for you that you called your lawyer."

Evenson continued to protest, becoming agitated, so Lei cuffed him and sat him on one of the chairs. "Stevens! Come see this!"

"On my way." Her husband's voice echoed through the warehouse.

Lei turned to look at the computer—an ancient, bulky Apple that hadn't been upgraded since the 1990s. She unplugged it. "We need to check your records."

"Go ahead. I don't know what you're looking for, but you won't find anything," the older man said defiantly.

Wouldn't surprise her if this dude were old-school and hardly used a computer, anyway. Lei turned to face a bookcase, spotting several ledgers. She reached for them.

"You can't take those! Those are mine, and I need them to run my business!" Evenson sputtered.

Lei found an empty cardboard box in one corner, dropping the ledgers into it. "You'll get them back when we're done."

Stevens poked his head in. "Find something?"

"Sure did." She pointed to the open drawer. Stevens walked over and glanced inside. "Whoa."

"I'm telling you I don't know anything about that box!" Evenson was red with agitation. "I swear!"

"Sergeant Texeira!" Bunuelos's voice, hollow with distance in the metal building, had gone high with excitement. "You have to see this!"

Lei left Stevens bagging the cigar box, while keeping an eye on the loudly protesting Evenson, cuffed in his chair. She hurried out into the dim, echoing depths of the metal warehouse with its faint smell of must and metal.

Bunuelos had his flashlight out and was shining it around the interior of a metal shipping crate at the bottom of a stack in the corner. "Check this out."

Lei pulled a powerful flashlight off her belt and flicked it on as she approached.

Torufu and Bunuelos had been opening the stacks of metal

containers. This one had been crudely made over into a cage. Holes were bored around the top of the box; bedding, still rumpled with use, rested upon a slowly deflating air mattress. A light source in the form of a small LED lamp as well as a few tattered magazines and paperbacks attested to a lengthy stay. Lei managed not to let her revulsion show at the sight of a paper plate, still crusted with food, and utensils in one corner. "Someone was kept in here."

"Here too." Torufu rumbled. He showed her another of the boxes.

"I also found some very incriminating evidence in the office," Lei said. "This supports that the girls were in transit here, at least some of the time."

"Look how small these are!" Bunuelos said. "The poor kids couldn't even stand up!"

"I'm glad they took out whatever they made the girls use as a toilet," Torufu said. "That must have been nasty."

"I'll call Nunez to come down here and check for prints, hair and DNA." Lei pulled her phone out of her pocket, ringing Becca Nunez, their head crime scene tech. "I want you to collect samples from the crates," she told the young woman. "Hopefully we can match them to something from our victims. We will also have hair samples we discovered for you to process too."

"Finally, a break in the case!" Nunez said. "I'm on my way."

Just then, Stevens came out of the office, wrestling Evenson in front of him. "I didn't do it! Whatever you're thinking—I didn't do it!" the little man yelled.

"That's what they all say," Lei said. "You'll have plenty of time to tell us all about it down at the station."

KEITH EVENSON's handcuffs had been clipped onto the metal table in one of Maui Police Department's interview rooms. Captain

Omura, called in despite the hour, was watching them through a one-way mirrored panel.

The lawyer that he'd called was familiar to Lei from other cases; Davida Fuller wore simple dresses and chunky art jewelry that set off well-developed arms. "I want to make sure that my client has been apprised of all of his rights," she said, seating herself beside Evenson.

Lei recited the Miranda warning a second time as she turned on the recording equipment, then sat down across from him with Stevens at her side.

A couple of hours had passed since their raid on the warehouse, and Lei's eyes felt sandy with fatigue and the aftermath of adrenaline overload; but, at last they had some evidence they could follow, and there sat Evenson, looking as guilty as a potbellied possible pervert could look.

The man continued to protest his innocence, claiming not to know anything about the boxes in his warehouse being used for human trafficking, or the cigar box in his desk. "I swear, I'm being set up! I have a legit business! I always wear noise-canceling headphones when I'm in the office because that damn building screeches and creaks in the wind like a cat in a room full of rocking chairs!"

"We're collecting DNA evidence and will soon have more information about whose hair we found in your desk, and who might have occupied those shipping crates," Lei said, when Evenson had finished his declarations. "We found two crates that had been occupied. We want to know everything about this operation and how it went down. Where are the girls now? Specifically, Stacey Emmitt?"

Fuller put a manicured hand on Evenson's arm as he opened his mouth to protest. "My client has no comment."

"No comment!" Evenson yelled.

That was the gist of the interview from then on, and it broke up in a half hour with Evenson booked into holding.

The MPD team and crime lab had combed through the warehouse, extending the search to the work trucks used in Evenson's business. The following day they would be executing search warrants on Evenson's home and personal vehicle.

Outside the interview room, Stevens and Lei checked in with Captain Omura, then headed out to the parking lot.

"I finally feel like we might be close to finding out what happened to these girls," Lei said. "I'll call Marcella and Harry and let them know about this break."

"You do that; take all the time you need. I'll head home and make sure the kids are fed, bathed, and tucked in if you get held up." Stevens leaned over and kissed her, a little longer than strictly necessary, but she wasn't going to complain. "I'll see you when you get home."

Lei got into her truck; her spirits had been marginally lifted by Stevens's loving gesture.

The hardest thing about this case had been the dead ends at every turn; now they finally had some solid evidence that they could really run down.

As Lei took her phone out to call Marcella and update the FBI on their progress so far, she pictured Evenson's adamant negations. The little man really had been oblivious to their noisy penetration of the building; perhaps he was telling the truth.

But *someone* had been using that warehouse to hold the girls, and someone had also been collecting trophies.

Lei shivered, thinking of the nine swatches of hair that they'd counted in that cigar box. "Please let them be alive," Lei whispered, shutting her eyes in a brief prayer, then took out her phone.

Lei phoned Marcella from the cab of her truck as she adjusted the windows to let in some of the cool evening air. Marcella answered promptly. "What have you got for me?" Her friend's voice sounded upbeat, considering the late hour.

"We have a break on the case." Lei told her friend what had happened in the last day or two, culminating in the arrest of Keith

Evenson. "But I am having doubts about whether this guy is actually behind it. He couldn't hear us when we came to search the place; he maintains that he wears his soundproof headphones when he is working at the warehouse. He couldn't even hear us blowing through the door with the cannon. It's possible that the victims might not have gained his attention." Lei fiddled with her keychain, a clear plastic fob with a picture of each of her children's faces on a small photo inside it. By flipping it back and forth, she could alternate between Kiet's handsome smile and Rosie's gap-toothed grin as a baby.

"Well at least you've got a location to follow up on, and some DNA to match against the missing girls," Marcella said. "We've been focusing on shipping as the transportation method here in Honolulu; in general it's so much less regulated and scrutinized than the aircraft industry. We hadn't been able to find any private craft or other clues around the airport through our contacts there."

"We were just working on that, too," Lei said. "We recently gained a confidential informant inside the Maui airport. We're just keeping an ear to the ground there through private enterprises, which are pretty small on Maui."

"So all you know for sure is that the girls were stored in that warehouse at some point," Marcella said. "But you have that box of hair samples. That's actually a big breakthrough, considering we virtually had nothing to go on until now, at least on your island."

"Yeah, that cigar box really turned my stomach," Lei said. "It reminded me of one of my first cases as a patrol officer—a serial. He would cut the girl's hair off and tie hanks of it on a keychain."

"Any connection?" Marcella's voice had gone sharp.

Lei rubbed the plastic fob, finding a degree of comfort in the way the surface warmed under her fingers and in looking at her children's faces. "No . . . but the guy who tipped us off to the warehouse was on parole. A very charismatic psychopath who uses his influence to capture runaways." Lei told Marcella about Keo Avila and her history with him on the previous case involving pirates.

"We've got Avila locked down with an ankle bracelet. Considering who's behind ownership of the warehouse, I wouldn't be surprised if there's some deeper connection to the Changs, beyond what we've uncovered."

"Even if Evenson isn't the guy, there are plenty of other leads to explore," Marcella said.

"Yep." Lei shut her eyes for a moment, remembering the face of Michael Stevens's former partner, a young man who had seemed like a great investigator . . . but who turned out to have a penchant for deviance that had led to multiple homicides.

Just then Lei heard Marcella's son's piping voice in the background, asking about dinner. "That's my cue. Stevens went on ahead to get the evening routine started, but I'd better go."

"Always a pleasure to hear from you, especially when the news is some kind of break," Marcella said. "But I agree. Get on home, Lei. Your babies need you."

"Thanks for the reminder, Italian mama."

Marcella laughed as she ended the call.

Lei inserted the keys into the truck's ignition but paused; she wanted to check in with Becca Nunez about the trace evidence collected at the warehouse. She took her keys back out, sent Stevens a quick text that she was delayed, and headed back into the station building, rubbing the scar of an old bite mark where it marred the skin of her neck.

CHAPTER SIXTEEN

M<small>ALIA</small> <small>WAITED</small> until almost bedtime to approach her mom. Harry had been shut in her bedroom on a work call, and now she wore a sleep tee and was tucked under the covers reading something official-looking in a binder. Beside her, Kylie was asleep, turned away from the light, a mound under the comforter.

"Mom," Malia whispered. "Have you heard anything new about Camille?"

"No, or I would have told you." Harry put a finger to her lips. "Quiet. Your sister's out already. She's had a hard day."

Malia forged on. "I need to check my phone and see if there have been any texts from Camille."

"Tell you what. I'll get that phone out and I'll check it for messages, myself." A little smile played around Harry's mouth, hinting that she didn't think Malia would go for that.

"If it means someone checks and sees a text from Camille, I don't care who reads it."

The sincerity in Malia's voice seemed to have convinced her mom, because Harry got up and opened the safe, making sure her body blocked Malia's view of the combination. Malia winced—but she deserved not to be trusted.

She glanced over at Kylie.

Her little sister was curled, shrimplike, with one hand outflung. Her mouth was ajar, and little snorting breaths showed that Kylie was deeply asleep. Harry smiled at Malia. "She really was tired." Their shared glance reminded Malia of what Kylie had been like as a toddler; she and Mom had both liked to watch her sleeping. Malia remembered holding her own tan arm against Kylie's baby pink skin, realizing that something was different between them. Harry had noticed and hugged her. "I love both my girls so much," she'd said. When Harry said that, the love in her eyes and the strength of her arms convinced Malia she meant it.

Harry handed Malia her cell phone.

"Thanks, Mom." Sitting on the edge of the bed, in full view of her mother, Malia logged into her text messages and scrolled through, but there was nothing new. She sighed, her head falling forward as she tried to think of what that meant as it related to the cry for help Camille had sent to the Wallflower phone. She handed the phone back to Harry. "Nothing. Can I check it again tomorrow?"

"Yes. I'll turn it off to save the battery." Harry did so and put the phone back in the safe. "At our family meeting with your dad tomorrow, we'll talk about when you can get it back."

"When does Dad arrive?"

"Midmorning tomorrow. I plan to meet him, and we'll have lunch and talk. I want you to be at the house at two p.m. for our family meeting."

"Okay. I've got no plans. Where's Dad going to stay?"

"I'm not sure. I'll see what he's comfortable with when I pick him up." A quiver in Harry's voice.

Malia hoped her mother wasn't hurt again. "Good night, Mom."

Harry trailed her hand over Malia's head, down the long waterfall of tousled curls hanging down her back. "Sleep well, honey."

"You too." Malia squelched a twinge of guilt. Her mom would freak if she knew what Malia and Blake were doing later. Waiting for eleven p.m. to roll around and her mom's light to go out seemed to take forever. Fresh guilt twisted Malia's guts: Harry would hate that she was sneaking out to spy on Leonard William; and yet—she might be able to find out something more, and at least she'd be with Blake.

Malia tossed and turned, steeling her resolve. *No more kissing. Period.* She was going to find Camille and clear things up with her friend before the relationship with Blake went any further.

At ten-forty-five, Malia crept out of her room and down the stairs. She dug around in the utility drawer in the kitchen and found the little penlight they kept there and sighed with relief that it still worked.

Malia exited through the kitchen to the garage door into the backyard, as that made less noise than the front door, slipped her shoes on, and stepped into the dew-cooled grass under the fat silver quarter of moon. She hardly needed the penlight with the moon so bright. She zipped up her black sweatshirt and pulled the hood up over her head, breaking into a jog as she moved down the driveway.

The little country road was a deserted ribbon bordered by tall grasses and wire fencing, all of it rendered monochromatic by moonlight. She continued down the road and spotted the Mercedes already in the pullout. She sighed with relief as she opened the door and slid in.

"Midnight raid on Lahaina Harbor, here we come." Blake was a black shadow in the driver's seat. He turned on the ignition and the lights on the panel lit his face.

"Thanks for doing this." Malia put her hands in her lap and squeezed them together to keep from reaching over to hug him.

"I hope it's worth it. Any trouble getting out of the house?"

"No. Surprisingly easy. Mom also let me look at my phone. No messages from Camille." She was still troubled by the message from Camille that she'd received on the Wallflower phone.

"What do you think that means?" Blake drove forward gently, slowly accelerating as they left Malia's house.

"I've been trying to put myself in her shoes. She's alone, disoriented. She grabs the guard's phone and texts me at the Wallflower number. Why didn't she just call 911?" Malia said, as they turned and headed toward the highway going into Lahaina.

"Maybe she did. But maybe she couldn't speak aloud without alerting the guard?"

"Why wouldn't she keep texting everybody she could think of, including me?"

"We're all used to having contacts and speed dial. It's hard to remember numbers you haven't seen in a while in the heat of the moment."

"Good point. She could have texted everyone's number she could remember, and we wouldn't know it. The Wal-Flwr number is set up so people can do it by the letters instead of numbers, so maybe that's why she sent the text there and not to my regular phone. But now I don't know whether it was a hoax or not, because of all those other goofy texts I've been getting." Malia told him about the texted "Camille sightings" in all sorts of places. "They're turning it into some crazy 'Where's Waldo?' game, like this is some kind of joke."

"I don't think anyone thinks it's serious anymore." A frown showed between Blake's brows in the reflected light from the dash.

"Yeah, because everybody thinks she's at a fat farm right now. I got on the blog enough to delete all the posts except the ones about finding Camille, but I haven't updated it since the post about her being at the camp. I've done all I can right now. I fished around with Mom to see if she'd heard anything new, but she said no. That makes me think MPD didn't take my phone-in call as Camille seriously, or they'd have notified her."

"Crap," Blake said.

They entered the outskirts of Lahaina. The former whaling village, now an enclave of art galleries and tourist shopping, sprawled along the coastal edge of the island. Blake turned down one of the side streets, empty after ten p.m. "Let's park and go to the harbor on foot."

"Sounds good."

They found a public parking lot, and Malia was glad of the moon overhead once again as they left the car to a town filled with rustling shadow. Coconut palms made a ghostly rattle overhead as thin clouds scudded across the moon. Malia shivered, and didn't resist as Blake took her hand.

"I still don't know what you're expecting to find," Blake whispered, as they walked briskly along the worn asphalt road toward the harbor.

"I just think Mr. William's in the middle of whatever's going on, and I want to check him out," Malia whispered. A nearby dog burst into barking. Malia jumped, crashing into Blake and clutching his hand tighter. "Let's hurry."

The marina was a small area of densely packed slips adjacent to a long stone jetty that blocked the surf and sea. A small, worn park facility, studded with palms, was rendered spooky by darkness. A tiny breeze strummed the lines of the tied-up boats, and the strange squeaks and moans of metal, wood and fiberglass rubbing against each other made Malia squeeze Blake's hand again. The floating traffic areas between the moored boats looked open and vulnerable.

"Everything seems so different at night." Malia hung back as Blake set foot on the dock. "Maybe this wasn't a good idea."

"Too late now. We have to find where the boat is tied up," Blake whispered.

They walked as quickly and quietly as they could up and down the aisles of boats, scanning the sides and sterns for names. Most of the craft were completely dark, but a few still had security lights on. "Look for a big yacht," Malia whispered.

"Still don't see any *Moonlit Mermaid*."

Finally, near the end of the last row, they spotted her. At least fifteen feet in height from up off the dock, the yacht was almost too big to tie up. Malia and Blake both jumped when a harsh voice yelled at them from the ship. "What are you doing out here? This is a private area!"

Malia clutched Blake. The nervous tremble in her voice was authentic as she called, "We're looking for friends. We heard there was a party on a boat out here?"

"No party. You kids get lost!"

Malia gasped at the sight of security lights gleaming on a rifle in the arms of a man clad in black on the deck of the *Mermaid.*

She turned and ran, and Blake wasn't far behind. They clattered down the planking toward shore. Malia ran into the park and ducked behind the small cinder block bathroom. Her heart was thundering like a taiko drum as Blake joined her in the shadow.

"You're really fast when you want to be," Blake said. "You should go out for track."

"Did you see the gun that guy was carrying?"

"Yeah."

"An armed guard? Seriously, on Maui? Leonard William is hiding something!"

"And I think we've established that we aren't going to be getting aboard that boat anytime soon," Blake said.

"I know. But we should wait a little, see if anything else happens. Do you think they can see us over here?"

"Doubtful. Even less likely that we can see anything going on over there."

That seemed to be negated as the yacht suddenly lit up with floodlights.

Once their eyes had adjusted to the bright halogen lamps, Malia recognized Regina William's silver-blonde hair moving down the dock. Camille's dad walked by her side, his white mane backlit.

Malia frowned; Camille had said the two hated each other.

"Just a couple of kids," they heard Leonard say, amplified by the surface of the harbor's water. "You can stay, Regina."

"No, I have to get home." Regina William's voice sounded strained. He walked her to the end of the dock, the guard following with his gun, and then Leonard William did something unexpected: he leaned down to kiss his ex-wife's cheek.

"Hang in there," he told her. "Matthew will walk you to your car."

Malia and Blake shrank into the dark against the back of the bathroom's wall as Regina William, followed by the armed man, passed by. Leonard returned to the yacht, while Ms. William walked to the parking lot and got into her SUV.

Malia and Blake stayed frozen until the guard who'd followed her went back to the *Mermaid,* his footsteps hollow thunder on the wood of the dock.

The bright lights went out.

Only then did the two hurry away. Back in Blake's car, Malia put her hand over her heart, only now settling back to normal. "That was way too close."

"Agreed."

"Don't you think it's weird that Camille's parents are together? From what Camille told me, they hate each other. Like, really hate each other. And then he kissed her on the cheek!"

"It does seem strange. An armed guard seems strange too."

"Something's going on."

"Maybe the ordeal of sending Camille to the fat farm brought them together?" Blake sounded doubtful. He turned on the vehicle. They drove in silence, and as the adrenaline from their adventure drained away, Malia's eyes grew heavy. She woke to a gentle shake of her shoulder. "Wake up, sleepyhead. You're home."

Malia sat up. "Oh, sorry."

Blake's hand remained on her shoulder. "Sure you haven't changed your mind about a good-night kiss?" He leaned temptingly close. "You don't know how much I wanted to wake you up with one."

"No. Yes. No. I better get out before I change my mind." Malia threw the door open. "See you Monday."

Blake looked up at her from inside the car. "Text me from the burner if you find out anything new."

"I will." She felt a physical wrench as she shut the car's door. She used the pain to get herself to jog back to the dark, silent house. "Oh, Camille. Where are you?"

CHAPTER SEVENTEEN

STILL AT THE station as full darkness fell, Lei suffered through the process of booting up her computer, using the time to give Harry a quick update about the raid via phone.

Somehow, by the time she ended the call, she'd navigated to Jeremy Ito's record. He had been a short, wiry mixed Japanese man in his early thirties. His narrow face with its sharp, intelligent brown eyes popped up quickly as she typed his name into the police department's database.

Just seeing him made Lei's stomach clench, even though DECEASED in red marked his status.

And Lei was the one to have killed him.

She didn't regret it. She'd rid the world of a man who might well have gone on killing; Jeremy Ito had possessed the earmarks of a psychopath. But just because Ito was gone didn't mean that whoever was involved with kidnapping these girls wasn't some kind of psychopath or deviant, too. Those hair samples were a good indicator of pathology; and God knows what the victims endured before they were shipped to their next destination. The clock was ticking even now.

Lei powered down her computer. She'd stop in on Becca

Nunez to see what progress the tech was making on the evidence collection from the warehouse.

Descending utilitarian metal stairs to Nunez's basement domain, Lei rubbed the bone hook in her pocket. Hopefully, she wouldn't have trouble getting to sleep tonight. The memories of Ito and that case were charged with old trauma and grief.

Nunez's hair was done in a bright purple spiked shag, and she perched on the tall stool that she preferred, hunched over her microscope. Lei tapped on the door's frame to alert the crime tech to her presence; Nunez turned, frowning. "You still here?"

Lei advanced into the room. "I might say the same to you."

"This case is really bugging me. I want to catch these perps," Nunez said. "After your team left, I crawled around inside those metal boxes looking for DNA. I came up with this," she pointed to a bloodied rag. "I think this was used as a restraint or a gag. I'm testing the blood on it and checking for any additional substances. I've got DNA samples and hair samples from several donors, but as you know we don't process those here. I've got to send them to Oahu. I'm trying to get as caught up as possible."

"Anything on the hair trophies?" Lei advanced over to where Nunez had laid each of the hair swatches on a long plastic tray, neatly labeled with numbered codes.

"Unfortunately, there were no bulbs available on the swatches for DNA trace," Nunez said. "But tomorrow, I'm going to match them visually with samples from the victims. I did a quick check first thing. Yes, these hair samples match our missing girls, but what's really troubling are the ones we don't have references for."

Nunez's confirmation unknotted a tiny piece of tension that allowed Lei's shoulders to drop and her breath to sigh out in relief. She'd unconsciously worried that they might have discovered a whole new case that they hadn't even known about.

"Good news for the most part," Lei said. "Now we know that warehouse is a solid link in the transport chain of the girls."

Nunez nodded, making a line of diamond stud earrings in the

shell of her ear twinkle in the light. "I think you've done all you can do today, Lei," Nunez said. "Why don't you get home to that family of yours? We're moving as fast as we can on this. A few hours one way or the other won't make much of a difference."

"Tell that to a girl stuck in a metal box." Lei patted Nunez's shoulder. "But yeah. You too. Wrap things up and get on home. That's an order."

"Aye aye, sir. Soon as I finish just one more thing."

"You're a woman after my own heart, Nunez."

The tech waved as Lei left.

Lei ascended the stairs and exited the building, mostly empty now, headed for the parking lot. Her mind ticked over a plan for the following day. At least, they had a trail to follow now, which was more than they'd had before.

CHAPTER EIGHTEEN

MALIA WOKE up to the sound of Kylie pounding on her door. "Get up, lazybones! Dad's coming soon!"

Malia threw the covers off. Bright Maui sunshine streamed in through the window, and her room was overly warm without the circulation of the open door.

"I'm up!" she yelled back at her sister. Kylie was clearly excited Dad was visiting, but Malia felt tired and grumpy after last night's adventure, not to mention worried about having the spotlight on her misbehavior. Mom had already gone to the airport to pick up their father, so Malia took a shower, trying to settle her nervous stomach.

She kept an eye on the driveway and tidied the house; a while later, Harry's Honda turned into the driveway, followed by an unfamiliar red Ford Focus.

Kylie sprang up from the couch and ran outside. Malia followed her sister and stood on the top step as Dad, even taller than Mom and dressed nice as always, got out of his rental car to catch Kylie in his arms.

Harry walked around and popped the trunk of the rental vehicle, and Malia came down to help her. She grabbed one of Dad's suitcases, surprised to see that there were two; that was all he'd taken when he left a year ago.

"Malia. No hug?" Dad had his arms open. He wore a pendant around his neck, an 'Om' sign in silver; so cheesy.

"Sure." Malia set the suitcase down, but her hug was the A-frame, non-touching kind. Dad was having none of that, and pressed her close. Malia let herself rest against him for a moment, inhaling his familiar Dad smell, but it had an odd herbal overtone.

"Where are you staying, Dad?"

"Why don't we have our family meeting?" Peter said. "And see where we are after that."

So, ten minutes after he'd pulled up in the driveway, the four of them were seated in the dining area.

Peter Clark put his hands on the table. He had broad hands with long fingers, and he spread them wide. The overhead light gleamed on his neatly barbered blond hair. "I want to start by saying I'm sorry. I'm sorry—for leaving each of you." He looked around the table and made eye contact, and to Malia's astonishment, he picked up Harry's hand, brought it to his lips and kissed it. Mom closed her hand into a fist and pulled it away, but her eyes were suspiciously shiny. "I'm sorry. I was wrong and selfish, and I'd very much like another chance to live on Maui with you, and be a family again." Dad had such a clear way of speaking that each word was complete, as if it could be set alone on a shelf; perhaps his work as a lawyer had honed that.

"I don't know what to say," Mom said. "This wasn't what we talked about at lunch."

"I know. But the minute I saw you, and the girls, now—I knew I'd made a big mistake." Dad's throat worked. "I've hurt this family more than I ever imagined. I should have handled things differently, and I'm sorry."

"I forgive you, Dad." Kylie got up and ran around the table to hug him.

Malia looked down. She picked at a scab on her arm. She was

swamped with feelings: hope, and love, and fear all at once. Hope that he meant it. Love she hadn't let herself feel in a year, for this man who'd been the gentle rock of their family for so long. And fear that her hope and love would be dashed again.

"Does this mean you want to get back together with Mom?" Malia wasn't sure what he meant by what he'd said, being with Mom as a couple was at the crux of the matter.

"I'm hoping she'll have me."

Malia glanced up; Dad and Mom were staring at each other with a kind of look that made Malia wish she and Kylie weren't even there.

"I'm willing to give it a shot." Harry's voice was thin and raspy.

A long pause. They all must be looking at her, but Malia kept her eyes down.

"Malia? What do you think of me coming back to Maui?" Dad finally asked.

"What does it matter what I think? I'm not really your daughter, anyhow."

"Malia!" Mom said. "It hurts to hear you say that!"

Dad put a hand on her shoulder. "You'll always be my daughter—the firstborn of my heart. It's okay if you need some time to think about it. To get used to the idea of having me back home."

"Yeah, I need time." Malia finally looked up into eyes the same shade as Kylie's. Deep lines around Dad's mouth showed her that he'd suffered too, on his quest for self-actualization. "I hope you mean what you're saying. I don't think we could take it if you don't. Kylie has to come live with you if you leave again. Ha ha."

"I do mean it. And, I'd like a chance to prove it."

Mom glanced at the clock. "Kylie has a doctor's appointment, so we'll continue this later."

Malia and Dad saw them off, standing awkwardly on the front step together. He turned to Malia when they'd gone. "Want to take a drive? I hear you're working on your permit hours."

"Yes!" Malia caught the key fob he tossed her, her mood immediately lifting. "I haven't gotten to drive in ages. You sure it's okay for me to drive a rental?"

"I didn't read the fine print too closely. Plausible deniability," Dad smiled.

"Let me run in and get my bag." How could she turn this opportunity toward her search for Camille? Nothing occurred, but it would be good to be prepared in case it did. "I'll be right back."

Malia ran back into the house and upstairs, unplugging the burner phone and putting it in her purse. She grabbed her big black hoodie and pulled it on as she hurried back outside.

Dad frowned as she got into the driver's side beside him. "Kind of hot for a sweatshirt." It was still balmy, though clouds gathered on the mountains in a weather pattern usual for Maui.

"It's a style thing."

Dad pushed Malia's sleeve back as she reached out to turn on the car. "Trying to hide something?"

Malia narrowed her eyes at him. "I'm sure Mom told you what's been going on, but I don't want to talk about it. Let's not go there."

Malia swiveled in her seat, carefully backing them down the driveway. Dad stayed silent as Malia mentally prepared to stop the car, get out and go to her room if he persisted trying to talk about her self-injury.

"Where do you want to drive to?" Dad finally said.

"I thought we could head into Wailuku town. Maybe we can get a coffee or something."

They ended up at the coffee shop on Market Street, sandwiched in between the vintage Iao Theater and a pawn shop. Once they were seated at one of the outdoor tables and had their drinks in hand, Malia met Peter's gaze. "Mom probably told you that I've been trying to find my friend Camille. She disappeared some days ago. Supposedly she's at a fat camp somewhere in Idaho—that's what her parents say, at least—but I don't believe it." Malia blew on her latte to cool it down.

"Why don't you think so?" Dad sipped a cappuccino. Foam made a little mustache on his top lip. "Your mom told me your friend's on a nine-day hike with no cell phones right now."

"Yeah, supposedly. Her parents are acting squirrely. This is going to sound drastic, but I believe Ms. William has fed Camille poison to make her sick at least once, maybe more times than that." Malia told him her concerns about Regina William. "One thing that could have happened is that Ms. William accidentally poisoned Camille too much, and Leonard is helping her cover up what happened while Camille gets better." As she spoke the words, Malia felt the truth of them. This theory covered both Camille's inability to communicate (except for that text, which was probably a hoax) and the strange sight of Camille's parents, together. Maybe Camille was even on Leonard's boat!

"Well, it seems like if you just wait and let the nine days she's supposedly on this tech-free hike play out, the truth will emerge." Dad's intelligent eyes were on hers as he brushed a tendril of hair off her face.

Malia sat back, out of his reach, and pointed a finger at him. "You better not let us down."

He sighed. "I don't plan to. I've missed you, Malia. Why didn't you come see me in California at Christmas? I loved having Kylie, but we both missed you."

"And leave Mom all alone? Having to deal with Gram and her drinking?" Harry's mom lived in Honolulu, and their annual holiday visit was something they all dreaded.

"I guess it wasn't fair to put you in that position."

"Why did you leave in the first place? And why did you do it the way you did? Not talking to us or giving us a chance?" The words burst out of her.

"Leaving wasn't anything about you girls; it was about your mother and me, and the rut we were in. I needed more from our

marriage—and your mother is married to the job. Still is, in fact."
Peter took too big a sip of his cappuccino, set it down hard, and
coffee slopped into the saucer. "I thought you'd go on without me
all right. I didn't realize how much we all needed each other."

Malia stood up. "Let's get back on the road."

Peter didn't argue.

Malia decided to go up through the Valley View Estates as they
drove out of Wailuku town. Her father made no objection; the
discussion they'd had seemed to have put him in a dark mood, and
he stared out the window silently as they drove past Camille's
house.

Malia blinked at the sight of Regina William's SUV parked in
the driveway. She never left the vehicle out unless she was leaving
shortly; maybe she'd be gone in a few minutes, and Malia could do
another search in the house for clues about Camille.

"You know what, Dad? My friend lives just up here." Malia
pointed to a lovely Asian-styled bungalow with a shiny new Beetle
in the turnaround. "We need to talk about a big school project. Can
you drop me off here and pick me up later?"

Dad's eyes narrowed. "I'm beginning to wonder if the turn into
this neighborhood was random after all," he said.

"No, really, we have a project," Malia said. "I didn't know
she'd be home but that's her car." It was amazing how good she
was getting at lying.

"That's fine, then."

Malia pulled up at the bottom of the driveway. Dad got out and
came around to the driver's side. "Call me when you need a
pickup. You know my number," he said.

"Of course. Thanks, Dad." Malia hugged him as a reward,
feeling guilty, still unsure what she was going to do, and wishing
Blake were with her with a sudden fierceness.

She watched Peter drive away, waving at his glance back in the
rearview mirror. She turned and pretended to head up the driveway,
then ducked behind the Beetle, glancing at the house—but nothing

moved. She turned and trotted back down the driveway when the Focus was out of sight.

Her familiar black sweatshirt felt overwhelmingly hot and claustrophobic, but it was important that no one was able to describe her if she were spotted, so she kept the hood up as she hurried toward the William house, then slowed as she approached it, glad of the shadows as she hunched down against the hedge below the house.

"Now what?" she muttered, staring at Ms. William's SUV.

Maybe she should go talk to the woman, beg to speak to Camille or something, and see what happened. Malia walked up the driveway, and, steeling herself, up the steps. She rang the bell; it was past time she spoke to Camille's mother face-to-face.

CHAPTER NINETEEN

THE SAME MORNING:

"Mama, wake up!" Lei woke to an assault on her head from toddler Rosie.

Lei grabbed her daughter's sturdy little body and nuzzled her round tummy through her nightgown, blowing and tickling. Rosie shrieked with delight.

Kiet joined the fun, jumping on Lei and trying to tickle her, too. The bed was a mass of giggling and pillow whacking as the three played, until Lei was able to hug both of her kids at the same time, wrestling them into submission. "That'll teach you to wake me up," she mock growled, kissing them.

Stevens appeared in the doorway with no shirt on, pajama bottoms riding low on his hips—just as sexy as he'd always been even after all these years. Lei smiled back at his lopsided grin that told her he was happy to see the three of them having fun. "You're on breakfast duty, Sweets," he said. "I prepped the pancake batter and I'm heading for the shower. All you've got to do is cook 'em up."

"Isn't Daddy the best?" Lei told the kids.

"Yes!" The two shouted.

Lei swung her legs out of bed and tucked Rosie under one arm, kicking and giggling, as she ruffled Kiet's hair. The three headed for the kitchen.

Soon the kids were digging into stacks of banana pancakes covered in guava syrup as Lei cooked scrambled eggs for herself and Stevens.

Stevens came out of their bedroom dressed for work. "Your turn for the shower."

"Here you go. I'll be out in a minute." Lei handed over the spatula and headed to their bathroom.

Under the flow of water, she thought through the day ahead. Hopefully this would be the day something shook loose, and she finally found one of the girls.

Lei's phone vibrated on the bathroom sink as she dried off and wrapped up in a towel. The name on the caller ID was Terence Chang. Lei's pulse bumped as she sat down on the closed toilet seat lid to take the call. "Terence! To what do I owe the pleasure?"

"An ironic twist of fate when a police detective considers it a pleasure to hear from me," Terence said. The intelligent young programmer had a long history with Lei that had culminated in becoming a confidential informant as he struggled to go straight in a notorious crime family. "I thought I would let you know that there's definitely an operation moving girls out of Maui. I didn't pay much attention until you twigged me to that, but it's being run by Harold Chang, who's been up to those tricks for some years now."

"Yes, we got on to him when the pirates were operating," Lei said. "But nobody was able to tie him to the actual trafficking on that case. How is he moving the girls off the island?"

"Shipping," Chang said. "Disguised as merchandise for an import/export business. They go from the outer islands to Oahu, then straight to China."

"Can you give us the names of the ships? Anything we can follow up on?"

"My cousin was super cagey about that information. People keep their distance from me since I have been trying to go legit, so I couldn't get the specific names of the ships they are using or the companies they're listed under. All I can tell you is that Harold Chang has a whole network underneath him, and you can be sure he's keeping the whole dirty business at arm's length."

"I bet they're making the transition of the human cargo out in international waters and other tricks that minimize our ability to track what's going on," Lei said. "But thanks for this. It confirms what we'd begun to think."

Lei ended the call and, standing up, winced at the sight of her bedraggled hair in the mirror. She squirted a handful of gel into her palm and squished it into her curls as she hurried into the bedroom to change; it was going to be another long day.

LEI DROVE towards the Kahului station, this time with Stevens in the truck; the kids were with their grandparents for the day. Her phone rang and she didn't have her Bluetooth in, so she handed the device to Stevens. "This is Lieutenant Stevens for Sergeant Lei Texeira. I'm putting you on speaker." Stevens hit the audio button.

Peg Roberts's voice came crackling through the phone. "Hey there guys! Got some disturbing news. Our perp, Keo Avila, has made a run for it. The alarm went off that his ankle bracelet was removed last night, and when I sent a unit by his last known address, he'd flown the coop. I've already called in a Be On the Lookout for him to be arrested if anyone can get their hands on him."

Lei and Stevens exchanged glances; Avila was likely the one behind the evidence they'd collected at the warehouse! "Thanks for the call, Peg!" Lei said. "We need to find Avila, and fast. We discovered evidence of the missing girls at the warehouse he told us about." She filled in the parole officer on the boxes and hair samples.

"The officer I sent out to Avila's apartment says it looks like he hasn't been there in weeks. He's got some other hideout he's been using this whole time," Roberts said.

"Did they find anything in his apartment that might give a clue where he went?" Stevens asked.

"I would have told you if they had," Roberts said. "Good luck!"

Stevens put away Lei's phone, and she pressed a little harder on the gas as they drove past Hoʻokipa, the famous surf and windsurfing spot. The early morning light was just striking the ocean as it came over the top of Haleakala, lighting the waves and surfers below, as they passed by. "I bet Jared's out there," Stevens said enviously. "My little bro has the best schedule as a firefighter."

"Can't disagree with that," Lei said, "Though you could take a surf break anytime you want to log off." She frowned, concentrating on the curve in the Hana Highway as it led past famous Mama's Fish House Restaurant. "My money is on that little psychopath Avila to be at the front of this. He's a deviant bastard."

"Agreed," Stevens said.

"Reminds me of our first case and Jeremy Ito, with those hair samples," Lei said. "Ito took hair trophies, too."

They exchanged another glance; Stevens set a hand on her leg and squeezed comfortingly. "Sometimes it's the ones you don't see coming that are the worst. I can just imagine those naïve teenaged girls going with Avila anywhere he asked them to."

"We got Ito. We'll get Avila too," Lei swore. "I just hope Stacey Emmitt is still alive when we take him down."

They soon pulled up at the Kahului station, and Lei ran into Harry as they were going in. "Harry! Good to see you. I want to catch you up on what's been happening."

Harry looked more put together than usual: her long thick hair was shiny and curled, and she was dressed in a red shirt and black jeans that made the most of her rangy figure and tawny skin. "Oh good. I had to take the morning off for personal family business. I'd love to hear what's happening."

"I just need a minute." Lei tugged her friend into an empty cubicle and gave her a quick rundown. "Our highest priority is finding Keo Avila. We're going to do interviews with the older guy we picked up at the warehouse, Keith Evenson, but I have a feeling he's out of the loop for the most part, even though he has a connection to the Changs. He claims he's being set up, and Avila would be the guy to do that."

"Makes sense," Harry said. "I don't like that thing with the hair samples. Sick."

"Nasty business." Lei shivered. "How are your girls?"

A shadow crossed Harry's light brown eyes. She looked down and rubbed her naked ring finger. "We're having problems, actually. I had to take the morning off because my ex came into town so we could have a family meeting. Malia has gotten into some trouble."

Lei frowned. "Oh no! Let me know if there's anything I can do."

Harry shrugged. "I doubt it, but thanks. That girl is way too nosy for her own good."

"You know, we have some teenaged CIs. Maybe Malia could be one. She could keep an ear out for youth-related crime and keep us informed. It could be a way to redirect her curiosity."

"I'll think about it. Maybe talk it over with her dad. But the last thing we need to do is encourage Malia's inquisitive side. Curiosity killed the cat, you know."

"Said the pot, calling the kettle black." Lei gave Harry a little punch in the shoulder. "Why do you think we became detectives?"

CHAPTER TWENTY

MALIA HAD NEVER SEEN Ms. William without makeup. The woman's face was almost gaunt, her skin grayish, and her usually vivid blue eyes must be contacts, because today those orbs were the tepid shade of a shallow wading pool.

"What are you doing at my house?" Ms. William frowned. A bulky black duffel bag rested beside her. She pushed it out of sight with her foot.

Tears welled in Malia's eyes at the woman's harsh tone. "Ms. William, I know you've never liked me, but I'm just so worried about Camille. I miss her so much. Is there any way to get a hold of her? Just to encourage her?"

"No, there isn't. I'm sure she's fine at Camp Willowslim, and it won't hurt her a bit to toughen up and lose a few pounds," Ms. William said, an eerie echo of Leonard William's comments to Malia on the phone.

Malia's temper ignited. "You thought it would be easier if everyone who knows and loves Camille was freaked out because you pretended that she ran away?"

"I don't like your tone, young lady." Ms. William straightened, angry color flooding her sallow face.

"And I don't like how you've been hurting Camille," Malia said, hands on her hips, eyes hot. "I'm onto you, you poisoning child abuser."

Ms. William's mouth opened and closed. She reached into her pocket and took out her phone. "You get off my property this minute, or I'm calling the cops! Your mother won't be able to protect you from a slander charge!"

Malia backed up, feeling for the step behind her. "Know this, Regina William: whatever lies you've told everyone else, even my mom, I'm onto you. I'm going to do whatever I can to find and protect Camille, no matter what it takes." Malia turned and ran, hearing the front door slam behind her.

Malia ran to the end of the driveway and hid behind the neighbor's hedge, panting with rage—but her knees were also shaky with fright. Hopefully, Ms. William wouldn't call the police.

No, she wouldn't; the woman wouldn't want more attention. Regina William was up to something, and Malia wasn't going to leave until she found out what.

"I hate her. I'm going to take her down," Malia growled. She trotted back up the driveway and circled around the outside of the house, staying below the sight line of the windows, until she reached Ms. William's office on the first floor.

Malia slowly slid to stand upright, where she could peek in the window. The window was open a couple of inches for circulation, allowing her to listen as well as observe.

Ms. William's desk light was on, and the woman was on the phone. She pinched her forehead with spread fingers, frowning. "Okay. I'm coming in a few minutes." She hung up the phone and straightened, dabbing her eyes with a Kleenex.

Malia stiffened and pulled away, flattening against the wall. "This will all be over soon," Ms. William muttered, and her footsteps sounded on the hardwood floor as she walked out of her office and through the house, headed for the front door.

What would be over soon?

Regina William seemed to be getting ready to go somewhere, and Malia was near the garage. Malia hurried to the outside garage door, which was locked. Fortunately, she knew where the key was. Frantic now, Malia hunched over and ran all the way back around the house to the Japanese garden, finding the extra keys under the rubber rock and running all the way back.

She was turning the key in the lock of the garage door when, just out of sight, Malia heard the front door closing. That front door was the noisiest thing in the house, Camille had always said.

That sound meant Regina William was heading for her car.

Inside the darkened garage, Malia hurried to Camille's Prius and grabbed the door's handle. Thankfully, the vehicle wasn't locked. Camille kept the keys under the sunshade on the passenger side, her idea of security. Malia reached up and fumbled for them.

Directly behind and to the right, outside the garage, Regina William's BMW roared into life.

Under the mask of that sound, Malia turned on Camille's much quieter car. It started with a happy purr, and she glanced backward at the garage's closed door.

How soon would it be safe to hit the door opener and try to follow Regina William?

Malia shut her eyes, counting aloud as she visualized Regina William reversing down the driveway, then moving forward to leave. Malia hit the garage door button clipped to the Prius's visor.

The metal door began an incredibly loud rumble upward as Malia put the vehicle in reverse, and when the door was halfway open, shot backwards. The Prius barely cleared the metal slider of the garage, but sure enough, Regina William's BMW was gone from view.

Malia braked hard when she hit the bottom of the driveway and then punched the garage door opener button to close it, before she turned to exit the Valley View Estates.

Hopefully, she could return the car somehow before the theft was discovered.

"It's not theft, it's borrowing," Malia said aloud. "Camille told me I could use her car any time I wanted to." Malia gunned the mostly silent Toyota down the winding road until she spotted Regina William at the entrance to the Estates; the SUV's left-hand turn signal was on.

Malia slowed; she couldn't follow too close or Ms. William would recognize the car. An older silver Toyota Prius was a common sight on Maui roads, except for strings of colored plastic Mardi Gras beads hanging from the mirror that made this car uniquely Camille's.

Malia pulled the beads off and tossed them into the glove box. Opening it drafted a waft of Camille's vanilla perfume into the interior. "I'm coming to find you, Camille," Malia said aloud, and slammed it shut.

Malia let Regina William dip out of sight down the hill before she followed, and finally a couple of cars filled in between the two vehicles as they approached Wailuku town.

The implications of what she'd just done sank in as Malia drove. Her whole body trembled—she'd just committed grand theft auto without even having a driver's license!

But if this reckless act led to finding Camille, it would be worth it.

She wasn't surprised when Regina William took the Pali highway, heading toward Lahaina. Whatever Camille's mom was up to, Malia'd bet money it had something to do with Leonard William and the *Moonlit Mermaid*.

Malia pulled the Prius into a stall in the parking lot as far as she could get from Regina William's SUV when the older woman parked at the Lahaina Harbor. Malia slid down, cracking the windows for some ventilation, and hiding in the shadow of a truck and boat trailer combo.

Should she get out and follow Regina William toward the yacht? Maybe this was the time to confront Camille's parents and see if Camille was on board the *Mermaid*, but remembering the armed guard dampened Malia's enthusiasm. Still debating, Malia was glad she'd stayed put when Regina William reappeared with Leonard William. Both were carrying good-sized duffel bags, and two men in army camouflage followed them. Malia's eyes widened when she saw the bulges of guns on their hips. She slid back down out of view. "Holy shit, what's going on? This is crazy!"

She fumbled the burner phone out of her pocket. *Only five minutes left!* She dialed 911 as the big black Cadillac Escalade Regina William had parked next to rumbled into life; they must be leaving in that car.

"911. What's your emergency?"

"This is Malia Clark and I'm in the parking lot at Lahaina Harbor. A man and woman, accompanied by two men in camouflage gear armed with guns, just got into a Cadillac Escalade. I think they are being kidnapped!" Her voice wobbled. "They are being forced to go somewhere!"

"What's the license plate number?"

Malia scooted up to see and recited the plate number as the big black SUV backed up and began to drive away. "I'm going to follow them." She started the Toyota.

"No, miss. Stay where you are," the operator said authoritatively. "We'll send an officer to check it out."

"Call Detective Harry Clark. This is related to the Camille William disappearance case, I'm sure of it." Malia was having a tricky time getting around the boat trailer with the phone against her ear.

"What's your name again?" The operator snapped. Malia hit the button that ended the call. She'd almost been out of minutes anyway, and she needed both hands to navigate out of the parking lot if she were going to keep the Escalade in sight.

Malia stayed a block away as the big vehicle moved down residential streets and turned onto busy Honoapi'ilani Highway, headed toward Ka'anapali. She reached down and fumbled around for the phone and called 911 again.

"They're headed for Ka'anapali!" Malia yelled the minute the operator came on. "Call Detective Clark! It's a matter of life and death!" Whatever else was going on, Malia was sure of that much. "Please, send someone now!"

The phone went dead—out of minutes.

Malia followed the Escalade, surprised when it passed the golf course and shopping mall that marked the last resort in Ka'anapali.

From those developments on out, the road narrowed to a two-lane track above steep cliffs that plummeted to black lava rocks crashed upon by a rough turquoise sea. The whole coastal area was a marine sanctuary bordered by former pineapple fields going to seed, dotted with scrub koa, boulders and overgrown bushes. The sky was streaked with hazy pinkish clouds as the sun went behind the long mauve slope of Molokai, a smaller island off the coast.

Whipping wind rocked Camille's little car as Malia hung back, trying to stay at least a curve away from the Escalade, but the powerful vehicle soon outpaced her. She lost sight of it entirely and had to concentrate on the narrow curves instead. She overshot the rough junction where the Escalade had turned off the road—only a puff of red volcanic dust alerted Malia to where the SUV had disappeared.

Malia hung a U-turn in the middle of the road, something she was sure would fail her forever from passing her license test. Red dust, the soil of the former pineapple field, still hung in the air as she followed an even narrower graveled drive leading along the edge of a cliff that plummeted down to a popular surf break, Shark Cove, now churned up by whitecaps.

Past the palm frond topped observation hut near the surf break, a cement block bathroom loomed, and beyond it, Malia spotted the parked Escalade. There was nowhere to hide but beside the bathroom, so Malia reversed and backed in behind it, hopefully out of view.

They had to have seen her, but hopefully they'd written her off as just someone using the restroom—a Prius wasn't exactly a threatening vehicle.

Malia rolled the window down and leaned forward so she could see what was happening at the Escalade.

Exactly nothing.

She glanced around the area. Because the surf was flat, the park, which was former pineapple land, was deserted.

What were they doing in that SUV?

Malia picked up the burner phone and checked it to make sure that her last minutes had been used on the second 911 call.

She had no way to get help. She had to hope the cops had taken her earlier calls seriously enough to contact her mother and send someone out here—because whatever the Williams were waiting for couldn't be good.

Malia heard another engine and slid down in the seat, out of sight, as a big tan Suburban SUV rumbled past and stopped directly across from the Escalade.

A window rolled down on each of the vehicles.

Malia sucked in a breath—because what appeared were guns, their black barrels seeming to absorb the light reflecting off the sea.

The back door of the Escalade opened at last.

Regina William got out, her pale outfit fluttering in the breeze, her hands held up. "Please. We did everything you asked, and we have the payment, too."

Leonard William climbed out behind her. His linen shirt billowed like a sail; his white hair gleamed. "Show us that our daughter is alive," he demanded.

So that's what had happened—*Camille had been kidnapped!*

Things would be over momentarily. The Williams would hand over those duffel bags, and Camille would be safe.

Malia turned on the Prius, thankful for the silent engine, and got ready to pull away. The last thing she wanted was to be caught in the middle of the William family reunion.

The back door of the Suburban opened. A man dressed in camouflage, wearing a black mask over his nose and mouth, got out. Shiny laced-up boots hit the soil and raised poufs of fine red dirt, quickly gone in the wind. He held a pistol in one hand. Reaching back into the SUV, he grabbed something and hauled it out.

That something was Camille, and the man held her upright, wobbly on her feet, by a fistful of long blonde hair. Her mouth was covered with silver duct tape, and her hands were bound in front. She wore the same clothes she'd worn the day she disappeared, and that, as much as anything, brought tears to Malia's eyes: her friend hated to be dirty, and she'd been held prisoner for days without even a bath.

The man tugged Camille against him and pressed the gun barrel to her temple. "You learn who's boss yet?" her captor demanded.

"I don't like your tone," Leonard William snarled. "Screw you."

The other doors of the Suburban opened. Three more guys, uniformed, masked and armed, got out.

In response, the Escalade's doors flew open too. The Williams' two men jumped out, brandishing weapons.

Regina William waved her hands, her voice shrill. "I told you, we have the money. Give us our daughter!"

"Tell me you agree." The man holding Camille addressed Leonard William alone. The kidnapper shook Camille, and even from where Malia was parked, she heard Camille's whimper of pain and fear.

Leonard reached back into the car—but he brought up a pistol instead of the duffel bag.

"I told you I won't do it. Give her to me. I can't miss at this distance."

Every man in the Suburban trained their weapons on Leonard as the man holding Camille laughed, a sound like knives clashing. "I can't miss, either. Give us the money, then. We'll start there and deal with you later."

Leonard turned back and brought out one of the duffels. He set it on the ground.

"I'm losing patience," Camille's captor said. "Where's the rest of it?"

With a gesture almost too swift to follow, he fired a shot into the back tire of the Escalade. The report was unbelievably loud, and the tire blew.

Regina William screamed.

Suddenly there was an explosion of gunfire. Camille wrenched away from her captor.

Everyone dove for the ground.

This was Malia's chance to save her friend! Malia hit the accelerator, and the innocuous silver Prius burst out from beside the bathroom.

CHAPTER TWENTY-ONE

L<small>EI WAS ON THE PHONE</small>, talking with Special Agent Aina Thomas of the Coast Guard about searching ships going out of Maui when Harry stuck her head into the cubicle she was using. "Lei! Dispatch forwarded a distress call from my daughter. She's somewhere outside Lahaina called Shark Cove. I need a partner, now!"

"Absolutely." Lei dropped the phone into its cradle, grabbed her weapon harness off the back of her chair, and stood up. "What's the situation?"

Harry was already striding for the doors of the station, and Lei trotted to catch up. "I don't know much, just that Malia called 911 with some garbled message about Leonard and Regina William and armed men in an Escalade. Dispatch already sent some uniforms that are stationed out there to check it out."

Lei shrugged into her weapon harness as she jogged to keep up with her long-legged friend. They soon reached Harry's vehicle, a Honda CRV with the license plate MAMACOP. Lei smiled despite the urgency of their mission, sliding into the passenger seat and slamming her belt buckle home.

Harry turned on a cop light and put it on the dash, reversed, and pulled out so hard Lei grabbed the side handle of the door for support. They screeched out of the parking lot and wove into traffic. Harry put on her siren, an exterior addition added to civilian vehicles, and they rapidly cleared the downtown Kahului traffic as they blazed through town.

"Now that we're on our way, tell me more about why there's a call from your daughter in the middle of the day, all the way out at Shark Cove. That's past Lahaina, almost an hour away. What's she doing out there?"

"I know as much as you do, at this point," Harry growled. "As soon as she's out of danger, I'm planning to ground her forever. I have no idea how she even got there. She doesn't have a car, or access to one that I'm aware of."

"I'm going to check with dispatch for current status." Lei activated her radio, checking in to let the dispatcher know they were en route.

"Units have been dispatched to the area identified by the caller," Iris said in her unflappably calm professional voice. "They are also en route to the disturbance and should be there in ten minutes."

"Tell us more about the distress call," Lei said.

"Two dropped calls, ten minutes apart, came in from an unidentified cell phone. Specific request was for Detective Harry Clark. Caller identified herself as Clark's daughter Malia. Caller said she was following Leonard and Regina William and suspected that they were being coerced. Two armed men were accompanying them. She said that the William couple was under duress."

"Roger that." Lei ended the transmission, glancing over at her friend.

Harry's hands gripped the steering wheel so tightly that her knuckles showed white; her jaw was tight and her eyes narrow. She gunned the Honda, swerving dangerously into oncoming traffic to pass cars slow to pull over. Lei bit her tongue on a request to slow down; imagining Kiet or Rosie, alone and in danger, made her own hands sweaty as she gripped the handle of the door to steady herself. They soon reached the sinuous curves of the Pali Highway.

"What kind of trouble is Malia in?" Lei asked.

Harry gusted out a sigh and took her foot slightly off the gas pedal. "She's involved with an online gossip blog, and she's been trying to investigate what has happened to her friend, Camille. It's frustrating, because there is something off about Regina's story: first Camille ran away, then she's at a fat farm, yada yada. You were there. Malia has refused to believe Camille's at that camp. From what I gathered has happened today, Malia got her father to drive her to Camille's house to spy on Regina; then, my guess is, she saw something suspicious, got a vehicle somehow, and followed Regina out to Lahaina."

"And why did your ex come to town?"

Harry's cheekbones reddened. "I asked him to come help me deal with Malia. She's been lying, and I'm afraid to find out how deep it goes. Kylie's having troubles, too. Won't sleep in her own bed, hoarding food in her room, clingy. I needed him to come back and deal." Harry flexed her hands on the wheel.

"Wow, that's a lot. Parenting isn't for sissies, is it?"

"No, it's not. Malia has other problems too, like self-injury when she is stressed. All of this developed after Peter left us."

"What brought that on? The separation?"

Harry slanted a glance at Lei. "He told me I loved the job more than I loved him."

Lei touched Harry's rigid arm. "I totally get how someone with a more normal job might get that idea. Fortunately, Stevens and I are both in this career up to our eyeballs, so any problems that come up because of it—we have to solve them together."

"Peter's a lawyer with his own business. He was never able to grow his practice the way he wanted to, because he was deter-mined that we parent the girls ourselves, and not "farm them out" to caregivers. He picked up the slack around my long hours for years. I should have taken his complaints more seriously, but I didn't. For too long. And suddenly, he was gone."

"Seems weird that he was all about parenting and then bailed on not only you, but the girls too."

Harry just nodded. They were approaching Lahaina now, so Lei let her friend focus on the complication of more traffic.

Iris from Dispatch's voice crackled through Lei's radio, asking for their location.

Lei hit the button and gave the street names they were passing.

"Two units nearing Shark Cove have reported multiple gunshots fired. Ambulances are on the way," Iris relayed.

Harry swore.

Lei bit her lip on a cry of alarm as her friend swung the Honda onto a sidewalk on the right, roaring past stopped cars and through a red light.

They headed for Shark Cove at top speed. Hopefully, they'd survive to give aid once they got there.

CHAPTER TWENTY-TWO

HARRY DROVE them on past Lahaina town way too fast, whizzing through an area filled with hotels and condominiums, developments that had filled the former pineapple and sugarcane fields that had once dominated the area. Harry hunched forward over the steering wheel, the siren and light going, as Lei clung to the sissy strap, shutting her eyes to pray for safety—both for them, and for Malia.

Lei pictured Malia's sweet round face with her striking, long-lashed dark eyes. She'd been such a lovely baby—and now, a pretty young woman who clearly possessed both a bright mind and a spine of pure steel. *What had that enterprising teen gotten herself into?*

They entered enough of a straightaway that Lei could let go of the strap and send a few texts: one to Captain Omura, apprising her of their situation, one to Pono, who'd been out on an errand when she'd left, one to Stevens, telling him she was with Harry on a mission to save her daughter . . . and finally, one to her father, Wayne Texeira, a lay minister in his church.

That text simply said, *"Prayer needed for a case."*

Though Lei had never formally joined a church, her faith in a higher power had increased over the years; at the very least, prayer brought comfort in stressful times and she'd seen it answered often.

They passed Ka'anapali and entered the stunning, narrow road that continued around that West Maui section of the island, all the way back to Wailuku.

The radio crackled again with a report of multiple gunshots reported in the parking lot above Shark Cove.

Harry groaned aloud, a terrible sound of pain, and Lei could do nothing for her friend but lay a hand on her shoulder. "We're almost there."

MALIA BARRELED toward her friend in the Prius, blasting the vehicle's horn as she directed the little car between the two embattled SUVs. "Camille!" she yelled through the open window.

Camille leaped to the side, away from the kidnapper, and Malia hit the man with the car. He fell backward, and his gun went off as it flew from his hand and landed on the ground. More gunfire exploded around them.

Malia slid down, below the dash. "Camille! Get in!" she screamed.

Camille grabbed the rear door handle and had barely jumped inside before Malia hit the accelerator again, this time in reverse.

Her friend lay flat in the back seat as Malia pushed the Prius's accelerator all the way to the floor. Malia ran over the kidnapper's gun with a satisfying crunch. She stayed low, her head barely raised enough to see out the back window, steering with difficulty from that awkward position. A thud and thunk of bullets hit the Prius as she jetted backwards down the narrow access road as it looped to join the main highway.

The kidnappers would probably be expecting her to go back toward Lahaina, so Malia would go the other way. That steep, curvy, mostly one-lane road around the empty windward side of the island plunged into deep clefts of untamed jungle or sheer drops to the ocean, and there was only one tiny village for miles in any direction.

Malia had to get them as far toward civilization as she could before the kidnappers caught up.

The Prius careened down the road as Malia clenched the wheel with both hands.

"Malia!" Camille's voice, raspy and dry, came from the back seat. She'd pulled the tape off her mouth.

"Are you okay? Are you shot?" Malia couldn't spare a glance behind her; the twisty route was too challenging at the speed she was trying to keep up.

Camille crawled between the seats into the front passenger side, attempting to free her hands but failing. "Holy shit, Malia! You saved my life!"

"I don't know about your parents, though," Malia said, with a quick grimace to her friend. "I hope they're okay."

Camille's eyes were huge and gray with shock, her mouth trembling. "I saw Mom dive under the Escalade, but Dad—they shot Dad."

Malia concentrated on driving, unable to think of anything to say. From where she'd been sitting, it'd looked like Leonard William brought the whole thing down on himself.

CHAPTER TWENTY-THREE

Lᴇɪ ʜᴀᴅ no attention to spare for Shark Cove's beautiful deep bay with its rocky beach and lush jungle entrance as Harry powered the Honda across the bridge at the bottom of the gulch where that beach was accessed, and up the road on the other side. The turnoff to the Shark Cove overlook's parking area with its bathroom and surf observation hut appeared abruptly; the Honda skidded onto the junction as Harry nearly lost control of the little SUV. The vehicle righted itself, surged forward, then screeched to a stop in front of two uniformed officers who were in the process of putting up crime scene tape, circling it ahead of where an ambulance was parked with its back doors open.

Harry leaped out of the vehicle, charging past the officer holding the sign-in log. "Where's my daughter? Where's Malia?"

Lei exited the vehicle more slowly, following her friend and signing in as Harry reached an area of total carnage, a scene like something out of a war zone. Fallen bodies lay everywhere between and around two large, bullet-riddled SUVs with their doors hanging open.

Harry stopped in the middle of the battle zone, her hands on her hips, her eyes wild. She spun to face Lei. "Where's Malia?"

Lei kept her voice calm as she confronted her friend. "She's not here. That must mean she's safe. Take off your 'mom' hat and put on your 'cop' hat. If you can't do that, leave now, before you screw up this crime scene."

Harry's full lips tightened, and her brown eyes flashed as she bit back an angry response. She turned to survey the bloodbath, then said deliberately, "Yes, sir."

Lei outranked Harry, and Lei had just given an order. Her friend brushed past Lei and headed toward the officer holding the log.

Maybe Harry would get herself together and stay; maybe she would leave to look for her child. That didn't matter—Lei had a job to do here.

Lei checked in on radio with Captain Omura, confirming that they'd arrived and updating her with the situation at the scene. Omura told her that Harry's partner, Pai Opunui, was on his way, as were Dr. Gregory and Dr. Tanaka, Maui's medical examiner team. Becca Nunez and a crime scene intern were also en route.

But Lei and Harry were the first detectives on the scene, and it was imperative to find out what had happened from the one witness left alive: loudly moaning Regina William, lying on a gurney near the black Escalade and being attended by paramedics.

Lei turned to one of the officers as he approached her, a man she recognized from the station. "All of these others are dead? She's the only survivor?" Lei confirmed.

"Yes, sir."

Lei took out her phone camera and began shooting reference photos; these weren't the official crime scene documentation, but for her own ease of recollection. She headed toward where Regina William lay. The woman's cream-colored outfit, covered in blood spatter and dirt, testified that she had taken cover under the Escalade. That had likely saved her life.

Lei studied the ground as she moved forward carefully.

A set of narrow tread, street type tire tracks led between the two vehicles that had faced off. Lei shot photos of the tracks. They stopped abruptly between the cars, then doubled back over themselves. Scuff marks near the Suburban indicated some sort of struggle on that side.

Lei photographed everything, including a masked, bullet-riddled male vic, lying face down just in front of where the tracks stopped.

Someone had zoomed right into the middle of the confrontation, hit this man, and reversed back out of it. That someone was no longer here.

Malia.

Harry's daughter had charged into the fray in whatever she'd been driving, and rescued someone—likely her friend Camille, because this scene had all the earmarks of a kidnap exchange gone wrong.

A smile lifted her mouth. *Malia was one badass kid!*

Lei had already gloved up in Harry's car, so she gently rolled the body that had been hit by the car Malia was driving onto his back. She pulled aside his mask, and gasped as she recognized the face staring sightlessly up at her. "Keo Avila. What are you doing here?"

Maybe this confrontation was about more than just one missing girl.

Lei turned back toward where Harry had gone, only to see her friend advancing with that rangy stride. Harry's light brown eyes were calm and sharp; only brackets of white around her lips indicated stress. "First responders confirm this was the scene when they reached it—no survivors but Regina William. Looks to me like a kidnap exchange that imploded."

"Just what I was concluding. I recognize this perp—Keo Avila." Lei prodded the camouflage-dressed body with her toe. "We'd recently interviewed him in connection with the missing girls. This guy's bad news, through and through. His intel led us to the warehouse where the girls were kept. But if this was a kidnap exchange, where is the Williams' daughter, Camille?" Lei caught Harry's eye, then pointed to the tracks on the ground. "I'm betting she's with your daughter, Malia, in whatever vehicle she was driving to follow the William couple."

The color abruptly left Harry's face and for a second Lei was sure she'd pass out; then, red flushed her cheeks. "That crazy girl barreled right into the middle of the exchange and got her friend!"

"Yep. She one *tita*, your Malia. She's probably taking Camille to the hospital via the backside road, as we speak."

A huge grin broke across Harry's face. "I'm going to kill her when I get my hands on her."

"Don't blame you a bit," Lei said. "Now let's grill Regina on what went down here."

REGINA WILLIAM WAS REMARKABLY unscathed considering the slaughter around her; she'd been grazed on the upper arm, though she moaned and cried as if mortally wounded as her gurney was loaded into the back of the ambulance.

Lei and Harry ousted the paramedics to help the recently arrived Dr. Gregory and Dr. Tanaka, who had a lot of bodies to deal with, and squeezed in beside Regina's gurney.

"What the hell went on here, Regina?" Harry demanded, grabbing the role of 'bad cop.'

"Now, Harry, she's probably in shock," Lei moderated. "Maybe we should wait until we get Ms. William to the station and use one of the interview rooms to take her statement."

"No, no. I can tell you what happened," Regina said hastily. "No need for all of that."

"Just to be clear—you waive your right to have an attorney present?" Lei showed her phone's record feature. "We're going on the record for this." She recited the Miranda warning.

"I did nothing wrong and I have nothing to hide," Regina said, combing her hair with her fingers. "I mean, I did hide something before, but I won't, now."

"Yeah, I'd say it's all right here, out in the open." Harry made a gesture that encompassed the seven bodies scattered over the area. "And both of our girls are missing, so you'd better start talking."

Regina mustered an indignant look as she met Harry's hot gaze. "Did you know your daughter stood on my doorstep and accused me of being 'a poisoning abuser?' And then, the little bitch stole Camille's car out of our garage and zoomed in and took her!"

"Malia probably saved Camille's life, you idiot!" Harry snarled.

Lei put a restraining hand on Harry's arm. "We're on the record here," she said gently. "Harry, do you need to take a break? I can have Opunui come in and join me."

"I'll stay just long enough to find out what she knows," Harry snapped.

"I don't know anything!" Regina cried. "Camille was kidnapped by these assholes who worked in shipping with Leonard. He was trying to get out of his partnership with them—something about the mob on Oahu—so these guys kidnapped Camille to force him to continue, plus wanting him to pay them for lost time! It seemed like everything was going as planned for the exchange, and then . . ." She shut her eyes. "Leonard pulled a gun instead of handing over the cash. And someone fired, and suddenly they were all shooting. I dove under the car, and the next thing I saw, Camille's Prius came zooming in with Malia at the wheel. She hit the main kidnapper and knocked him down. Camille jumped in the back seat, and then Malia backed up to the road and took off!"

"I thought that's what might have happened," Lei said. "Did you see what direction the girls went?"

"I couldn't see from where I was lying under the car."

"You were too busy saving your own skin to see what happened to your child," Harry said. "I've heard all I need to. I'm driving the backside and looking for the girls."

"Good idea," Lei said. "Send Pai in here."

Harry gave a brief nod and jumped out of the ambulance.

Lei looked around and spotted a water bottle. "Can I get you something to drink while we wait for Detective Opunui?"

"Please." Regina's eyelids fluttered. "I'm not feeling well."

"You're in shock," Lei said sympathetically, handing the woman the bottle with the cap removed. "Drink this. Just try to relax."

Regina shut her eyes; she'd gone as pale as the sheets on the gurney. She gulped the water, her teeth chattering against the bottle's opening.

A few minutes later, Pai Opunui jumped up into the cramped vehicle. "Sergeant Texeira. I got here as soon as I could. What's going on?"

Lei turned her recorder back on and took the water bottle from Regina's trembling hand. "Ms. William was just telling us that her daughter Camille was kidnapped," Lei said. "Regina, can you repeat to the detective here what you told us? Again, we're on the record now."

Regina caught Opunui up to speed when Harry had left. "I hid behind the tires as best I could with my arms over my head. The shooting was so loud . . ."

"How did you know that the kidnappers were associated with your husband's shipping business?" Lei asked.

Regina frowned, her mouth pursing. "Leonard knew from the beginning that Camille had been kidnapped. I called him right away when she disappeared, confused by Camille's runaway note and wondering if she'd gone to his boat. But he lied to me at first."

"How did you find out what was really going on?"

"He told me Camille had come to him on the *Mermaid*, which was anchored in Lahaina Harbor. He said Camille was angry with me about all the treatments I was making her do and wouldn't speak to me." Regina licked her lips. "Can I get some more water?"

Lei handed her the bottle again, removing the lid since the woman's arm was injured. Regina drained it, handed it back. "I didn't believe that Camille wouldn't speak to me. I told Leonard I was coming down there with my lawyer to bring her home. That's when Leonard told me she'd been kidnapped. He said he'd had a ransom demand but had no idea who did it." She shut her eyes. "I'd already alerted the cops—sorry, Sergeant Texeira— so we had to have an explanation. I came up with the fat camp idea. I even had a brochure because I'd been trying to talk Camille into going." She sighed. "It was so stressful. You can't imagine."

"You must have been crazed with worry," Lei soothed.

Opunui rolled his eyes, but fortunately Regina didn't see that as she continued.

"Leonard and I'd had a bad divorce. We could hardly stand to speak to each other, and now here I was having to cover up our daughter's kidnapping with him, when I suspected she'd been targeted because of him."

"That must have been awful," Lei said.

"When did you become aware that this was more than a simple kidnapping?" Opunui asked.

"I went out to the boat to talk to Leonard in person about the money, and the exchange meeting—all the details. I saw his armed guards on the *Mermaid and* realized something more was probably going on. While I was in the head, I overheard him talking to someone on the phone—Leonard was threatening the guy, and the caller was threatening him right back. When I came out, I confronted him." Regina shook her head, a tear slipping through the dirt on her face. "Leonard said he did some shipping of illegal goods, and the mob on Oahu were forcing him to continue after he'd refused to do it anymore. They had taken Camille to show him who was boss."

"That's pretty cold, right there," Opunui said.

"Isn't it?" Regina dashed the tears away. "Poor Camille, a

pawn in all of this. And then, the cops sniffing around, tearing my house apart . . ."

"You should have told us what was really going on," Lei said. "We could have helped you from the beginning."

"Leonard said they'd kill us all if I did."

The EMTs reappeared. "We've helped Dr. Gregory all he will let us," one of them said. "Are you done? We'd like to transport our patient now."

Lei looked at Opunui, and he nodded. "We'll follow up with you soon," he told Regina.

The two of them got down out of the ambulance. Shortly afterward, it pulled away. Opunui went over to join the ME, inspecting one of the bodies. The full crime scene team was now on-site, everyone busily working around the bloody scene.

But Lei only had one thing she wanted to do: identify where the kidnappers had hidden the remaining missing girls.

CHAPTER TWENTY-FOUR

CAMILLE CONTINUED to pick at the duct tape on her hands, not making much progress. "Got anything sharp in here?" she asked Malia in a voice that was muffled by chewing on the tape.

"I don't know. This is *your* car!" Malia blew out a breath as the Prius was hit by a gust of wind off the ocean far below.

Camille's eyes widened. "Oh yeah. I guess I knew that—I'm not thinking straight." She used her bound hands to fumble open the glove box. The Mardi Gras beads tumbled out onto the floor as she scrabbled through, eventually holding up a pair of nail scissors. She waggled them in her fingers. "Any chance we can pull over and hide somewhere and you can get this off me?"

"Not a bad idea. Then you can drive. I'm sure you're a better driver," Malia said, slowing around yet another blind corner.

"I don't know about that. You're doing great." Just as Camille said that, Malia swung a little too wide around another curve. A passing car blared its horn at them, swinging dangerously close to the edge. "Okay, that's it. Find somewhere to pull over while we change places."

"It might be a good idea to stay there and hide a while, when we do find a spot." Malia's heart hadn't stopped its rabbit-like thumping since she charged out from behind the bathroom to save Camille. "Both of those big SUVs can go faster than this car. I barely kept up with the one your parents were in on the way to the rendezvous."

"I can't believe you did all that," Camille said.

"I just knew your mom was up to something, so I followed her." Malia spotted a small, rutted dirt turnoff tucked behind a massive boulder outcrop.

She put on the brakes, and the Prius jerked to a stop; she reversed and turned so hard that Camille was flung against the door. Then she gunned the engine to get over a berm like earthen mound she was pretty sure was supposed to keep drivers out.

They lurched over that barrier but were only able to go another hundred feet or so before they reached a cliff encircled by boulders. Malia pulled as far to the right as possible, out of view of the main road. The paint job of the Prius screeched in protest as she took cover behind an overhanging bush. "Oops," Malia said. "Sorry."

Camille flapped her bound hands. "Don't worry about it. Car's already going to the shop because of all those bullet holes."

The girls glanced at each other.

A bubble of hysterical laughter rose, bursting out of Malia's mouth at the same time as one did from Camille's.

The two flopped toward each other, laughing and embracing.

Malia hugged Camille close and felt the moment Camille's laughter turned to shaking, then to tears.

She rocked her weeping friend as a storm of emotion broke over them and slowly abated.

"Let me get this crap off you." Malia took the nail scissors and cut the tape loose at Camille's wrists. Her friend winced as Malia wrestled the sticky adhesive away, leaving reddened patches of irritated skin on her arms.

"You wouldn't happen to have a phone, would you?" Malia asked.

Camille cocked an eyebrow. "Really? A phone? I spent the last week in a metal box with a bucket for a bathroom."

"Holy crap. Did you ever get hold of one, and text me for help at the burner number?"

"No." Camille got out of the Prius. She stretched her arms above her head, spread them wide, and sucked in great gulps of air. Her friend's ribs showed clearly under the filthy tee she wore, a fragile bony arch. "It's beautiful out here."

"Well, someone pranked the Wallflower then." Malia frowned. Far below them, just outside the boulders that defined the area, waves crashed the black lava rocks at the foot of the cliff. A passing squall off the coast made a rainbow that scudded by, trailing over the whitecapped sea. "My phone is out of minutes. We need to call MPD and tell them where we are."

"I can't walk far," Camille said. "I feel really weak."

That was all the warning Malia had before her friend keeled over into the grass. "Camille!" Malia hurried over, squatting down beside Camille's crumpled body.

Had she been shot?

No, it just looked like Camille hadn't eaten the whole time they'd held her prisoner: her cheeks were hollow and her hip bones pressed up in sharp angles against the fabric of her jeans. Her face was white, her lips bloodless.

She'd fainted.

"Your mom should be happy, the fat camp certainly worked," Malia muttered. "Poor baby."

Malia had no food, no water, no actual way to help her friend. She sat in the grass beside Camille and slid her friend's head into her lap. She chafed her hand, then smacked her cheeks lightly. Camille came to, eyelids fluttering. "What's going on?"

"You're here, with me—Malia. We're safe now." Hopefully, that was true.

Camille slowly sat up as Malia kept an arm around her for

support. "They tried to make me eat, but I wouldn't. I was on a hunger strike."

"Geez, Camille. What did you have to prove? You were kidnapped!"

"I didn't want to be helpless." Camille burst into tears. "It was the only thing I could do."

Malia pulled Camille in for another hug. "No offense, but I think we need to get back to civilization so you can get a bath."

"I know I stink. It's so gross . . . Just give me a minute, out here in the sunshine." Camille lay back in the wind-tossed grass, her eyes shut, her arms spread.

"Tell me what happened," Malia said. "When we get back, I probably won't get to see you for days."

"I wish you could stay with me all the time. You make me feel safe." Camille kept her eyes shut as she spoke. "I got home from school like usual, and that man who was holding me at the rendezvous was in the house already, waiting. He made me write that runaway note—for some reason, they wanted Mom to think I ran away, maybe to buy time. A second guy grabbed a bunch of clothes to look like I'd left, and stuffed them in a backpack. They put tape on me and a pillowcase over my head and marched me out to a car. Made me lie down in the trunk." She shuddered.

"What happened next?"

"Like I said, they put me in a toolshed kind of thing. It got hot during the day, and cold at night. I could tell it was somewhere isolated because there was no street noise, just mynah birds and doves, and a dog that barked sometimes, far away. They put food in once a day and a gallon jug of water and took the bucket out. I decided not to eat on the first day. I wanted to make them return me." Camille looked down at her transparent-looking fingers.

"Well, this is really ironic, because your mom said you were shipped off to a fat farm to lose a few pounds."

"What the heck?" Camille frowned. "What do you mean?"

Malia told her about the course of her own investigation,

including the part about Blake blackmailing her to let him help. She watched her friend's face carefully as she told Camille about Blake's involvement. "He really seems to care about you. He helped me a lot."

"Oh, Blake," was all Camille said, and Malia heard a sigh in the words, but wasn't sure what that meant. "Can we get going? I'm sure the coast is clear by now, and I could really use a burger —or three."

MALIA AND CAMILLE pulled up at Jack in the Box in Kahului in the bullet-riddled Prius, which had begun to make ominous hissing noises accompanied by clanking. Malia called her mom's cell from a pay phone, while Camille scarfed down a plain burger, all they could afford with the change Camille had in her ashtray.

"I'm on my way with a squad car," Harry said, the minute Malia finished her breathless explanation. "Does Camille need medical attention?"

Malia glanced in the window, where Camille was polishing off the last of the burger. "Probably, because she fainted—but I think she was just hungry." Malia blew out a breath. "What happened to her parents and the kidnappers?"

"More when I meet you." Harry hung up.

A few minutes later, Malia and Camille were alerted by the cry of sirens. They went outside the fast-food joint to wait as two squad cars pulled up, lights flashing, followed by an ambulance. Harry jumped out of one car and Regina, her arm bandaged, jumped out of the other. The two women converged on them.

"I'm glad we had a little time together," Malia told Camille.

"Me too." Camille's worried eyes were on Regina William as her mother advanced. "I wish you could stay with me."

"I'll try."

Two med techs came over from the ambulance. They insisted

Camille be examined at the hospital and said that only her mother could ride in the ambulance. Camille seemed resigned. She gave a little wave as she and Regina climbed into the vehicle, and it took off.

Harry frowned at Malia. "I'm glad you're alive, but you're in big trouble right now, young lady."

"Can I at least get a hug?"

Harry scooped Malia in close and squeezed her hard. "You crazy brave girl." She kissed Malia's forehead. "I'm taking you to the station to give your statement."

"Okay. Whatever I need to do." They got into one of the squad cars as the other officer dealt with calling an impound tow to take the Prius in. Harry pulled the phone off her belt and handed it to Malia as they drove. "Call your dad. He's been worried sick."

Malia grimaced. She couldn't help feeling guilty for ditching Dad to help Camille. "Am I going to be charged with stealing Camille's car?" Malia asked as she scrolled to find Dad's cell number in her mom's contacts.

"Not sure." Harry stared out the windshield, letting Malia feel the weight of her displeasure.

"What's the latest, Harry?" Peter asked tersely when the call connected.

"Dad, it's Malia."

"Oh, thank god." He caught his breath. "Honey—are you okay? I heard from your mom that you were involved in something to do with Camille's kidnapping."

"Something to do with rescuing her. It's a long story."

"You can tell me when you get home." His voice went steely. "And by the way, not cool to use me to get a ride to her house."

"I'm sorry, Dad. I had to do it." Malia's voice wobbled as Harry shook her head, frowning. "I know I'm in a lot of trouble." She covered her eyes with a hand. "I hope you understand that I was trying to help Camille."

A long pause. The MPD headquarters building loomed in the

twilight—a large brightly lit fortress. Malia'd only been inside once or twice before and she wasn't looking forward to this time even a little bit.

"Kylie and I will be here when you get home. I love you," Dad said. Malia sighed with relief as she ended the call. He, at least, was going to forgive her.

"Will this take long?" she asked her mom.

"I don't know." Harry still wasn't making eye contact. Malia swallowed her other questions.

Sitting in the ugly interview room with its bolted-down Formica table and metal chairs was as intimidating as cop shows depicted. The walls were dingy and one of them sported a one-way mirror. Malia hated seeing her frazzled hair and blotchy, scared face. She looked away, pulling up her hood and zipping up her sweatshirt.

"Want something to eat?" Harry asked. "I can get you something from the break room."

"Yes, please." Malia's stomach rumbled loudly in agreement. Her mom left.

Malia pulled her knees up to her chest and wrapped her arms around them.

She felt like a criminal. She hadn't done anything wrong . . . Well, okay. She'd done a few things. Breaking and entering. Car theft. Cyberbullying.

She leaned her forehead on her knees, wishing herself somewhere far away.

CHAPTER TWENTY-FIVE

Lᴇɪ ᴘᴜʟʟᴇᴅ into the parking lot of the Lahaina Harbor. Pai Opunui pulled in beside her in a dark Ford pickup.

She had called Special Agent Aina Thomas to meet them at the *Moonlit Mermaid's* slip, and she glanced toward the mouth of the mooring area, as he would be arriving in one of the Coast Guard's fast-moving inflatables.

No sign of the craft yet.

She got out of her truck, checking her weapon, and making sure her badge was clearly displayed on her belt. Pono was also on his way from the Kahului station, now that they had what looked like a solid lead. Her partner had asked their go-to judge for an emergency search warrant for the yacht and was bringing it with him to the harbor.

Keo Avila had to be at the heart of what was going on with the disappearances; maybe they'd find something on the William yacht that could move things forward.

Opunui came toward her, his eyes narrowed, a crease between sun-lightened brows. "Are you sure these cases are related?"

"You heard what Regina William said about why their daughter was kidnapped. We have a solid connection between Keo Avila, found dead at the scene, and the missing girls, because of the metal boxes we found that were stored in that warehouse he sent us to. Now that he's gone and so is Leonard William, we need to find the girls before they die in whatever container they're being held in. We don't have time to dick around."

"I get it. I just feel a little behind the eight ball on this, since I wasn't on your case," Opunui said. "Harry is up to speed, but she's occupied with finding the girls."

"I know. Sorry to throw you into the deep end of the pool . . . My team has been working this for months now, along with a task force at the FBI. Speaking of, I'd better bring our agent over there up to speed while we wait for the Coast Guard to arrive."

Lei and Opunui walked through the parking lot towards a beach area that rimmed the marina. Kiawe trees provided welcome shade as Lei put a call through to Marcella on Oahu, leaving a message about the events at Shark Cove and how they'd led to the current search of the William yacht.

As she was finishing the call, Pono drove up in Stanley, his purple lifted truck. Even after all these years, the sight of the little yellow and red replica Hawaiian war helmet dangling beneath Stanley's rearview mirror brought a smile to Lei's face. Pono was getting out of the truck when they heard the powerful roar of the large outboards on the rigid inflatable Coast Guard vessel as it entered the harbor.

Lei and Opunui quickly briefed Pono on the events at Shark Cove as they walked toward the pier, where the Coast Guard Defender was docking, its lights flashing.

Special Agent Aina Thomas, handsome in his uniform, jumped out onto the dock with another agent right behind. Lei and the two detectives approached. "Regina William told us the yacht's name is the *Moonlit Mermaid*, and this is where she's berthed," Lei said by way of greeting.

Agent Thomas nodded briskly. "I looked her up on the way

over. She's a big girl, so she'll be at the end of the mooring." He led the way down the floating dock, a-bristle with vessels tied up on either side of it. The clang of the breeze in the rigging, the squeak of the hulls against the rubber bumpers they were moored to, and the slap of waves created a backdrop of urgency.

The *Mermaid* was huge, almost too big for its slip, but its graceful lines spoke of power and speed. Lei didn't know much about boats, but this one looked expensive.

Special Agent Thomas knocked on the side of the vessel, then called out. "US Coast Guard Investigative Service. We're here to board your vessel. Is anyone here?"

No one answered. The yacht appeared deserted.

He called out again, then held a hand up for Lei and Pono to wait below. He and the other agent proceeded up a short gangplank to the *Mermaid's* deck and the aperture to the main cabin. No one responded to his hails, so he and the other agent explored all of the entries on board, finding them locked.

Agent Thomas came back to the gangplank. "Doesn't look like anyone's here. Do you have reasonable suspicion that these missing girls could be on board?"

"It's a definite possibility," Lei said. "And time is of the essence. The perps involved with their capture might be dead, and I'm worried they will be in danger from neglect in whatever container they're in."

"In that case, we should perform a thorough search belowdecks," Agent Thomas said.

"I agree. The owner of the yacht, Leonard William, is dead, and we have a search warrant," Lei said.

"I've got a door cannon in the back of my truck," Pono said.

Agent Thomas gave him a nod, and Pono jogged back up the pier and soon fetched the heavy metal door breaker. Agent Thomas and his fellow officer made short work of knocking in the yacht's shiny main cabin door.

They drew their weapons as they went into the luxurious interior of the yacht, the CGIS agents in the lead. Agent Thomas and his fellow agent checked all the rooms and pronounced them clear while Lei and Pono waited in a beautifully appointed sitting area.

Lei put her hands on her hips. "William wouldn't keep the girls somewhere easily accessible where Regina or others might come across them. They'd be out of the way, in some sort of cargo area, if there is one."

Agent Thomas's fellow agent was already pulling up the handle of a large hatch into what looked like a lower deck area. He flicked on a light and peered down a ladder into those depths. "I don't see anyone in here."

"They would be in some kind of soundproof box or storage," Lei said. "Maybe even something built-in to fool searches."

They all went below into a utilitarian space separated into a storage area and simple cabins, perhaps for crew.

Lei shone her flashlight over every surface, slowing herself down, taking deep even breaths.

She put herself in the mind of Leonard William.

If he were involved with human trafficking, wouldn't he want to keep an eye on the cargo? If so, what was the best way to do that? Probably one of those nanny cam video monitors, hooked into his personal laptop or phone.

But if he was having a dispute with the traffickers and refusing to move the human cargo, the girls were likely somewhere else, wherever Avila was storing them. Lei and her team had already thoroughly searched the warehouse at the Kahului docks, so that wasn't the location.

They had to find Keo Avila's bolthole.

Meanwhile, if she were Leonard William, wouldn't she keep the smuggling information somewhere hidden, but accessible?

Lei went back up the ladder and into the master stateroom with its distinctively masculine dark blue king-sized bed and teak furnishings. An office suite was separated from the bedroom by a movable partition wall. Lei rifled through the drawers of the neat desk and used her combat knife to pop the lock on a lower drawer.

At the back of the drawer, she found a small leather book, filled with initials and phone numbers. She held the booklet up triumphantly as Pono came in. "This could provide the names of the other people involved with the trafficking!"

"I hope so, because we haven't found anything below except for metal crates full of weapons," Pono said. "He was weapon dealing, too."

"Did you see anything down there that looked like it could have held human cargo?"

"Nothing." Agent Thomas had come to the doorway.

"Well, I found something." Lei showed him the notebook.

The agent washed his hands, which had picked up dirt in the explorations belowdecks, then wiped them on one of the pristine monogrammed towels in the head. "This is a dirty business," Agent Thomas said, pointing to the towel, marked by his hands. "I'll look for any watercraft that are underway associated with William's operation. We will search them all."

Lei picked up a ledger she'd spotted and handed it to him. "Vessel names and registration numbers. All you need to find William's ships." She turned to Pono. "But *we* need to find out who goes with these phone numbers, and any addresses associated with Keo Avila and the Changs. That's where the girls might be."

LEI AND PONO parted ways with Opunui, who headed back to the Shark Cove crime scene—but a sense of urgency in finding at least the most recent victim, Stacey Emmitt, pounded a drumbeat in Lei's veins.

Lei and her partner headed for their trucks. She held the little black book she'd taken from Leonard William's desk in its evidence bag; it could yield evidence useful in tracking down the entire human trafficking ring if she could find who owned the phone numbers, but it wouldn't help any girls who might be trapped in a metal box right now with no one alive who knew its location.

Lei stopped in her tracks and addressed Pono. "We have to find these girls, now. We can't just go back to the station and track down phone numbers while we wait for some new clue to pop up. I'm worried about what's happening to them."

Pono rubbed his mustache vigorously, a fierce frown drawing his brows together. "Let's talk it over with Agent Thomas and see if he's got any ideas."

They returned to the *Mermaid* at her slip. Agent Thomas was running KEEP OUT tape around the yacht as the other agent worked to secure the door they'd knocked in.

Lei and Pono approached the CGIS agents, and by then Lei had an idea. "Aina, any chance we could meet at the Coast Guard Station and use your computers to look for any connection between Leonard William, Keo Avila, and the Chang family?" Lei asked. "I'd like to search for two locations where the girls might be held: one on land, and the other aboard a boat, some craft that's associated with Leonard William and his business. I don't want to drive all the way back to Kahului station just to follow up on phone numbers when time is of the essence."

Agent Thomas's intelligent brown eyes sparkled with excitement. "Sure. If you can give me a ride, we'll go back to the Coast Guard station at Ma'alaea Harbor and my teammate can take the Defender back by sea. If we all work together on this, and time is of the essence as you say, that should be the priority right now."

He gave orders to the agent with him to take the inflatable back around the coast, and he and Lei got into her Tacoma with Pono following in Stanley.

Lei used the time on the drive to Ma'alaea to talk through the different leads they'd discovered. "There's a connection with the Chang crime world through the warehouse owner, Keith Evenson.

Keo Avila, who I identified dead at Shark Cove, is a major player in this human trafficking operation. Avila was working for the Changs on our last case, though we were never able to bust that connection."

"It shouldn't be too hard for me to identify where any vessels associated with Leonard William and his business are currently located," Thomas said. "All owners are required to register their boats, and when they are at anchor, they're supposed to be logged in locally with the harbormaster in charge of each marina. We can track the location of William's cargo vessels using the AIS Automatic Identifications Systems transponders through vessel traffic services. Unless William was hiding a craft in some unregistered docking area, we should be able to find possible hiding places relatively quickly."

THE COAST GUARD station on Maui was a modest building surrounded by a chain-link fence for security. Located at Ma'alaea Harbor, a popular port for whale watch tours, fishing, and other sport or recreational boat traffic, the fenced, reinforced cement block structure overlooked its own dock area.

Ma'alaea was not a commercial harbor, however, so even though Lei ran an eye over the many sport and fishing boats tied up in the marina, she knew better than to hope it would be that easy to find the victims.

They logged into the Coast Guard office with Special Agent Thomas, then ascended to the open loft cubicle on the second floor where Thomas shared space with another agent. That staffer was away, so Lei and Pono drew up chairs in front of his computer. With Thomas's help they logged on to use it to search for tax maps associated with any land owned by the Chang family or their known enterprises.

As they conducted their search, bumping shoulders and arguing good-naturedly, Thomas worked his search of William & Company craft. Soon, Agent Thomas looked up from his monitor, his eyes flashing. "William has a small interisland freighter docked at Kahului Harbor," he said. "Can you come with my team to search it?"

Lei tapped her monitor. "There's a fifty-fifty chance the girls will not be on a boat, but on land, since Avila and William were in conflict over their transportation, but I can have Detectives Torufu and Bunuelos meet you there with a search warrant. Pono and I have spotted a piece of property out in a remote neighborhood outside Wailuku that looks like a possibility; I don't see any building permits for it, so we need to do a drive-by to check if there are any outbuildings that might be suspicious."

"Sounds like a plan."

All three of them stood, then Pono frowned at Lei. "Do you think we should get bulletproof gear on?"

"Nah. Let's just go check out this acreage. If there's nothing on it, we know they're not there. The lot's only five acres, so our side trip shouldn't take long."

Lei and Pono followed Thomas out of his office as the other agent issued orders briskly over a radio, gathering a search team to head to Kahului harbor to meet Torufu and Bunuelos. The rigid-hulled inflatable had just pulled up, and they would be taking that craft, swinging around the island to approach from the sea.

Lei and Pono walked out of the Coast Guard building and headed for their vehicles. Pono flipped a coin about which of their trucks they'd take, and they ended up climbing into Stanley.

Lei patted the familiar chrome skull gear shifter fondly as she settled into her seat. "I can't believe Tiare still lets you drive around the island in this ridiculous thing."

"She never sets foot in it unless she has to," Pono admitted. "You know my wife—all class. She's driving a Mercedes SUV that she paid for with her wedding business."

"You're one lucky man," Lei said.

"I never forget it."

They drove out of the harbor, taking a right and circling through downtown Kahului to head past it to the small village of Waihee, the last bit of civilization before the route that wound its way back to Lahaina.

Lei frowned. "I sure hope Harry has found Malia and Camille. They would have had to come down this way from Shark Cove. Maybe I'd better call her."

"Can't hurt." Pono swung around another vehicle on the busy road.

Lei called Harry's cell and was relieved when her friend picked up right away.

"I was about to call you," Harry said.

"Any news?" Lei asked.

"As a matter of fact, the girls turned up at Jack in the Box," Harry said. "Camille is alive but weak from dehydration and lack of food. She's at the hospital with her mother. I've got Malia down at the station, waiting for you to get here to take her statement."

"Might be a while," Lei said. "We are running down some leads to try to find the remaining missing girls. I'm afraid they might be stuck in some cage or container, with no one alive who knows where they are."

"You don't have to tell me," Harry said. "Don't worry about making her wait. I'm glad Malia has to sit in the interview room and cool her jets. Hopefully it scares her straight from doing any more amateur sleuthing."

Lei chuckled and shook her head. "Not likely to help, if she's got that curiosity gene. I'll get back to you about my ETA as soon as we've checked the area we're headed for."

༄

THE SIDE ROAD to the Chang property was one of those tiny one-lane thruways off the main highway. The narrow route wound into foothills that buttressed the stunning West Maui mountains, robed in green jungle that mantled dramatic cliffs carved by erosion and revealed famously in Iao Valley. Java plum trees, coconut palms, strawberry guava, and stands of wild ginger gave the area a unique character.

"This is it." Lei tapped her phone's GPS when they arrived at a fenced area marked by a large NO TRESPASSING sign, a high barbed wire fence, and an impenetrable-looking stand of guava trees. A padlocked steel gate blocked a muddy dirt track leading into the trees. The whole property had a dank, overgrown, forbidding feel about it.

"Looks like we'll have to go on foot," Pono said, parking in long grass beside the gate. "Good thing I've got my junk shoes on."

Lei pointed to the huge combination lock, thick chain, and shiny metal of the gate. "This is all-new, top-of-the-line stuff. Why the expense for all this if it's just an empty lot?"

"Let's find out."

They helped each other clamber over the slatted metal gate, then walked up a muddy dirt road. The thick guava grove gave little visibility on either side. Lei studied the track made by two wheel-shaped gouges in the turf, but tread marks at the edges looked fresh. She pointed. "Someone came this way not long ago."

Pono nodded. They drew their weapons, holding them in the low-ready position as they moved forward alertly.

The tracks curved sharply to the left, causing Lei to suck in a breath at what she saw as they came around the last of the sheltering grove of trees into an open, grassy area.

A long metal Matson shipping container, often used for storage in the islands, nestled at the edge of the fenced lot, close to the guava grove. The rest of the property was an open pasture.

Lei and Pono scanned carefully but saw no sign of humans— though a camera node was mounted to the top of the container, overlooking the door.

They'd probably already been spotted.

"No one around to hear you call for help," Lei said grimly.

They approached the container carefully, staying out of direct line of sight from the door, which appeared to be padlocked shut, but there was no telling if someone was guarding the merchandise by hiding inside the container.

Once they got within range. Pono lifted his weapon. "Should I shoot the camera out?"

"No. We want to find where that surveillance is being monitored from. That will end up being part of the case," Lei said. As time went on in her career, she was more and more aware that it wasn't enough to simply catch a criminal in the act or stop a crime from happening; she had to try to set up the rest of the case for the prosecution, or things could fall apart even at the booking stage.

Lei and Pono split up and approached the container from the sides. Once they reached the huge metal box, Lei reached over to knock on the fitted, padlocked metal door at one end of the container. "Maui Police Department! Is anyone inside?"

A hollow, metallic, but distinct thumping came from within. "Help me!" a faint voice called.

Lei's eyes grew wide as she met Pono's gaze. "Shit!"

She holstered her weapon and advanced to the padlocked door. She pounded on the door again, calling out, "We're here to help! We'll get you out of there!"

Three loud thumps came back.

Lei tugged at the big padlock, looking over at Pono. "In the movies, they shoot these things off."

"Asking for a dangerous ricochet, and usually doesn't work, anyway," Pono said. "I'll call for backup and have the guys bring bolt cutters. They have to open the gate with those, anyway."

He tugged his radio off his belt as Lei moved around the side. She walked around the length of the twenty-foot container. A window air conditioning unit had been mounted high on the wall on one side. The device was attached to a large solar panel, set on the ground and angled to catch the maximum sun.

When Pono joined her, Lei pointed at it. "Looks like they found a way to give the girls some fresh air out here off the grid. This place is the perfect setup for what they've been doing; we're just lucky we found a connection to it through Harold Chang's ownership of the property. Maybe we'll finally be able to really bring down a part of their operation by connecting him to the trafficking."

"We can hope." Pono rubbed his mustache in a troubled fashion. "The Changs always seem to wriggle out from under whatever we try."

Lei stood ready as the backup police officers broke through the padlock on the Matson container with a pair of long-handled bolt cutters. An officer swung the heavy metal door open; the scent of unwashed body and the smell of human waste hit Lei's nose. Her eyes almost watered as she stepped into the gloomy interior, her heart squeezing with compassion as she glimpsed a pathetic figure in the far corner.

Stacey Emmitt, aged fifteen, still dressed in the clothes she had been kidnapped in on her way home from school, huddled on a mattress. The lidded toilet bucket in the corner was overflowing. A gallon jug of water was tipped over, empty, and her hands were tied behind her back. The only mobility she appeared to have had was that her feet were free.

The moment Stacey's eyes met Lei's, tears welled and rolled down the grime on her face.

Lei hurried over to her, squatting down to work at the knots on her bindings. "It's okay, Stacey. We're here to help. You're going to be all right."

The girl trembled as Pono lost patience and cut the fabric ties that held her arms back. He had already called for an ambulance, and Lei could hear the distant wail of its arriving siren. "Thirsty . . ." Stacey's voice was a ragged whisper.

One of the backup officers nodded. "I'll get you something from my car." He trotted off.

"Can you stand up?" Lei asked.

Stacey shook her head. "I don't think so."

The officer soon returned with a water bottle and handed it to her. "Try not to drink too fast. You don't want to get sick."

Stacey nodded, but quickly drained half of it. Her voice was stronger when she spoke. "I haven't had food in a while either."

"We have a granola bar or two somewhere, I'm sure. It's probably okay for you to eat something on the way to the hospital." Lei nodded to the officer to fetch whatever he could find, then crouched down beside the shivering teen. "Do you have any other injuries? Did they . . . abuse you?"

Stacey shook her head so vigorously that her greasy hair flew around her cheeks. "No. I was afraid he was going to, but he didn't."

"Can you tell us anything about who took you?"

"This guy, he told me he'd give me a ride home from school. I knew I shouldn't, but he had a nice car, he was young and cute . . ." Tears filled her eyes. "It's all my fault."

Keo Avila. Had to be. Anger tightened Lei's belly. "No, it's all your kidnapper's fault. Never forget it. This was done to you. That man who picked you up?" *Keo Avila's glib tongue was stilled forever.* "He will never bother you again."

Stacey raised wet eyes to meet Lei's gaze. "He's dead?"

Lei tightened her lips. "I don't know if I should be telling you this, but yes. He is."

"I'm glad. He kept me in another box, even smaller, with hardly any food, water or changing the bucket." Stacey indicated the receptacle with her chin. "Then he brought me out here. I hope he burns in hell." She choked on an angry sob. "I hate him!"

"Anger is good right now," Lei said. "Just don't direct it at yourself." She patted the girl's shoulder. "There will be a counselor at the hospital to talk to you." She scrolled through her contacts and sent a text to make sure that someone met Stacey when she arrived.

"What else can you tell us? Did you see anyone else?" Pono asked.

"No. I was in a different place for the first few days—smaller, just a box really, like I said. But at least I had magazines and I wasn't tied up." Stacey licked her dry lips. "I tried to get away when he moved me here, and he tied my hands after that."

She'd likely been in Evenson's warehouse until Avila was forced to spill the beans and set up Evenson by planting the hair samples—then he'd moved her here. But where had he kept Camille? "You didn't see another girl?"

"No. But I could tell someone was here before me—the smell. She had blonde hair, too." Stacey indicated the filthy pillow.

Avila had limited contact with the girls himself, and had kept them separated—that blonde hair on the pillow likely belonged to Camille William.

Pono was on his radio, calling into the station with the information that Stacey had been rescued to be routed to her parents. He approached, a big grin on his face. "Your parents will meet you at the hospital. Let's get you to the ambulance."

Lei hooked an arm under one of Stacey's and lifted the girl to her feet. After not being able to move much for so long, with so little nourishment, Stacey's legs wobbled as she tried to help Lei and Pono carry her out of the filthy container.

All three of them sucked in a deep breath of fresh air once they got outside. The backup officers had cut the lock on the gate, and the ambulance trundled into view.

Stacey blinked in the bright sunlight, then smiled, looking at Lei on one side and Pono on the other as they supported her to the vehicle. "If I don't get a chance to thank you again . . . Thank you.

Thank you. Thank you." The girl spoke her gratitude aloud with each step she took.

Lei's eyes prickled. She glanced across Stacey to Pono, and her partner smiled back as tears rolled freely down his fierce brown face.

CHAPTER TWENTY-SIX

LEI AND PONO got back into Stanley once the ambulance had pulled away and radioed Agent Aina Thomas at the Kahului Harbor. "We found one of the missing girls! Any luck at your end?" Lei asked.

"As a matter of fact, yes! We found another girl on the freighter in the harbor. She looks like she's been here for a good long while. We're giving first aid, and Detectives Torufu and Bunuelos have an ambulance and a trauma social worker from the hospital on their way. They're making plans to interview her later." Lei met Pono's eyes—*this had to be the girl who had gone missing before Stacey!*

"Perfect." Lei blew out a breath. "Listen. Now's the time to move on the Chang operation connected with Leonard William's shipping platform. Can you radio to Oahu to have them search and seize any William craft that are underway on the open sea over there?"

"Copy that," Agent Thomas said. "I'm on it."

"I'll get a hold of the FBI to locate any William craft that are moored on Oahu and for some higher level warrants for Chang properties on the other islands," Lei said, with satisfaction. "We'll have those searched, too. Catch up soon."

Back at the station, a flurry of phone calls and other updates followed—but Lei had another priority.

She took time to shower and freshen up in the station's locker room, eager to wash the stench of Stacey's prison off her skin and hair. Her heart still squeezed every time she thought of that fragile girl in that awful metal container with the overflowing sewer bucket.

What had Camille William been through? The same, or worse? Hopefully, Malia Clark would know.

Lei headed toward the interview room where Harry's daughter waited.

"HEY, MALIA!" Sergeant Lei Texeira let herself into the room, carrying a clipboard. Malia's mom's friend looked slim and pretty in black jeans, a green tank shirt, and a tan cotton jacket, her face shiny and makeup-free, her curly hair still damp from a shower. "I'm so glad you're okay. I'm here to take your statement."

Malia made herself smile—she'd been waiting a long time, and it had been scary to sit alone in this grim room with its bolted-down steel table. "I'm glad it's you to talk to me, Lei."

"This interview is going to be recorded. Is that okay?

"Sure."

Lei flicked a switch on the wall that turned on a camera mounted in the corner, then took a seat across from Malia. "Sorry it took so long for me to get here." She blew out a breath that made a curl on her forehead lift comically. "We had a break in the case and were able to rescue two of the missing girls."

"Really?" Malia sat up in excitement. "Where were they?"

"Unfortunately, I can't discuss an active case with a witness, but I thought you deserved to hear the good news. Anyway, the police scanner was going nuts after your calls from Shark Cove asking for help. I'm really interested in how you got involved with what went down." Lei clicked her pen and poised it above the yellow legal pad in front of her expectantly. "Why don't you start at the beginning?"

"Sure." Malia let go of her knees, which she'd pulled up under her hoodie, and slid her feet to the floor. "But I don't really know where to start."

The door banged open. Harry strode across the room, dropping a granola bar and a couple of juice boxes in front of Malia. "Malia's a minor. I have a right to be here." Harry yanked another chair out and sat next to Malia, eying Lei. "Hope you didn't ask my daughter anything without me present."

Lei grinned and held her hands up in a "surrender" gesture. "I wasn't sure where you were, Harry. We were just getting started. I'm glad you're here."

Harry pushed one of the juice boxes over to Malia in a silent gesture of support. "I take it this is all being recorded."

"It is. Saves Malia having to tell her story over again."

Malia unwrapped the little straw, stuck it in the hole, and sucked thirstily. The taste and smell of apple juice reminded her of being a little kid; she'd never been so grateful to her mom. She leaned against Harry. "What do you want to know?"

"Only everything." Lei smiled. "Why don't you begin at the beginning?"

"I'm not sure where that beginning is." Malia glanced at her mother. "I've basically been looking for Camille since she went missing. I never believed she ran away, *or* that she was at the fat camp."

"I gathered that." Lei leaned back slightly. "Tell us why."

Malia pierced the second juice box and sucked it dry. "I know Camille. She would have found a way to communicate with me if she could have. From the beginning, I thought something bad happened to her, and that her mom had something to do with it." Malia proceeded to tell Lei about her theory about Ms. William and the rat poison.

Lei frowned, meeting Harry's eyes. "I remember when we searched the house. You were looking for that."

Harry nodded. "We never found the yellow box of poison you described," she told Malia.

"She must have got rid of it." Malia shrugged. "The other person I suspected was Leonard William. I know he's her dad, but he seemed fishy, too." Malia left out how she'd come to get his number but described the content of their phone call and how it had made her more worried and suspicious. "Then I tracked the IP of his computer and found his boat at the Lahaina Harbor." Malia fiddled with the straw, uncomfortable with leaving Blake's involvement out, but unwilling to name him.

"Let's move to today's events. How did you come to be driving Camille William's car?" Lei's brows rose. "Regina told us you came to her house and confronted her."

"Yes. Dad dropped me off near their house." The part about getting Dad to do that was best left out. "I went to talk to Ms. William—I wanted to push her a bit and find out if I could contact Camille at the fat camp. I ended up telling her off. After we had words, she threatened to call the cops." Malia spared a glance at her mother, who shook her head. "I left, but I still thought she was up to something and I wanted to find out what. Her car was parked in front, which usually means she's going somewhere, so I went around the back of the house to see what she was doing."

"You're very observant and curious." Lei smiled.

"You mean good at spying on people," Harry said.

Malia flushed but forged on. "I heard Ms. William on the phone outside her office. She told someone she'd be there shortly. She seemed really stressed out. I thought she might have done something to Camille and was covering it up."

Lei's eyes widened. "Really. What did you think she'd done?"

"Like I said, I thought she was medically abusing Camille. I thought she maybe did something really bad to Camille and she and Camille's dad were . . . um . . . hiding her or something, probably on the boat, but maybe at a house somewhere in Lahaina—I don't know. So, after she got in her car, I borrowed Camille's car and followed her."

"Borrowed?"

"Yes. Borrowed." Malia didn't look away. "Ask Camille. She'd given me permission to drive her car."

"Perhaps. But you didn't ask Camille this time, did you? Nor Regina William, either, who's the actual owner of the car. In fact, you don't have a license to drive alone at all."

"Don't answer that," Harry said.

Malia folded her lips and looked down. "I thought Camille was in danger."

"We'll put that aside for now." Lei's tone softened. "Please go on."

"I followed Ms. William out to Lahaina, and she met Leonard at the marina. When they left his boat, it looked like they were being taken somewhere in that Escalade by two armed men. I was scared. I called 911 for help, and I didn't have many minutes, so after I told them what I saw, I hung up. You probably have that recorded."

"What happened next?"

"I followed them onto the highway. As soon as I knew which direction they were going, I called 911 again and used the last minutes on my phone to tell the operator where we were headed." Malia wiggled the straw in the juice box; now her mom knew she had a second phone. Oh well, she had bigger worries. She filled in the rest of the story. "I was watching from behind the bathroom. No one pays attention to a Prius. It seemed like things were going okay, that it was a kidnap exchange—and then, suddenly they were all shooting." Malia didn't realize she was crying until a hot tear landed on her hand. Harry squeezed her arm. "I just hit the gas and zoomed out. I ran into the kidnapper who had Camille and knocked him down. I yelled at her to get in the car, she jumped in, and I drove her out of there. They shot up the car but didn't hit us."

A long pause.

"Anything else?" Lei asked.

"Not really. Camille was bound with tape. I found a place to pull off the road and hide so I could cut her loose, but she fainted because she hadn't been eating. Then we drove to Jack in the Box. The car was having problems by then."

"Did you see Leonard William or any of his men shoot at the kidnappers?"

"Leonard William pulled a gun first, but I don't really know who shot first. There was a lot of shooting. I was just focused on getting Camille out of there."

"Where was Camille held captive? Did she tell you?"

"She said it was a boxlike metal place. That there were no other people around. She was given food and water, but she refused to eat. She was on a hunger strike, she said." Another hot tear hit Malia's hand.

Lei led Malia through the story again. And again, gently teasing for details about that final confrontation.

Several people had died in that shootout; Malia could tell. She was going to end up being a witness. Malia repeated what she remembered as truthfully as she could, but suddenly she was drooping with fatigue.

Harry held up a hand. "That's enough for today, Lei. You can get in touch with me if you need anything further and we'll schedule an interview."

"Sure. Thanks for hanging in there, Malia." Lei stood up and turned off the recording equipment. She patted Malia's shoulder as they walked to the door. "You're a very brave girl."

"Don't give her any ideas," Harry said. "The news is already all over this, and I don't want her getting a puffed-up head."

"What?" Malia looked around frantically. "I don't even know what's happened!"

"Let's get you home and hope the reporters aren't camped out at the house," Harry said. "I'll fill you in on the way."

Malia trotted after her mom's long legs as they strode to the parking lot. They got into the Honda. Harry slammed the door and turned to Malia. "You have a second phone. How long have you had it? What do you use it for?"

"Oh, geez, Mom! Who cares about my phone? People died out there. Please, just tell me who!"

Harry turned on the ignition. "Everyone except Regina died. And Camille, thanks to you. We're trying to piece together what happened. Regina William's version of events pretty much matches yours."

"I didn't run over that guy." Malia's heart pounded at the memory of how he'd thumped into the bumper. "I did hit him, and he fell down. That's how Camille was able to get away. But I don't think I killed him." Malia had begun to shiver; the reactions she hadn't let herself feel were catching up with her. "Did he die from getting hit by the car?"

"We don't know yet. The ME's still examining the body, but from what I saw, it looked like he'd been shot." As they drove home, Harry told Malia how she'd dispatched squad cars from Lahaina to intervene, and driven "like a madwoman" from Kahului, following Malia's last call to 911. "Honey, that scene was bad. A bloody mess, literally. I'm so glad you got out of there safely and got Camille out of there—but my God, girl! What were you thinking?" Harry put her signal on, pulled over, and turned in her seat to yell at Malia. "Don't you ever—I mean, ever—put yourself in danger like that. Call me! I'm trained to handle situations like this!"

Malia covered her face with her hands. "I was afraid to call you. I hardly had any minutes."

"Back to that phone. That's what you use for that damn gossip site, isn't it?"

Malia froze.

She couldn't answer.

Couldn't look at her mom.

Couldn't remove her hands from her face.

Shame swamped her. Shame, and *terror.*

"You know what? I don't want to know. If I did, I'd have to do something about it, and that would be bad at your school and for the case, because your credibility as a witness would be ruined." Harry drew a long, shaky breath and blew it out. "Here's the thing. You may well have saved your friend's life. You're going to be called a hero. You now have a responsibility to act like one. I don't want to hear one more bad thing about that Wallflower site, now, or ever. If I do, we will have that conversation, and to hell with the consequences."

"Okay," Malia said. "I'm sorry, Mom."

Harry turned on the CRV, pulled back onto the road, and they drove home in silence.

CHAPTER TWENTY-SEVEN

LATER THAT AFTERNOON, Lei and Pono, driving Lei's truck, pulled up and parked near the long, curved turnaround drive that led to importer Harold Chang's house in Wailuku. Torufu and Bunuelos got out behind them. All four were dressed for the raid in protective gear. They stayed silent, trotting up the drive with its silky tufts of golf course grass growing up between the bricks, past the man-sized bronze dragons guarding the entry, and all the way up to the fancy front door.

As Lei reached the portal with its long silken tassel of a bellpull, she remembered the first time she had come to question Chang about his involvement in their pirate case.

They hadn't been able to get him then; his lawyers had blocked any involvement.

This time, they had more evidence tying Chang to the girls: Keith Evenson, who technically owned the warehouse where they'd found evidence of the girls' captivity, had finally admitted that Harold Chang was its real owner, and that he suspected "everything Chang imported and exported wasn't legal."

Still thin, but enough for an arrest warrant.

Pono and Bunuelos split apart and ran around the sides of the house to block any other escape routes. Lei pounded on the glossy front door. Torufu bellowed, "Open up! Maui Police Department!" The same maid Lei had encountered before appeared, her eyes wide in astonishment.

Lei and Torufu brushed past her, their weapons drawn.

They found Chang seated on a gold-plated toilet, wearing a magnificent satin robe and fuzzy bedroom slippers. The man slowly raised his hands as Lei and Torufu approached. "Don't shoot! I surrender."

Dad had pulled his rental onto the lawn so Harry could hit the garage door opener and drive straight inside, past the cluster of news vans lining the road outside their driveway. Malia gasped at the sight.

"I told you everyone wants to talk to you about what happened. When you're ready to talk to the media, I'll schedule a press conference. That way we can make sure you say what you want to, it's controlled, and it's over with quickly." Harry closed the garage door behind them.

"I can't even—I feel sick." Malia ran into the house, past her dad, his mouth open and spatula in hand, past Kylie setting the table, and up the stairs to the bathroom. She paused long enough to slam the door before she fell to her knees, dry heaving into the toilet.

Nothing came up because she hadn't eaten in so long—she never had eaten the granola bar Harry had dropped on the steel table of the interview room.

If only she could disappear down the pipe somehow. She didn't want to be in the spotlight—everyone seeing her, asking her questions, maybe even uncovering the Wallflower.

Malia battled the temptation to scratch her arms in reaction to the stress. Instead, she flushed, shut the toilet's lid, and laid her head down on it, wrapping her arms around the cold porcelain, her teeth chattering.

Her mom entered and knelt beside Malia, rubbing her back. "You're in shock. You had a traumatic experience. These are all normal reactions to an event like this. You're going to be okay."

Harry's calm voice of authority was just what Malia needed. She turned to hug her mom and sobbed in her arms. When she wound down, Harry turned on the bath.

"Soak in here as long as you need, and when you come down, dinner will be waiting for you."

Malia ended up eating off a plate in bed, with Mom on one side, Dad on the other, and Kylie wedged in at their feet with her bag of popcorn. They watched Kylie's favorite movie for the umpteenth time. Malia didn't remember when she fell asleep.

MALIA WOKE up to the sense that she was being smothered. Buried alive in a hot, dark metal box, with her hands bound—*like Camille*. She flailed her arms, trying to get out, and heard "Ow!" from beside her.

She sat up, blinking and pushing hair out of her face. Kylie was holding Doodlebug up to fend her off. "You hit me, Malia!"

"Bad dream. Sorry."

Dad had gone during the night, but Harry, tousled with sleep, glanced at the clock from her side of the bed. "Time to get up, anyway."

Malia slid past Kylie, who'd settled back down wrapped around the stuffed bear. "Do you really have to go in to work on the weekend?" she whispered as she and Harry exited the room.

"Yes. Thanks to our big case, we have a lot to do at the office. Your dad's in Kylie's room. You were so sound asleep last night I just let you both stay in bed with me."

"Can I have my phone and laptop back?"

Harry pinned her with a narrowed gaze. "You must be kidding, Miss Grand Theft Auto."

"Worth a try," Malia said.

She turned to go downstairs as Harry went into the bathroom. In the kitchen, Malia busied herself making coffee. As soon as it was going, she used the house phone to call Camille's number. No answer.

She tried the William house phone next. It rang and rang, and then Regina William's voice mail came on. Malia glanced at the clock—well, it was early. She'd try again later. She needed to call Blake too, and catch him up on all that had happened.

Dad came in, rubbing messy blond hair. He was tan and more toned than he used to be and looked good, for an old guy, even in old sweats and an undershirt. "Coffee ready?"

"Mugs are over there." Malia pointed. "You're looking buff, Dad."

"Thanks. I took up Bikram yoga. Great for the body and detoxification." He removed a mug, filled it, handed it to her. "I know you're drinking the devil's brew now."

"Well, it's not going to stunt my growth any more than this," Malia said, making a gesture that encompassed her shortness.

Dad snorted a laugh. "Yeah, you're on the petite side."

This time Malia snorted. "Petite? More like short and fat."

"Not true, honey, and you know it. But then, don't all teenage girls have body issues?"

Malia shrugged. Her dad wasn't going to talk her into believing something she wished were true. *Petite?* With these boobs? She crossed her arms over them, remembering she didn't have a bra on. "So, what's Bikram yoga? As opposed to other kinds?" she asked, to change the subject.

"An hour of structured poses done in a hundred-and-five-degree room."

"Sounds like hell. Literally." Malia grimaced as she sipped the black coffee. "I still need some half-and-half. Trying to do without because of the calories, but I'm not there yet." She took the carton out of the fridge and splashed some into her mug.

"Let's go outside for a minute before your mom comes down." Dad indicated the door with his head.

Malia followed him, mentally bracing herself to apologize for getting him to take her to Camille's house. She followed him to the back stoop, a cement slab outside the garage that looked out at their empty, forlorn backyard, with its sagging chain-link fence and view of scrubby wild java plum trees. Beyond that, richly green, corrugated West Maui mountains began to light up with the day, garlands of morning-lit cloud draping their peaks.

Tears prickled her eyes—with her dad standing beside her and all four of them together under one roof, the rental house felt like home for the first time. They sat on the splintery bench facing the backyard. "Dad, it's so good to have you back. I'm sorry again for what I did yesterday—for getting you to take me to Camille's. For not being honest with you."

"I get it. You needed to help a friend; you couldn't ask permission for something I'd never let you do because it was too damn dangerous." Peter circled her shoulders with an arm and squeezed. "Please don't ever scare us like that again. That said, I'm proud of you. I hope you'll be that loyal to me, someday."

"Are you going to stay with us, Dad?" Malia's voice was a ragged whisper.

He kissed the top of her head. "If your mom will let me."

"She still loves you," Malia said. "But don't skimp on the romance. Mom deserves it."

"Is that so?" Her father squinted at her, the sun in his eyes. "How do you know she still loves me?"

Malia couldn't say anything about the anniversary date access code on Harry's laptop. "I just know. And Mom is awesome. She could have anybody. Don't let her get away." Malia stood up. "It was tough on all of us, you leaving. None of us saw it coming. It's going to take a while to be able to forget."

Peter's mouth tightened in remorse. He reached out, caught her hand, and squeezed it. "I will give it my best to earn the trust of each of my girls again."

Back in the house, Malia punched in Blake's number on the house phone. He sounded raspy, as if she'd just woken him. "Hello?"

"Everything went down yesterday," Malia said. "Camille's safe now, but Leonard William got killed. Can you come over? I'd like to tell you what happened in person."

"This I gotta hear. On my way. Meet you at our spot." He ended the call.

Harry came down the stairs, brushing her long brown hair. She'd put lipstick on, an unfamiliar touch of red, and she looked beautiful in a scoop-necked tee and tight jeans.

"Where you going?" Harry asked, slipping a pearl earring into one of her lobes.

"Just for a walk. I'll be back in an hour or so. Dad's outside and he'd like to see you."

Malia hurried to grab her shoes by the front door, peeking out to make sure the reporters were gone. Thankfully, they were. She walked down to the turnout and paced back and forth, missing her phone and worrying about Camille. *Why hadn't her friend called yet?*

She heard the Mercedes's engine, and Blake drove up.

He'd taken time to shave and his hair was wet from a shower. He smelled minty and delicious when he opened the door for her. Malia wanted to throw herself into his arms and kiss him. Instead, she closed the car's door quietly as she sank into the soft leather seat. "Thanks for coming."

He moved a swath of hair out of her eyes. "Tell me what's been going on."

Malia pulled her legs up under her hoodie, turning to face him as she folded in on herself. "A lot. But you can't talk to anybody about it until they say we can. Promise?"

"Of course."

Malia told him everything about what had gone down at Shark Cove.

"So, while I was at football practice, you were stealing Camille's car and chasing kidnappers around the island?"

"Borrowed. I *borrowed* Camille's car. And even though I saved her, I had a totally scary interview down at the station, and I'm a witness in the case. Apparently, Leonard William, some other guys, and the main kidnapper I hit with the car died. Mom's going to be at the station all day today, working on the case."

"Holy shit," Blake breathed. "You're a hero."

"What was I going to do? Sit in the car while Camille got shot? What surprises me about the whole thing was how easy it was for me to run that guy down. How much I wanted to drive right over him and finish the job." Her teeth had begun to chatter again.

Blake pulled Malia over, pressing her close against him, his arms tight and strong around her. Her ear rested over his heart, the slightly accelerated thud of it matching hers, and for a long moment that was enough.

Slowly her arms loosened from around her legs as the tension melted from her body. She unfolded, sliding her hands up the muscles of his arms and around his neck, turning her head toward his, extending her legs for support. The shivering stopped, leaving a blooming warmth in its place that drove darkness out of her thoughts and anchored her in this perfect moment.

For long moments, nothing but *now* happened, and that was all, and more than enough.

Malia pulled back. "I haven't talked to Camille about us yet. I tried to call her this morning from the house phone, but she wasn't picking up. I don't have any minutes on the burner, and I'm still grounded from my own phone."

"I told you I'd talk to her. Let me try now."

Malia's throat went dry—*would Camille be devastated?* Was

this the right time to tell her she and Blake were together, with the trauma from the kidnapping so fresh?

Camille might be even more hurt by hearing this from Blake, at a time when she needed all the support she could get. Malia opened her mouth to tell him to let her talk to Camille first, but he'd already called. "Camille? It's Blake. Are you okay?" His voice was warm and soft.

It was wrong to sit here listening to him. Malia felt sick again, wishing she'd found some way to talk to Camille herself. She opened the door, gave Blake a little wave, and walked rapidly back down the road and back to the house.

WHEN MALIA GOT HOME the house was silent, and the red rental car was gone. She hurried into the kitchen.

"Mom?" No one there. She peeked into the garage—her mom's car was gone, too.

She found a note by the coffeemaker: *"Malia: I had to go to work, and your dad's got some errands. I'll call later. ~Mom*

Kylie came downstairs, pushing snarls out of her eyes as she headed to the pantry cupboard and got a box out. She shook some Lucky Charms into a bowl. "Hey."

"Hey yourself." Malia looked at the clock—would Camille be done talking to Blake yet? As if on cue, the house phone rang. She ran over and snatched it up. "Hello?"

"Malia?" Camille's voice sounded hoarse, thready. "When can I see you?"

"I'm so glad you called. I've been worried sick! But I'm stuck at the house with no wheels, and I can't leave Kylie here alone even if I could get a ride." Malia paced back and forth, brought up short by the beige phone cord.

"You can leave me here," Kylie said, digging into her bowl of cereal. "I'm almost twelve, and that's legal to be left alone."

Malia ignored this. "Can you come over here by any chance?"

"I'm at the hospital." Camille was crying. "They admitted me when I came in, said I was dehydrated. I'm calling you because—Mom's trying to send me to a mental institution."

"What?" Malia looked around wildly. "No way!"

"She's got the doctors convinced I have PTSD and an eating disorder, just because something is wrong with my stomach and I can't keep anything down. Malia, you have to help me! I think Mom might be behind this whole thing!"

"Wait a minute. Why would she have her own daughter kidnapped?"

"She'd do anything to get back at Dad. Her gallery's been struggling and needs cash. I bet she thought this would be a nice two for the price of one: stick it to Dad, and cream off a couple mil of his money for herself in a kickback from the kidnappers. And boy, she stuck it to him, all right." Camille wept in great sobbing breaths.

"Your mom seemed so upset when I followed her yesterday. What makes you think she's behind it?"

Camille struggled to stop crying, gulping and blowing her nose. She finally said, "I should have told you yesterday when we were alone. I was just in shock or something, but I overheard the kidnappers talking about whoever had paid them. They were going to double-cross "her" and they said "she." What other "she" is there, other than my mom?" Malia pictured Camille in the hospital bed, white as the sheets she lay on, terrified and alone. "And don't forget Mom fed me rat poison!"

"You knew about that?"

"I suspected. I've suspected a lot of things."

"Oh man. I'll call my mom. She'll know what to do. Did you talk to Blake about this?"

"No. He was too busy trying to tell me he had a crush on you, and frankly I couldn't care less. My mom's trying to get me put away!"

Malia squelched the tiny surge of relief she felt at Camille's words—now wasn't the time to get into any of that. "I won't waste another minute. I'm calling my mom. She can stop this."

"Please! You have to do it now. They're moving me to the mental ward any minute, and I won't be able to see anybody or call anybody once I'm locked up!" Camille broke down again.

"I love you, Camille. I didn't save you from kidnappers to see you shipped off to a rubber room. Hang in there." Malia hung up.

"Wow," Kylie bugged her eyes theatrically from her side of the table.

"You can't talk to anybody about this," Malia said.

"I'm not a baby."

Malia rolled her eyes and called Harry's cell phone. *No answer.* She called the station, asked to be put through to Harry's office. The voice mail picked up.

"Dammit!" Malia paced and finally called 911.

"What's your emergency?" the operator said.

"I urgently need to speak to Detective Harry Clark. This is her daughter."

"This is a public emergency help line, not a message service, young lady."

"It's an emergency! She's not answering her cell or office line, and the girl I just rescued, Camille William—is being put in the mental ward!"

"I understand you're upset, Malia. I heard about you on the news this morning. You were very brave." The dispatcher's voice was too calm.

"Please, can you just get hold of my mom and have her call me?"

"Malia. Calling 911 for nonemergency is a serious offense; I'll let your mother know you called this number as a favor. I'm sure she won't be happy about it because it'll be going into her employee file." The operator hung up.

"That didn't go well," Kylie said.

"I have to get to the hospital. I have to do something." Malia thought of calling Blake, but an adult was a better idea. She called her dad's cell.

"What's up, Malia?"

"Dad! It's an emergency—Regina William is having Camille put in the psych ward, and then shipped off to a facility. I need you to drive me to the hospital and get it stopped!"

"What about your mom? She seems in a better position to help with something like that."

"She's not answering her phone!"

"Okay. I still have a license to practice law in Hawaii, so perhaps Camille can retain my services as legal counsel."

"Oh yes, thanks Dad!" Relief surged through Malia. "Though I thought you practiced estate law?"

"I can pinch-hit on any kind of legal problem in an emergency," he said. "On my way."

Malia ran upstairs. She dragged a brush through her hair and braided it, pulled on her 'Camille jeans' and a dark purple button-down shirt that Gram had given her for Christmas. She threw on a little makeup. She looked almost pretty, and a lot older than sixteen. That might help the adults at the hospital take her more seriously.

Kylie hung in the doorway. "I'm coming with you."

"I'd rather you didn't."

"Too bad."

Both girls were waiting on the front steps of the house when their father drove up in the now familiar red Ford Focus. Malia got in the front as Kylie climbed in back. Malia handed her father a one-dollar bill.

"I'm retaining your legal services on behalf of Camille William."

Her father's smile lit up his face; he'd really wanted to help. "I'll do my best."

Kylie thrust her tousled head between the seats. "What's going on?"

"Yes, I could use a recap," Dad said. "Tell me more about this phone call you got from Camille."

The remainder of the drive was taken up with Malia's description, including what Camille knew about the rat poison and other things Regina William might have done.

They parked at the hospital. Dad told Kylie to play on her phone and wait in the lobby as he and Malia went to the information desk and asked about Camille. Fortunately, she hadn't been moved to the psych ward yet, but on the way up to her room, a white-coated doctor intercepted them in the hall.

"I'm Dr. Gelanno, Camille's emergency care physician. I was paged by the front desk that you're providing legal representation to Camille?"

"Yes. She called me for help to prevent a transfer to the psych unit and further transition to a mainland facility."

"Can we speak privately?" Gelanno glanced pointedly at Malia, who folded her arms and thrust out her chin.

"Malia, why don't you go see Camille while I talk to the doctor," Dad asked. "She can do that, right?"

Dr. Gelanno nodded. After a moment spent considering her options, Malia walked toward the room number they'd been given at the information desk.

Camille's door was shut. Malia knocked and pushed it open.

Her friend was lying in bed, hooked up to an IV. Pale, with purplish circles under her eyes, Camille's moonbeam-blonde hair was still greasy and lank from captivity, and she looked so skinny that her body hardly lifted the sheet. Worst of all, one of her hands was attached to the rail of the bed with a padded restraint.

"Oh no, Camille!" Malia ran to hug her friend.

"They shot me up with something after I called you." Camille's speech was thick. "I can't think straight, but I feel better." She giggled helplessly as tears welled in her eyes.

"I brought my dad. He's representing you as your lawyer, so if anyone asks, say you called him and hired him. I paid him a dollar on your behalf, so it's official."

"They're telling me I have post-traumatic stress disorder, and that's why I think my mom is behind all this." Camille's eyelids fluttered shut as if it were too much effort to keep them open. "Thank you. Peter Clark is my lawyer. Yay. I can go to sleep now."

Malia held Camille's hand, sitting close in one of the plastic chairs. Camille's breathing changed, slowing down to barely discernible—she'd passed out, or was deeply asleep.

The door opened. Two burly orderlies rolled in a gurney.

"No! Stop! You can't take her!" Malia jumped to her feet. "I won't let you!"

"Sorry, miss. We're just here to transport Camille William to the psychiatric side for observation and stabilization," one of the men said soothingly.

"No!" Malia threw herself bodily over Camille. She grabbed the red button attached to the frame and pressed it repeatedly. They tried to grab Malia; she fought and kicked, screaming, "Fire! Fire!" Her mom had told her nothing got people moving to help like a cry of 'fire.'

The two men pried Malia, still screaming "Fire! Help!" off Camille, just as her dad appeared in the doorway.

"Let go of my daughter!" Peter yelled.

This gave Malia a second to lunge over and pull the fire alarm on the wall.

The hospital corridor erupted in flashing lights and beeping noises, and the two attendants let go of Malia, shaking their heads.

"I don't get paid enough for this shit," one of them said. "We're calling security." They rolled the gurney back out.

"You might have bought a little time, but it seems as if, according to Dr. Gelanno, he might be justified in trying to put Camille in psychiatric care. He says his assessment has nothing to

do with Regina William. Camille's been trying to hurt herself."
Peter held up one of Camille's bandaged wrists.

"She's traumatized and grief-stricken because her dad was
murdered. Putting her in a padded room and shooting her up with
drugs is terrible! She needs familiar places and loving people to get
over this!" Malia gulped back a sob, hugging her unresponsive
friend. "Let's take her home to our house!"

The door opened, and this time it held two uniformed security
guards.

"We need to clear the room," one of them said. "And you need
to come with us, young lady. Pulling a hospital fire alarm under
false pretenses is a police matter."

Peter Clark took out his wallet and handed the security guy his
card. "This is my client, Camille William, and this is my daughter,
Malia, her best friend. She got a little hysterical finding out that
Camille is going to psych. Her mother is a police detective. We
will certainly deal with her behavior at home."

"Afraid that's not good enough," the security guard said. Malia
looked frantically at her dad as, one on each side, the men took
hold of her arms.

"Don't fight. Go with them." Her dad squeezed her shoulder as
he met Malia's frightened eyes. "We'll handle this legally, the right
way. I'll stay with Camille and keep her safe."

Peter already had his phone out, calling someone, as Malia shut
her eyes and went limp, dropping to the ground, making the men
drag her down the hallway.

The security men took her in the elevator down a couple floors
and pushed her into a small conference room with nothing in it but
a table, chairs, and a trash can. One wall held a whiteboard
and pen.

"What are you doing with me?" Malia cried, but they just
walked out. Malia heard the door locking.

She sat down at the table, then got up and paced. It felt weird
and awful to be trapped in here with nothing to do and no way to

communicate. She hadn't realized how seldom in her life that had happened to her; and she flashed to the missing girls' ordeals. "Oh, Camille. How can they be doing this to you?"

Malia mentally scrabbled over her options—there were none. She tried the door handle. *Locked.*

She'd write out her concerns about what Camille had told her with the erasable marker on the whiteboard for something to do; maybe someone would read it.

Malia wrote out all her suspicions and what had led to her rescue of Camille.

It took a long time.

Standing back to look at the board, holding the pen in her hand, Malia felt better somehow. Hopefully, someone would read it before they scrubbed it off.

She sat down at the table and leaned her head on her folded arms, exhausted by the drama. She must have dozed off because she woke up to the sound of the door unlocking.

Detective Harry Clark stood in the opening. Her mom looked pale but resolute, her jaw set. "Malia, for goodness' sake! Can't you stay out of trouble for five minutes?"

"They're taking Camille to psych!" Malia wailed. "Her mom's having her committed to an institution!"

Harry held up a finger to the security guards in the hall, entered the room, and shut the door. Out of view of the little glass panel in the door, she pulled Malia close and spoke quietly into her ear.

"You couldn't reach me because I was in the interview room with Regina William. A witness we found turned on her, bargaining with us by telling us that Regina tried to set Leonard up by inciting Camille's kidnapping. Phone records to a burner we found in her possession confirm this. She's been arrested for conspiracy to commit murder, kidnapping, and medical child abuse. She won't be making any decisions about Camille's welfare anytime soon."

Malia hugged her mom desperately tight, tears flooding her eyes. "But what's going to happen to Camille now?"

"Regina is an only child with no relatives, but Leonard William has a sister who lives in California. Camille's Aunt June is flying out now. Camille's quite an heiress and will need someone to take care of her and look out for her interests. Your dad told me you suggested she come home with us—she can, of course, but only for a few days, and only when Dr. Gelanno decides that she is safe to be released from the hospital. I can't have a suicidal teen who's lost both parents in our house."

"I get that, but I think it would be good for all of us to have her."

"It's not an option right now, and I have to take you down to the station for a citation—at least make it look like I'm slapping you with a consequence for pulling the fire alarm."

"I just wanted to stop what was going on!"

"I know, honey." Harry sighed. "We did stop the transfer to a long-term institution Regina was working on. We think she was doing it to get control of Leonard's assets that come to Camille. But right now, Camille has to go to the psych unit. With all that's happened to her and her self-injury, Dr. Gelanno won't allow her to be released until he's sure she's safe and going into a supportive situation. Until her aunt gets here and signs guardianship papers, Camille's a ward of the state."

"Poor Camille. This is so horrible. I can't even imagine what she must be feeling. Where's Dad?"

"After Camille was transferred to the psych unit, which went through after you pulled the fire alarm, he went back down to the lobby and got Kylie and took her home. He's acting as temporary 'guardian ad litem' for Camille. Don't worry, you'll get to visit her right away in the unit."

"Oh, good."

"Kind of puts things in perspective, doesn't it?" Harry tipped Malia's chin up to look into her eyes, and Malia saw love and grief in her mom's honey-brown gaze. "Whatever is happening in our family is nothing compared to what's happened to Camille."

"I know. Are you getting back together with Dad?"

Harry turned away. "Now's not the time. Let's go."

They were escorted all the way to Harry's SUV by the security guards; Harry took a call once they were in the car. "We're having that press conference at the station. You better do something about your hair," Harry said, when she ended the call.

"Oh no!" Malia's braid had come undone in the struggle with the orderlies. Malia frantically redid her hair with her mom's comb and put on a little lipstick. Thankfully, she'd put mascara on earlier and worn that nice purple shirt.

Soon Malia was standing in front of hot TV lights, microphones bristling at her. Her mom took up one side, and Captain Omura stood on the other. Lei and her partner Pono stood just behind her.

Malia was asked by reporters how it felt to speed into the middle of a kidnapping exchange to rescue her friend.

"I didn't think about it, because it was the only thing to do," Malia said. "I had to save her."

Captain Omura stepped in and made a statement about the case wrapping up with "significant arrests."

Way in the back of the conference room, Malia spotted her dad and Kylie. Peter Clark had an arm around her little sister, and when they caught her eye, both gave Malia a thumbs-up. That gave Malia a boost of energy that straightened her spine, and she was able to tell the harrowing story of Camille's rescue for the news.

THE NEXT DAY, late in the afternoon after school, Malia met Camille in the "rec room" at the Molokini Youth Ward of Maui Memorial Hospital.

Harry had dropped her off. Malia was nervous through the

process of signing in, showing ID, being checked for contraband, and finally, buzzing into the locked psychiatric ward.

Once inside, efforts had been made to make the unit homey; there were rugs on the floor, artwork, and comfortable couches around a TV bolted to the wall in a living room area. Camille jumped up from a table where she was working a jigsaw puzzle with another girl.

"You made it!" her friend exclaimed. They hugged.

Malia held Camille's shoulders and looked at her. A fog of medication still clouded her friend's pretty eyes, but Camille's hair had been washed and brushed and she was clean. She wore an outfit from her "coordinated" closet—an aqua shirt with capri pants. She looked a hundred times better than the day before.

"I'm so glad to see you're okay," Malia said. "I was so worried."

"I think they'll let me out tomorrow. With my aunt."

"I hope you'll come stay with us for a few days."

"We have to see what Aunt June says. She's staying in a hotel. She wants me to join her there, and that's fine because I never want to go to my old house again."

Malia touched the sleeve of a shirt she'd never seen Camille wear. She tugged her friend's hand and led her over to the couch. Camille drew a deep breath and sighed, leaning her head on Malia's shoulder after they sat down. "My aunt wants me to come to California with her. Thinks it will be better for me to start fresh, not have all the memories to deal with."

"No!" Malia pulled back. "She can't do that to you! My dad can block it."

"Your dad has been great. He was here this morning, interviewing me about what I want. It's hard to think about it, but my life has changed forever. And . . . maybe for the better." Camille's soft mouth firmed into a line. "Mom, for instance. I never want to see her, ever again. And the thought of going back to that house—I can't even handle it. Aunt June was right about that."

Malia tried to sort through how much of her own reaction was selfish: wanting Camille to stay so she'd have her friend in her life. "I can see not wanting to go home. But I also think that starting over in California seems like a lot to take on after what just happened."

Camille's shoulders sagged. "I think so too. You know what my auntie suggested? A trip for a few months. I'll get a correspondence course, and we'll travel all around the world for the rest of the school year. By the time I start school again next fall in Orange County, I'll be ready to get back to a routine."

"Wow," said Malia faintly. "That sounds amazing. I've never been farther than the mainland."

"I told Auntie June I'd do it if I got to take you with us, for the first two weeks, when we go to Paris."

"Holy crap, really? Paris?" Malia clasped her hands together.

"Yeah. We're starting in Paris, then taking a cruise around Europe. What do you say to doing that for spring break?"

"I'm packing, is what I say to that," Malia grinned.

"You saved my life. You deserve it," Camille said.

"I don't, not really. I went behind your back with Blake. We kissed." Malia felt her eyes fill. "I feel so bad about it. I want to die for betraying you."

"Blake told me all about how he fell for you when he saw how much you cared about finding me. He thinks you're brave. He went on and on." Camille's lip wobbled. "He and I might have been something, a little something, but it wouldn't have been much. I only liked him because you'd made him such a big deal on the website, and I couldn't tell you because I knew how you felt about him."

"I don't care if you've decided it's okay. It was wrong, and I won't be seeing him anymore. You're the one that matters to me." Malia felt a knifelike pain to the chest at the thought of only seeing Blake from afar, and she'd changed through all of this. She wasn't sure she could go back to her observation posts and hoodies.

"I'm telling you, I'm over him." Camille flapped a hand. Malia could see her exhaustion. "Are you going to Paris with me, or not?"

"If my parents say I can, yes. And if I can get a passport in time."

"Yes, to both. I told your dad, and he called your mom. They think it's a great idea, and your dad is going to get the passport started with a rush order."

Excitement bloomed under Malia's sternum. "Wow, this is amazing!"

"Now. What's happening with the Wallflower site?"

"My mom is trusting me to retool it. I'm going to use it to help people, maybe be a confidential informant for the Maui Police Department." Lei had asked Malia if she was interested, and she was.

Camille's smile was sad. "Too bad it took what happened to me to get you to see that doing good was what Wallflower Diaries should always have been about."

Malia could only nod in agreement.

MALIA STILL DIDN'T HAVE her phone or laptop privileges back, so after she got home, she took the house phone and carried it upstairs, plugging it into a jack in her room. Dad was out doing errands and Mom had taken Kylie to counseling, so Malia was on her own. Being alone in the house felt good, but what she had to do did not.

She steeled herself, and phoned Blake.

"Hey. I was hoping to hear from you. I saw you on the news last night. Impressive." His voice was neutral, hiding something, but the words were polite.

"I wanted to call you a thousand times, but I didn't have my phone, didn't have privacy, and wasn't ready to tell you what I have to tell you." Malia pressed her fingers against her eyes.

"It's about Camille, isn't it?"

"I can't do this to her. I can't do 'us' to her."

"Me neither." Blake's immediate agreement made Malia's heart constrict.

"Oh. That's good, then." Malia made herself say the words, but they came out small.

"Yeah. Camille told me she doesn't care if we go out, and she understands how we got to liking each other—but I can't spend time with you knowing it might hurt her, not when she's lost so much." Blake sounded firm and sad.

Malia's heart broke with a feeling like the soft cracking of ice cubes melting under hot water. "I couldn't have said it better myself," she whispered. "She's invited me to go to Paris with her and her aunt. Maybe we'll both be over it when I get back."

"Yeah, that would give us a good break to think about things." A heaviness in Blake's tone conveyed doubt. Awful as it was, Malia's spirits lifted at this evidence that she mattered to him, that this was as hard for him too. "I'd better go, then," he said. "I was sitting in our spot, working up the nerve to call you."

Malia jumped up from the bed and ran to the window. She moved the curtain, and a few hundred yards down the road from her house, pulled over in 'their spot,' she saw the rounded lines of the old Mercedes.

"Don't leave," Malia said. "Wait there. I just want to say good-bye." She hung up the phone and hurried down the stairs, out the front door, and down the driveway.

Evening was soft charcoal gathering under the shadows of the trees as Malia ran all the way to the car. The window was down, and Blake sat inside. His eyes were dark and startled and his mouth a little open in surprise as she leaned in to touch her lips to his. She kept her eyes open until the last second.

A moment later, she felt his hands awkwardly steadying her

arms, and realized she was hanging halfway into the car. "Dang it, I'm sorry." Malia pulled back and covered her cheeks with her hands. "I totally overdid that. I just wanted a kiss goodbye."

She stepped back as Blake opened the vehicle's door and got out, shutting it with a soft click. She'd never been so aware that he was at least a foot taller. "Then let's have a real one," he said.

He drew her in and bent his head to hers, his arms winding around her until she didn't know where one ended and the other began.

CHAPTER TWENTY-EIGHT

LEI, Pono, Torufu, Bunuelos, Harry Clark, and Special Agent Aina Thomas of the Coast Guard sat around the meeting table at Kahului station with Captain CJ Omura and District Attorney Hiromo. Special Agent in Charge Ben Waxman and agents Marcella Scott and Ken Yamada were tuning in from Oahu.

Omura passed a platter of cut-up fruit and vegetables in one direction, and a box of Komoda's malasadas in another.

"We're jealous of those snacks over here," Marcella said. "Where's ours, boss?"

Waxman raised a brow. "Let's get started."

Omura tapped her shiny red nails together. "This multiagency gathering is to recap the latest developments in the human trafficking case as it has played out on Maui. We've arrested Harold Chang, and his warehouses and properties have been seized. We have a fight ahead of us in prosecuting him; he is already out on bail and his lawyers are claiming that his properties were used for the trafficking without his knowledge or consent."

"The Changs are a wily and well-connected bunch," Hiromo said, stroking a swatch of goatee on his chin. "But I am hopeful, this time, that we will find something more to connect him directly to the trafficking. Detectives?"

"We're focusing on his bookkeeping and computers," Lei said. "We've taken all of the units we could find, along with the phone list and records we found on the William yacht, and given them to the FBI."

"Yes, and our tech department is hard at work," Marcella chimed in. "Agent Bateman, our tech specialist, has run down the numbers in the black notebook Lei found on board the Leonard yacht. Many of the numbers were burners, but some have been traced to Chang-connected businesses or family members. We're tapping their phones now and spreading our net wide."

"Here on Maui, to follow up, we're working on a better support system for runaways," Bunuelos said. "If kids had more safe options, they wouldn't be as vulnerable."

"Yes," Lei said. "Elizabeth Black, a social worker with Child Protective Services, and I have applied for a million-dollar multiagency grant to provide housing and wraparound services for teen runaways. We're hoping to set up a healthy version of the Runaway Railroad for kids with problems at home to be able to access."

The group discussed that for a few minutes, then Agent Thomas wiped a bit of powdered sugar off his chin. "As for the Coast Guard, we've searched and seized all of the registered William vessels and they will be auctioned off. His illegal empire is being disassembled, as we speak."

"Will his daughter, Camille William, inherit anything?" Harry asked. "She's innocent in all of this."

Hiromo harrumphed. "Regina William's property is also being confiscated. After the state's expenses for services rendered are reimbursed, Miss William will be entitled to the remainder. She may be innocent of wrongdoing, a victim even, but her parents were not."

"No one is arguing with that," Harry said. "Per usual, the sins of the fathers are visited on the children."

"That's always been true," Omura said. "Now, is there anything else?"

The meeting wrapped up.

Afterward, Lei caught Harry by the arm in the hall. "Everything okay? I know Malia and Camille are close . . ."

Harry sighed. "Mind if we step outside for a break? I could use a smoke."

"Not at all."

Lei trailed her friend out the double doors of the station and over to a patch of lawn shaded by a flowering rainbow shower tree, where a picnic table and refuse bin served those who liked to go outside for their noon meal. Harry sat atop the table, her feet on the bench, and lit up as Lei unslung her backpack purse and stretched jean-clad legs out into the sunshine.

"Do you ever think about that time in Mexico?" Lei hadn't meant to say that, but somehow it popped out.

"Yeah. Of course." Harry blew smoke off to the side. "I try not to dwell on it but if that craziness hadn't gone down . . . I wouldn't have my daughter. I can't regret it."

"That trip was a turning point for me. I was already on my way to being a cop, but . . . it sealed the deal. And what happened with those traffickers in the desert made me realize I didn't want to be judge and jury ever again, no matter how hard it is to make charges stick sometimes. No offense."

"None taken." Harry's eyes narrowed. "Do you have any regrets, in hindsight?"

"Nope," Lei said. "Especially not about what happened with Cruz." Lei would never forget the unusual experience she'd had with Harry's mysterious martial arts trainer.

"What about Cruz?"

"His training was . . . unique." Lei felt an old betraying blush. "But very effective."

"I wondered if he'd used some of his tantra magic on you." Harry grinned at Lei. "He wouldn't do any of that with me, no matter how I tried to provoke a reaction."

"Sometimes, people come into our lives briefly, but it's a moment that will change everything. And sometimes, a person turns up again, just when they're supposed to, to be there always." Lei gave Harry's knee a smack. "You, sistah. I want you and your family to be in my life, always."

"Absolutely," Harry said. "You're stuck with me now."

EPILOGUE

ONE MONTH LATER . . .

Sitting on the plane on the way back to Maui, Malia put a period on the end of the sentence of the newest Wallflower Diaries post and scanned through it one more time.

The new design of the site was much more serious than the old one: a black border with a grunge font that spelled out *When Wallflower Watches* and signaled a more serious tone—but the subtitle "The Wallflower is everywhere because it's YOU" was the same.

Malia had created her latest post as a cartoon: a stick figure, representative of a student, leaned tiredly on his desk with a thought balloon over his head: *SO TIRED. How am I going to get through that calculus test?*

Next frame: **lightbulb!** *I heard someone on campus has some ADHD meds that will wake me up.*

Next frame: Stick figure texting with conversation bubble overhead: *Text the secret number for prescription of choice, pay online, and pick up behind the toilet in stall #3 of the Boys' Restroom. Got it.*

Final frame: *"Is this happening on our campus? Text the Walflwr if you know for sure!"*

Lei had asked Malia to be registered as a 'confidential informant' for the MPD. In discussing it, Harry had told Malia she could keep the website if she tipped her mom off when and if crimes were taking place in the community. "If you can turn that site into something good, it could be training for you as a journalist or even a detective in the future," Harry said. "And if you're ever identified as the Wallflower, being a CI could help protect you legally."

Spying on her classmates to share gossip was one thing, turning them in to the cops was another; but on the other hand, Malia was concerned about growing prescription drug problems at school, and a series of robberies of lockers she'd heard about at Maui High.

She'd decided to go ahead and become a CI and keep the site going, expanding her info to cover all the county's schools, and this tip about a prescription drug ring had come from the Wallflower burner number. She was eager to sink her teeth into who was behind it—because if prescription drugs were being sold to kids, not far up the supply chain was an adult with medical privileges.

Malia got off the plane after it landed, stiffness from the long flight home from France tightening her neck. The familiar windy warmth of Maui enfolded her as she stepped out into the baggage pickup area. Palm trees outside the airport gyrated in their usual afternoon dance, and off in the distance, the blue-purple folds of Iao Valley created a dramatic cloud-topped backdrop welcoming her home even more than the rainbow-colored sign over the receiving gate. "No place like home," she said aloud.

"Lucky girl." One of her fellow passengers overheard her and smiled in passing.

"Yes, I am."

Being with Camille and her aunt in France for the last few weeks had been wonderful, and probably the best possible therapy Camille could have had. Even so, there had been many nights her friend had trouble sleeping. Bouts of tears took them by surprise during the day, triggered by the sight of a father and daughter together, or something that reminded Camille of the family and life she'd lost.

Aunt June had the look of her brother Leonard William—big and brash, with a chin like the prow of a ship, and thick, prematurely white hair. She was practical and funny and her theme for the trip had been "walk it off."

So they'd walked all over France.

They'd put miles on their shoes walking through Paris's narrow, cobbled streets, exploring street fairs, museums and architectural wonders, and when they left the city, they'd driven outward to explore the countryside, and hiked through the Pyrenees.

Malia had toned up despite indulgence in everything from cheeses to chocolates, and her favorite 'Camille jeans' only stayed on because she wore a belt. She'd tired of her long hair, and Camille had convinced her to cut it in Paris. Freed from the weight of its length, carefree curls tossed around her shoulders.

Malia picked up her luggage at the carousel and waited at the curb until the Honda, with its MAMACOP plates, wove through traffic to pull up at the curb. Harry jumped out from the front with Dad close behind, but Kylie reached her first, throwing her arms around Malia's waist. "I missed you!"

Harry and Peter joined the hug. "That was too long for me," her mom whispered into Malia's ear. "And where did all your hair go?"

"I was ready to lighten up."

"You look great." Kylie hugged her again.

"I think I want a recording of my first-ever little sister compliment," Malia laughed.

"I hope you're hungry." Peter helped Malia heft her suitcase into the back of the car. "I'm cooking tonight."

"You're at the house?" Malia asked. They'd limited phone

contact due to high rates and made do with texts and e-mails while Malia was gone. She felt out of the loop with whatever was going on at the house.

"Your mom and I are in counseling, but we're working it out and back together," Peter said.

Malia let out a breath of relief as she and her sister got into the back seat.

"How's Camille doing?" Harry asked.

"A lot better than if she'd stayed here. Aunt June kept us moving. Literally. They're on a cruise now." Malia turned to smile at her sister. "I brought you something." She dug in her bag and pulled out a chocolate bar the size of a small baseball bat. "That ought to fix your sweet tooth for a while."

"All right!" Kylie grabbed the bar and hefted it. "What's this? A pound or so?"

"Yep."

"Thanks," Kylie said. She tore open the bar, broke off a piece, and handed it to Malia.

ALL THROUGH THE pleasant family evening, at the back of her mind, getting stronger and stronger, was the need to call Blake. She'd e-mailed him the date she was getting home, and she had something to give him from Camille, plus a gift she'd picked up at a store in the Pyrenees.

Finally, alone in her room, Malia shut the door, sighed with relief, and checked her phone.

He'd called. *Twice.* But hadn't left a message.

Malia flopped on the bed. Everything in her space seemed small and worn after the luxury hotels of the Williams' accommodations in France, but all the sweeter for it.

She pressed Call Back and Blake picked up. "Malia?"

"Blake, hi."

A long pause. She shut her eyes, put her hand over her heart, feeling its accelerated beat, and braced herself.

"I'm not over it," he said.

Malia let her breath out in a whoosh. "Me neither."

MALIA HAD NEVER BEEN out to this eastern side of the island, with its thick green jungle, tall fern trees, and lush landscape. The address wasn't easy to find, nestled as it was far in the country along a windy road, but Blake had followed Mom's car which led their way to the fenced compound with its retracted gate. Malia looked around the property with interest as Blake tried to find a spot to park amid a jumble of cars.

Lei's daughter Rosie's third birthday was apparently a big deal.

Off on the right of the compound, a small cottage surrounded by red ti plants was where Lei's father and mother-in-law lived, according to what Lei had told Malia. Back behind the larger house that they approached, an adorable tiny house could be seen—and that was where Lei's grandfather Soga resided. Scattered around the property were tropical trees: macadamia nuts, large round Hawaiian lemons, mangoes, Surinam cherries, avocados, and even lychee.

They found a place to park and joined her Mom, Dad, and Kylie, who were hanging back waiting for them.

Blake squeezed her hand and whispered in her ear as they walked toward her family. "You look great."

"Thanks. And thanks for coming with me." Malia smoothed the fabric of a silky bronze-colored blouse that she'd bought in Paris.

Peter clapped Blake on the back. "Glad you could give Malia a ride."

"I wouldn't miss it, sir."

Mom laughed, and elbowed Dad. "Sir! Oh my!"

"He can keep calling me 'sir.' I'm fine with it," Dad said with dignity.

Kylie rolled her eyes, and Malia squeezed Blake's hand. "Watch out, or you're going to give my dad a big head."

Blake flushed. "Just trying to be respectful, sir."

Dad slung an arm around his shoulders. "And I appreciate that. We have to stick together around these ladies; they've got us outnumbered."

They trooped up to the wide veranda where Lei was waiting to greet them. The birthday girl, adorable in a tiara and puffy princess dress, sat on her hip.

"Happy Birthday, Rosie!" Kylie handed Rosie a wrapped package.

"Mahalo!" Lei exclaimed. The little girl wiggled to be put down, then plopped onto her bottom to tear into the package immediately. Lei clapped a hand to her forehead. "This kid has the self-control of a gnat."

"Thank you!" Rosie squealed with delight at the reveal of a new Barbie; Kylie grinned. "I used to love those when I was her age."

"She has a huge collection," Lei said. "Never too many Barbies!"

Malia handed her wrapped gift to Lei. "This one is a little more sophisticated." She'd bought Rosie a music box to put jewelry in when she got older.

"I'll take it to the present pile. Come on in, everyone. It's past time you met the rest of my 'ohana." Lei addressed that comment to Harry, who slid her arm through Peter's as she followed Lei into the noisy, crowded house.

Butterflies of happiness fluttered in Malia's stomach as she joined the party, Blake's hand warm at her back.

Mom and Dad were making a go of it again, and now they were part of a real community of friends on Maui. She finally had a place to belong.

Turn the page for a sneak peek of, *Wired Revenge*, Paradise Crime Thrillers book 13.

SNEAK PEEK

WIRED REVENGE, PARADISE CRIME THRILLERS
BOOK 13

Six months after Wired Strong

FASHION WEEK in Paris could be deadly.

Pim Wat retrieved her name card from the brocade seat, and sat carefully on the tiny gold imitation Louis XIV chair facing the runway of the show. "Pleased to see they gave me a front row seat," she told her companion in French, tweaking the folds of her flowing white silk pant suit so that it draped beautifully over her legs.

"Of course, they did, *ma petite*," Pietro said, settling in his place beside her. "They wouldn't dare do otherwise."

Pim Wat didn't contradict him. The reason for her favored status was quite different than it had been in the past, but getting a front row seat for the Dior show was always a big deal.

The long black runway, currently unlit, was surrounded by draped, ruched tulle in luxe purple. Pim Wat's heart beat with excitement that echoed the thumping bass of the heavy techno music. *How she loved her new identity!*

She'd come up with it ten years before, but had not actually used it until her complete facial overhaul and departure from Thailand six months before. Fortunately, she'd had all the photos in her identification documents updated before she'd had to go on the run.

No time to dwell on that unfortunate series of events. She'd landed on her feet, as she always did. "More lives than a cat, my Beautiful One," the Master's voice whispered in her mind.

Thank the gods, Pietro had responded to her contact when she'd arrived in Paris. He'd helped her build that identity out into the fully-fleshed woman who sat beside him now. Pietro's loyalty was a weathervane that swung to the highest bidder, but she'd been able to secure that from her hidden source of funds. Besides, he knew her history—and was aware that saying no to her would likely have deadly consequences.

Pim Wat adjusted the square-framed, tortoise shell glasses perched on her nose, scanning for threats. The glasses, embedded with a facial recognition program, circled each face briefly and flashed identities and employers in the upper left corner of the clear lenses. She'd learned, through many hours of practice, to be able to monitor as she looked about in a normal way. "A good crowd so far."

"And an even more exciting collection." Pietro scrolled through his social media feed on a diamond-encrusted phone. Dressed in a lavender silk suit and taupe fedora, he played the part of gay man about town flawlessly, hiding a shark-like constitution that Pim Wat found comforting—she always knew where she stood with her old friend Pietro.

The lights dimmed. The runway lit up with lines of embedded lighting and strobes encircled the ceiling. Spontaneous applause broke out as the first model strode out in that ground-eating way they affected. Pim Wat checked the rapt faces turned up to watch the progression of the model down the runway, the spin-turn, spin-turn at the end, a hand on a protruding hipbone, the outfit shimmering under the lights.

No one she needed to worry about was watching the show, at least so far. She'd do another scan before it ended. Pim Wat stowed the glasses in their case in her golden clutch purse. She sat back to enjoy the spectacle; phone ready to photograph the outfits she might want to try.

SOPHIE SMITHSON, CEO of Honolulu-based Security Solutions, gestured to the small round conference table in the corner of her office. "Welcome to Security Solutions, Dr. Ka'ula. Please have a seat."

The headmaster of prestigious Kama'aina Schools pulled out a chair and sat. Sophie's colleague and friend, Pierre Raveaux, seated himself as well. Raveaux, an elegant blade of a man, spoke in his accented voice. "I'm pleased Stuart thought to bring his problem to us, Sophie, after the way things went on our last case."

Dr. Ka'ula wore a frown that seemed stitched onto his forehead in deep furrows. "Actually, it was Security Solutions' good work finding that embezzler at the Schools, that brought me back with our current situation."

Sophie hefted herself out of her office chair to join them, carrying her tech tablet. At almost nine months pregnant, just maneuvering from one side of the room to another was a bit of a project. She wore a simple black A-line shift that minimized her girth, but still, Dr. Ka'ula's eyes widened as she approached. "I didn't realize you were expecting."

"And yet, my brain remains unimpaired." Sophie forced a smile. Reactions to her pregnancy, especially at a male-dominated security firm, continued to irritate her. "Let's get down to business. What can Security Solutions do to help?"

Wired Revenge, **Paradise Crime Thrillers #13, will continue in spring of 2021 :** tobyneal.net/WRwb

ACKNOWLEDGMENTS

Aloha, dear Readers!

This book was such a treat to write during the pandemic year of 2020! Squirreled away at home, unable to visit friends or family due to social distancing and serious travel restrictions, it was a joy for me to return to Lei's world on Maui, where old and new friends form a close-knit community. These characters have come to feel like friends to me as well—and in a place and time where no one must wear masks or worry about hugging each other at a birthday party!

I'm excited to integrate the Clarks into upcoming books in the Paradise Crime World, and I hope you enjoyed getting to know Malia as a teen sleuth. (Hint: our intrepid sixteen-year-old may get into some trouble again in the future.)

One of the things I enjoy, in case you haven't noticed—is involving all generations in the story: from Great-Grandpa Soga down to the littlest, Rosie. Lei and Stevens's "compound" is based on my sister's place in Haiku, where multiple generations of friends and family enjoy gathering together, having holidays, and picking up macadamia nuts and Hawaiian lemons out of the grass before they can break the blades of the lawnmower!

Though this story had its dark moments, I hope that, overall, it gave you a break from the trials, turbulence, and uncertainties of our current world. *Hang in there; better times are coming!*

As always, thanks to Jamie Davis, business manager extraordinaire, who helps my business run smoothly so that I can spend the most time possible writing; thanks again to Angie Lail, my "Eagle Eye Angel" who copy edits and keeps the many characters and settings of the Paradise Crime World straight in our series bible. Thanks also to my advance reader team, who help us keep typos to a minimum and give my books those important first reviews!

A special thanks to the U.S. Coast Guard Motion Picture, Television and Author Liaison Office for providing input and feedback about Coast Guard standard procedures and protocols related to scenes in the book involving the Coast Guard's CGIS agents.

Most of all . . . THANK YOU, my readers, without whom I would not be able to write stories for a living! Your love of these characters keeps me coming back, book after book, to create a world we can all enjoy where Lei, Stevens, Sophie, Harry, Malia, Marcella, Dr. Wilson, CJ Omura, Gerry, Abe, Ken, Aina and Pono, just to name a few, bring justice to those in need. (One day, I'm almost certain, I'll turn a corner and run into Lei in Costco or playing with her kids on the beach . . . they're that real to me!)

If you enjoyed this, or any of my books . . . *please leave a review*! They help other readers discover the stories. Even a few words matter SO MUCH! I read them and appreciate you all.

Until next time, I'll be writing!

Much aloha,

Toby Neal

FREE BOOKS

Join my mystery and romance lists and receive free, full-length, award-winning novels *Torch Ginger & Somewhere on St. Thomas.*

tobyneal.net/TNNews

TOBY'S BOOKSHELF

PARADISE CRIME SERIES

Paradise Crime Mysteries
Blood Orchids
Torch Ginger
Black Jasmine
Broken Ferns
Twisted Vine
Shattered Palms
Dark Lava
Fire Beach
Rip Tides
Bone Hook
Red Rain
Bitter Feast
Razor Rocks
Wrong Turn
Shark Cove

Paradise Crime Mysteries Novella

Clipped Wings

Paradise Crime Mystery
Special Agent Marcella Scott
Stolen in Paradise

Paradise Crime Suspense Mysteries
Unsound

Paradise Crime Thrillers
Wired In
Wired Rogue
Wired Hard
Wired Dark
Wired Dawn
Wired Justice
Wired Secret
Wired Fear
Wired Courage
Wired Truth
Wired Ghost
Wired Strong
Wired Revenge
Coming 2021

ROMANCES
Toby Jane

The Somewhere Series
Somewhere on St. Thomas
Somewhere in the City
Somewhere in California

The Somewhere Series

Secret Billionaire Romance
Somewhere in Wine Country
Somewhere in Montana
Date TBA
Somewhere in San Francisco
Date TBA

A Second Chance Hawaii Romance
Somewhere on Maui

YOUNG ADULT

Standalone
Island Fire

NONFICTION
TW Neal

Memoir
Freckled
Open Road

ABOUT THE AUTHOR

Kirkus Reviews calls Neal's writing, *"persistently riveting. Masterly."*

Award-winning, USA Today bestselling social worker turned author Toby Neal grew up on the island of Kaua`i in Hawaii. Neal is a mental health therapist, a career that has informed the depth and complexity of the characters in her stories. Neal's mysteries and thrillers explore the crimes and issues of Hawaii from the bottom of the ocean to the top of volcanoes. Fans call her stories, *"Immersive, addicting, and the next best thing to being there."*

Neal also pens romance and romantic thrillers as Toby Jane and writes memoir/nonfiction under TW Neal.

Visit tobyneal.net for more ways to stay in touch!
or
Join my Facebook readers group, *Friends Who Like Toby Neal Books,* for special giveaways and perks.

Made in the USA
Monee, IL
28 May 2021